C000162918

MURD~~ER BY~~
THE SHORE

An addictive crime thriller full of twists

GRETTA MULROONEY

Detective Inspector Siv Drummond Book 4

JOFFE
BOOKS

Joffe Books, London
www.joffebooks.com

First published in Great Britain in 2022

This paperback edition was first published
in Great Britain in 2022

© Gretta Mulrooney 2022

This book is a work of fiction. Names, characters,
businesses, organizations, places and events are either
the product of the author's imagination or are used
fictitiously. Any resemblance to actual persons, living
or dead, events or locales is entirely coincidental.
The spelling used is British English except where fidelity to
the author's rendering of accent or dialect supersedes this.
The right of Gretta Mulrooney to be identified as author
of this work has been asserted in accordance with the
Copyright, Designs and Patents Act 1988.

Cover art by Nick Castle

ISBN: 978-1-80405-312-6

For Tim Stollery with heartfelt thanks

CHAPTER 1

A quarter to four and all's well, Tom Pullman told himself. Lyra had changed into her party gear and was running around in the garden. He supposed he should have let her play out in her old togs and put her fancy dress on at the last minute, but it was a dry day and she'd said she'd be careful.

It was a long time since he'd been involved in a children's party, but if he could chair the occasionally heated meetings of BSS — Berminster Senior Students — he could keep a bunch of tots in line. He'd suggested only half-heartedly that he could start the revelry, but his daughter Kay had jumped at the offer. She had a responsible job and worked hard, so he had to step up. He'd gathered from the cold tension in the air that her marriage was going through a sticky patch — and no wonder, given what had happened — so he'd do his bit.

There was no love lost between himself and Ryan, his son-in-law. Nothing in particular he could put his finger on. Ryan wasn't much of a conversationalist, not the kind of man who'd put himself out to be sociable. They'd always avoided talking when they could, and when they did speak it was stilted, forced. It was like that with some people. It didn't help that after Kay had confided in him, she'd insisted

1

he keep his knowledge of their marital problems to himself. Tom had to tread carefully around Ryan now, in case he let something slip.

Tom watched Lyra through the window. She was a strapping girl for her age. He called her 'chunky monkey' to himself, but he'd never admit that to anyone. She always brought a smile to his face, but it didn't last long this afternoon, because he started ruminating about his problems again.

First, there was the man who'd contacted him a couple of months ago, bearing astonishing news. Tom's blood pressure hadn't been right since and he'd had throbbing headaches. What to do? He'd never faced such a dilemma in his life. The timing was as bad as it could be, and he worried about the impact the situation might have on Kay and her sister, Nell. Kay was already worried sick about her own predicament, and Nell was so erratic, prone to hissy fits or, even worse, anxiety attacks. Just yesterday, she'd flared up at him.

The man who'd appeared in his life had become pushy, too keen, wanting to up the pace. In the end he was a stranger, come to cause trouble and disruption. After sleepless nights, the latest incident with Nell had decided Tom and he'd given the only answer he could. It was final.

Then there was BSS. He'd been considering resigning, not just as chair but from the organisation. He'd miss it, but he wasn't enjoying it much these days. Too many hassles — and he was obsessing about them, letting them dominate his life. When he'd helped to launch BSS, there'd been a real buzz and he'd been proud of the achievement. And yes, he'd got a kick from seeing his photo in the local press and hob-nobbing with the mayor and councillors. Nowadays, being in the organisation was often too much like hard work.

And there were all the complications regarding Belinda. It was difficult to believe how much she'd come to feature in his life, how big a part she was playing, and not just on the BSS committee. She stalked his dreams, and every morning he woke feeling startled by the turn of events. Tom wished he could dodge speaking to her, but she was always in his face. He thought of the letter sitting in his printer. Writing it had helped, if only for a few hours. Anxiety over Belinda made his mouth go dry, so he tried to push it down and turned to his party duties.

Come on, Tom, forget about your troubles for now and focus. This is Lyra's day.

Kay had made him a meticulous list and he'd checked everything off, or so he hoped. She'd decorated the house last night and the caterer had delivered the food earlier, setting it out on the kitchen table. The children's entertainer would be here at half five, so they could spend the first hour marauding in the garden and stuffing themselves. Then they could collapse on the living room floor and watch the antics of Dotty Debbie and her Magic Miracles.

Tom surveyed the laden kitchen table: fresh fruit kebabs, tiny sausage rolls, mini veggie burgers and pizzas, cheese muffins, crudités with dips, one-bite samosas, oriental snacks and a plate of gluten-free savouries. There was a stack of napkins and hand wipes for sticky fingers, recyclable card plates and cups and little boxes for take-home slices of cake. Most of the food, of course, would end up on the floor or half-eaten and cast aside. At least none of the guests had a nut allergy. One was gluten-free — *tick* — and one couldn't have dairy, so there was a plate of suitable cupcakes for them instead of birthday cake.

Tom was proud of the mermaid-themed cake, which stood centre table. Lyra, the birthday girl, had breathed, '*It's so beautiful*' when he'd brought it in from the car and revealed it with a *ta-da!* He'd ordered it from a woman in Brighton and it had cost an arm and a leg, but it had been worth it to see the delight on his granddaughter's face.

He checked that the gift bags were ready, filled with tiny toys and balloons. Kay had bought them all online, together with the bunting and other decorations, from that company run by the future king's in-laws. She seemed to believe that added extra cachet, but to Tom, a card-carrying republican, it

3

was just posh tat rather than pound-shop tat. Kay must have spent a fortune, what with that and the catering. Companies that serviced this 'keeping up with the Joneses' in the complex whirl of kids' parties must be minting it. Tom doubted that he'd had a fourth birthday party. If he'd had any kind of celebration it would have been peanut-butter sarnies and a bowl of jelly and ice cream with his sister. Now, it seemed that kids' get-togethers were up there with Ascot and the Henley Regatta as social events. Kay had mentioned something called *party-shaming*, where you were criticised if you didn't fulfil expectations regarding birthday festivities.

Tom glanced up at the garden and saw Lyra, resplendent in her party dress, sitting in the doorway of her playhouse, head bent over a daisy chain. Good. She was a terrific girl for keeping herself amused. That should occupy her for a bit and allow time for a mug of tea to gird the loins before the onslaught at half four. He turned up the radio — Cher, singing 'Chiquitita' — switched on the kettle and reached for a teabag, humming along with the song and tapping on the worktop while he waited for the water to boil.

He took milk from the fridge and became aware of a figure at the back door. Surely not a guest this early? When he turned around, his heart sank. Not again. This was yet another intrusion and too much on Lyra's special day. He'd made it clear that the matter was over and he was going to be busy with the party.

A few sharp words, he decided, leaving no room for doubt and emphasising that he didn't want any further discussion.

* * *

Meg Sterling was the first to arrive for the party, a quarter of an hour early, parking behind the grey car outside the double garage. Meg was always early for everything. Her mother said it was because she'd been a premature baby. Better than being late, she'd say in self-defence. So here she was on this warm late-April day, turning up too soon in the drive of the impressive house called Seascape. Elsie, her daughter, kicked the back of her seat in excitement.

'Go in, Mummy!'

'We're early, sweetie. Best wait a little bit.'

'I want to go to the party!'

'And you will very soon.'

'I want to go now!'

'Just a few minutes.'

Elsie had been building up to this party for days, wearing her fairy wings around the house. In the rear-view mirror, Meg observed the pink spots in her daughter's plump cheeks. Excitement could turn to tears in the blink of an eye.

'I want to see Lyra!' Elsie waved the present they'd brought for the birthday girl, a personalised book about a trip around the world — *Can you see Lyra, swimming with the dolphins in Hawaii? Look, there's Lyra climbing Annapurna!* The spotted wrapping paper was now the worse for wear.

'Very soon now,' Meg said soothingly, turning round and stroking Elsie's arm. 'Sing me that song about the bear.'

Elsie obliged, to her mother's amazement. She wasn't usually so cooperative. While her daughter warbled, Meg retrieved the present from her hot little hands and smoothed the wrapping. She and her husband had been mimicking the book's breathless style. *Can you hear Elsie having another tantrum on the stairs? Look! Elsie's parents are opening the wine in desperation!* Meg would have preferred to buy a more meaningful present, such as an 'Adopt a Penguin' gift, garden seeds to encourage bees and butterflies, or a nature detective set. She'd suggested all of these, but Elsie had been set on the Lyra-centred book. Maybe she had a crush on her friend. Was it possible at that age?

The sun was intense. Still no other arrivals. Surely someone else would get here soon. It was twenty past four now, and if Kay had been at home, Meg would have gone to the door and waved Elsie inside. Kay wasn't the type to be fazed by a kid arriving early. Meg thought of her slot booked at the fitness club. All day, she'd been anticipating the freedom this party was going to buy her. She'd finally get to use her Christmas voucher on a sauna and a massage. A whole hour and a half of peace and 'me time'. But Kay's dad was hosting the start of the party until she got back from work, and Meg didn't want to impose. She'd met Mr Pullman once and he'd been genial, but even so, Meg didn't like to presume on the goodwill of an older gentleman who was about to cope with a bunch of excited kids.

Meg could glimpse the glimmering bay beyond Seascape. It must be lovely to live here and wake up to that view every day. The sun on the water, winter storms, huge waves rolling in below, sea birds wheeling across the Sussex coast. Always something to watch, never a dull moment. She was a tad jealous, although it was six miles out of Berminster, so not that handy. Meg lived in a semi on an estate, her view the back of a neighbour's house with its huge satellite dish, but she could walk to Elsie's nursery, the supermarket and the fitness club.

Thank goodness, another car arrived just as Elsie got tired of singing, stuck her lip out and kicked the seat again. Why were little kids so utterly relentless?

Meg said, 'Hey! Who's this?' *Look, Elsie, who is this coming for Lyra's party?* She didn't recognise the man driving.

'Manda!' Elsie shouted. 'Party!'

When they'd been released from the cars, the two little girls ran to each other, bobbing up and down with excitement and then headed to the front door. Elsie's gossamer-like fairy wings opened and closed as she gyrated. Manda was in a white-and-yellow gauzy layered dress, printed with glittering butterflies.

Meg stepped towards the smartly dressed man. 'I'm glad you're here. I was early and hanging about. Hello, I'm Meg Sterling.'

'Sim Costa,' the man said abruptly. 'Let's go in. I have to get back to work.'

'I suppose it's nearly time now,' Meg said, but he was already striding to the door and pressing the bell.

After a minute, Costa rang the bell again. No response. He knocked on the door and Elsie banged it with her little fist. Manda insisted on being lifted up to press the bell, which she kept her thumb on. They could hear it playing.

'Ding dong ding dong,' Elsie sang.

They waited. Nothing happened. A couple of gulls called overhead. The sea breeze ruffled Meg's hair.

'Where's Lyra?' Manda grumbled.

Costa muttered and frowned at Meg, as if this was her fault. 'Have you been here before?'

'Just once.' It had been last December, Christmas drinks for the nursery group parents. She'd got squiffy, but could vaguely recall a large living room and kitchen, and what Kay had referred to as an orangery but she'd call a conservatory. Meg moved away from Costa's grumpy presence and peeped through the front window. The slatted blinds were open enough to show that the living room was empty. Clusters of balloons hovered near the ceiling and candy-striped bunting festooned the walls: *Happy Birthday to Lyra! 4 Today!*

Costa was peering through the letterbox. 'No sign of anyone.'

Elsie whined, 'Mummy, I want to go *in*!'

'And me,' Manda added.

'In a minute,' Meg told them, baffled. Was Mr Pullman deaf? Even if he was, Lyra would hear them.

'This is ridiculous,' Costa said. 'We have got the right day, yes?'

'Definitely. Maybe Lyra and her grandad are in the garden. It's big, so they might not hear the bell.'

'Ridiculous,' Costa said again. 'I have a conference call at five. Who can we contact?'

'I've got Kay's number. Let me just check round the back before I disturb her at work. Elsie, stay here with Manda and her daddy.'

Elsie glowered but did as she was told for once. A couple more cars were drawing up, depositing parents and little kids clutching gifts, so she and Manda were distracted.

Meg went to the side gate at the right of the house. It opened when she pressed the latch and she walked down the path, calling Mr Pullman's name. A flowering currant brushed against her hand as she turned the corner to the kitchen. Through the glass doors, she saw the table set with plates of covered party food and jugs of squash and juice.

She knocked on the glass and tried a door handle, calling, 'Mr Pullman, hello!' The door opened and she stepped in. The radio was on, Shirley Bassey belting out 'Goldfinger'. In the centre of the table was a tall birthday cake in layers of blue, green and coral, with four pink candles. Kay had said that her dad was having it made. It was stunning, but as she approached the table, Meg saw that a slice had already been cut from it, nicking off a portion of the number 4 shaped from mermaid tails. The sticky cake knife lay beside it. Strange.

'Hello!' Meg called again, walking around the table, puzzling over that cake. Maybe Kay had taken a piece to work — but no, that would have spoiled it for the party. She wouldn't have marred the anticipation of the candles being lit, the singing of 'Happy Birthday' and the applause as Lyra blew out the tiny flames.

The sun blazed through a window, dazzling Meg. She shielded her eyes and moved into shadow by the sink.

She saw him then, a shape by the huge, six-burner cooker. Mr Pullman was lying on his back, staring sightlessly at the ceiling. The side of his head was split, soaked in matter and blood, with rivulets streaming around his shoulders. Meg gasped and put a hand on the cool enamel of the sink, noting hazily that the blood was almost the same shade as Mr Pullman's socks. His mouth had been smeared with birthday cake in a blur of colours.

Meg opened her own mouth, but no sound came out. There was a buzzing in her head and she swayed, clutching the sink with both hands. She was dimly aware of the doorbell ringing insistently, of running and children's voices. They mustn't see this. She stumbled to the doors and saw

Elsie and Manda chasing towards her from the garden, waving their gifts. Her daughter's wings, threaded with gold, flashed in the sun's glow.

'Mummy!' Elsie called anxiously. 'Why is Lyra sleeping?'

'Sleepy,' Manda echoed.

Meg croaked, 'What?'

'In the little house. There, Mummy! She won't wake up.' Elsie pointed to the timber playhouse on the lawn.

Costa appeared, bristling with annoyance. 'What's going on? There are loads of kids now at the front, champing at the bit.'

Meg's heart was pulsing hard and fast. She heard it in her ears. *Boom boom.* 'Take the children away. Hurry. In there . . . it's dreadful, dreadful.' Meg stepped out and closed the door behind her, stretching her arms across it. 'I have to find Lyra. Take the children. I'll call the police. Elsie, go with Manda, NOW!'

Costa went to speak, then stared at Meg. 'Come on, kids.'

Meg wanted to buckle, but something gave her grit and the sense to keep the party arrivals away. She called after Costa, 'Don't let anyone back here, guard the gate!'

She ran along the soft lawn to the playhouse, her chest tight, her throat parched, and peered through the open door. Lyra lay with her head on a cushion, her honey-coloured hair caught up in a scrunchy. Her pale-green dress had a pleated skirt with orange and blue sequins on the bodice. A crumpled daisy chain was by her side. Her eyes were closed, apparently in sleep. Meg fumbled with her phone, pressing 999 as she knelt down, calling Lyra's name and shaking the lacy sock on her foot. When the little girl didn't wake, Meg touched her wrist for a pulse. There was none.

The operator answered. Meg sank back on the grass and whispered. 'There are people dead. Murdered. They must have been murdered. A man and a little girl. We need help.'

The operator asked her calmly for her name and the location she was calling from.

For a panicky moment, Meg couldn't think. 'By the coast . . . out of town . . . Seascape.' Then she managed to stumble through the address. The operator said that the police would be there very soon.

The call ended and she sat, unable to move. Daisies sprang all around her. She picked one and pressed it to her cheek. A horrible thought whispered insistently in her head.

Elsie has seen Lyra's dead body.

CHAPTER 2

DI Siv Drummond was having a day off. The station had been quiet for a week or so — although she rarely used the Q word, aware that it could summon disaster, just as actors superstitiously referred to 'the Scottish play'.

She unclipped her little fold-down table from the kitchen wall, and placed plates of poppy seed crackers, gruyere and taleggio cheeses, pepper salad and tomato relish on it.

'Tuck in,' she told her friend.

'Lovely nosh,' Hope Merrick said.

'It should be good. Most of it comes from Gusto in town. It's the one thing I have in common with my mother, or at least I hope just the one thing — a dislike of cooking and a penchant for high-end deli food.'

'I'm not complaining,' Hope said. 'My usual lunch is at my desk. Variations on sandwiches from the Tesco on the corner.' She put crackers, wedges of cheese and salad on her plate and took it to the window seat of the wagon.

'Glass of wine? I've red and white, in your honour.'

'I'll stick with fruit juice, if you've got any. Or water's fine. I've got to finish a report later. Clear head needed.'

Siv debated whether or not to open a bottle of sauvignon but decided against it. It was always awkward if the other person wasn't drinking and it would be best not to start this early in the day. She poured them both orange juice, helped herself to food and sat at a right angle to Hope. 'Here, you can put your juice on the window ledge.'

'Ta. I still can't get over how amazing this little home is. Dinky and cosy.'

After Ed, her husband, died, Siv had moved back to Berminster from London and into the converted circus wagon. It sat at the bottom of a meadow, by the River Bere. Some people found it isolated and off the beaten track. That was exactly why it suited her. She'd been able to grieve in peace, weeping unnoticed under the trees by the river.

Siv balanced some cheese on a cracker. 'I can clean it in ten minutes and it's almost always warm. The wood burner sees to that.'

'You never feel cramped? I mean, it's great, but you can only just turn round.'

'I have neat habits.'

Hope had a cheeky smile. 'I remember that about you at school. Your books and your pencil case were always immaculate.'

'I suppose a shrink would say it was my way of compensating for my chaotic childhood.'

'*How* many schools did you say you'd been to before you came to ours?'

'Eight, including one in Biarritz.'

'Your mum was a nomad.'

'Restless legs and *cherchez l'homme*. It was useful experience in a way. I learned to gauge other people and situations at an early age.'

'Very useful in a detective.'

'I like to think so. Enough about me and my rackety childhood. How are your anniversary plans?'

Hope had married at twenty, to a man Siv vaguely recalled from school. She hadn't met Hope's husband yet. They were having a crystal wedding celebration soon. She'd bumped into Hope, an old school friend, earlier in the year and this was their second get-together. Hope was the only person she'd invited into her home so far. She was a social worker with bitten fingernails that spoke volumes about the stresses of her job.

She shook her mulberry-tinted hair and groaned. 'I wish we'd agreed to go away somewhere now. I'm discovering that an anniversary party has a lot in common with a virus. It replicates silently, until one day you realise it's out of control. Did you and Ed celebrate anniversaries?'

Siv recognised that her grief must be less raw, because she didn't flinch when Ed was mentioned. 'Not our wedding, but the day we met. It always seemed more significant to us. Every twenty-ninth of June we'd take a boat on the Thames and have a meal as it cruised along the river. That's how we met, at a birthday party on a boat at Southwark.'

'Sounds amazing. You will come to our party, won't you? And bring your friend, Bartel. I'd like to meet him. He sounds fascinating, larger than life.'

'He'll probably want to wear his Polish national costume. I've seen him in it and he looks stunning.'

'Good, I'd love that. My father-in-law's the most awful bigot and I'd like to watch his face drop.'

Siv wasn't sure if she was up to attending an anniversary party yet. She'd done a funeral and that had been hard, but a wedding anniversary might be even trickier. She made a vague noise and busied herself with salad, aware that Hope had noted her avoidance. They'd clicked at school, grown close. Siv had never had many female friends other than Rik, her older sister, who had dominated her childhood. Rescued it in many ways. When their mother had tired of dragging them around rented flats and a series of 'uncles', she'd despatched Siv and Rik to Berminster to live with their bewildered father. Hope's boisterous, cheerful family had provided thirteen-year-old Siv with a much-needed compass point.

'Bartel's a platonic thing, right?' Hope asked, fork poised in mid-air.

'That's right. A good friend.'

'Any other kind of man on the horizon at all, or is it too soon for you to consider that?'

Siv appreciated the way Hope always came straight out with what was on her mind, even if the questions might cause discomfort. There was a man who might be the vague shadow of a possibility, but she didn't want to tell Hope, who would enlarge the subject and pick over it.

'Bit soon,' she said offhandedly and asked about Hope's job.

She was cutting lemon cheesecake when her phone rang. It was Detective Sergeant Ali Carlin, sounding cheerful. He always took pleasure in delivering bad news.

'Guv, sorry to disrupt your day off, but we've a double murder. I'm on my way now.'

'OK. I'll be there as soon as. Where?'

She scribbled the address, glad that she'd chosen not to have wine, and turned to Hope. 'Sorry, that was work. I have to go.'

Hope rose and brought her plate and glass over. 'No prob, I'd finished. That was delicious.'

'Take some cheesecake with you.'

She shoved a slice in a bag for her friend, picked up her jacket and followed Hope down the wagon steps to their cars.

The sun was high, the breeze soft and fresh, rustling the trees.

Hope paused and breathed in. 'I can see the attraction to living here, I really can!'

* * *

Siv stood by the man who'd had part of his skull caved in and birthday cake shoved in his mouth. The red of the blood and the vibrant icing made quite a canvas of colours. Tom Pullman was of slight build, neat grey beard, plain gold wedding ring. *Dapper* came to mind.

Steve Wooton, the crime-scene manager, pointed to a large, bright-blue griddle pan on top of the cooker. It had a crust of blood on the side.

'We don't need to search for the weapon. This is iron and incredibly heavy.'

'Aye, Polly has one of those at home,' Ali said. 'Feels like a weight at the gym when I pick it up.'

Steve pointed at Ali's comfortable stomach, which was straining through his protective suit. 'Not sure you spend much time at the gym, mate. Mr Pullman's wallet and phone were in his jacket, his smartwatch is still on his wrist and his car's outside. No evidence of a break-in.'

'I took a gander around the house while I was waiting for you,' Ali told Siv. 'No obvious sign of disturbance or any kind of struggle. There's a mug by the kettle with a teabag in and a carton of milk beside it. Looks like Pullman was interrupted while making a cuppa.'

Siv turned, taking in the crowded table. 'There was quite a party in the making. What did you get from the woman who called it in?'

'Meg Sterling,' Ali said. 'Twelve kids were invited for Lyra Turton's party at half four. Mr Pullman, Lyra's grandad, was on duty until his daughter Kay Turton was due back from work around five thirty. Ms Sterling and another parent couldn't get a reply at the door, so she came round the back and found Mr Pullman. Then she went up to the playhouse in the garden, because her daughter Elsie had seen Lyra in there. The little girl was dead.'

Siv grimaced. 'Elsie saw the body?'

'Aye, and her friend Manda. Awful, but they'd run up there before anyone could stop them. All excited about their wee friend's birthday and wanting to hand over her presents.'

'That's rough. Where's Ms Sterling now?'

'She was in a right state, but holding it together. I got uniform to take her details and allow her to go home. Same with the other parents. No point in keeping a bunch of restless kids hanging around here.'

'And Kay Turton?' Siv asked.

'Upstairs, in her bedroom with a constable.'

'She tried to go in the garden to see her daughter and got very distressed when we explained she couldn't,' Steve said quietly. He was usually cocky and upbeat, but this evening he had a grave expression. He had a son Lyra's age.

'And is there a partner?' Siv asked.

'A husband, Ryan Turton. On his way home from Canterbury.' Ali consulted his notes. 'There's also Ms Turton's sister, Nell Pullman. She's been contacted. I explained that the Turtons would need to stay somewhere until we've finished examining the house. She said that they can go to her.'

Siv's phone buzzed and she read the text. 'Patrick's on his way.' DC Hill, her youngest team member. When he was fully alert and engaged, he was good, and he'd upped his game recently, after a few sharp comments from her.

A constable put her head around the back door. 'Sorry to interrupt, guv, but there's a children's entertainer still outside. Dotty Debbie's Magic Miracles, according to her van. She was booked to do a magic show at the party. Shall I send her away?'

Magic and miracles wouldn't do much good here, unless Dotty Debbie could raise the dead. Siv said, 'Please, once you've taken her details.' She stepped over to the table. 'Cutting a slice of cake for the dead man was a nasty gesture.'

Ali followed her. 'Gorgeous though, isn't it? Like a work of art with the layers of sponge and jam. Those mermaid tails are intricate.'

Siv glanced at him. With Ali, stomach and head were always in competition. He'd be imagining the cake's cream and icing dissolving on his tongue. 'OK,' she said, 'let's see the little girl.'

The long garden sloped gently towards the sea. It was mainly lawn, with borders of shrubs. At the far end was a wall of pale brick, covered with ivy.

'Cracking spot this, lovely and quiet,' Ali said. 'That house must have cost a bit.'

Siv nodded. 'Money buys you privacy. It's the kind of area where the neighbours might not see or hear much. Good for them, not so good for us.'

16

The playhouse was a fair way down, on the left-hand side. Rey Anand, the pathologist, was on his knees outside it and waved as they approached.

He sat back on his heels, his brow slicked with perspiration. 'From an initial look, I believe that Lyra was smothered. There were several cushions in there, including one beneath her head, which I've bagged. No immediate signs of any sexual activity.'

'Two of her friends saw her in here,' Siv said. 'We don't know yet if they touched her or entered the playhouse. We'll have to arrange for interviews with them.'

'Poor kids. Let's hope they're not too traumatised.' Rey got to his feet, his protective suit rustling. 'I've seen Mr Pullman. On first inspection, I'd say that they've been dead no longer than a couple of hours. I'll get the bodies removed shortly. Over to you.' He shook his head. 'Such a dreadful thing to happen. The big bad wolf come calling at a kiddies' playhouse . . .'

Siv was taken aback. Unlike Steve, who never shied away from offering his opinion, Rey didn't usually make personal comments at crime scenes. The death of such a young child unnerved everyone, and he was also a parent. He walked away slowly, head bent.

The playhouse was large, almost a small shed, and painted duck-egg blue. It was in the style of a Dutch barn, with a central door and two windows on either side, complete with curtains. Siv crouched and looked inside while Ali peered through a window. It was warm in there, and the air smelled slightly stale and sweet. The girl lay on a striped rag rug, arms by her sides, a daisy chain beside her. The sequins on her party dress winked in the evening sun. She was tall for her age, with fleshy legs and solid arms. Behind her was a red plastic table with a red-and-white gingham tablecloth and a toy tea set, with miniature plates of pretend food that bore an uncanny resemblance to the spread on the kitchen table. A fly balanced on the rim of a little jug filled with purple fruit squash. A teddy, a fluffy dog and a cloth giraffe sat on three green stools, in front of plates bearing cardboard sandwiches. The house was furnished with a miniature cupboard, an armchair, a toy TV, a cooker with saucepans, a bookcase and a barbecue set. A wave of heartache washed through Siv. She pressed her nails into her palms.

'The poor wee girl,' Ali said. 'I'm glad her mother didn't see her like this.'

Siv inched towards Lyra. 'I can't see any bruising on her arms, suggesting she didn't struggle.'

'Someone she knew?'

'Perhaps, or she was just taken by surprise.' Maybe she'd been telling her animals to tuck into their food when her assailant struck. Although she was no lightweight, it would have been easy enough to hold her down.

'Some birthday,' Ali said.

Siv backed out of the structure to let him look. She knelt on the grass, running her palms across it and smelling its fragrance.

He poked his head through the door. 'She must have been excited about her party, in her lovely dress and all. Quite a set-up in here, I wouldn't mind moving in myself.'

Siv closed her eyes for a moment, letting the rich warmth of his Derry accent soothe her. 'It must have cost a fortune, furnished with all mod cons.' She was most affected by the fact that, despite all the expensive toys and paraphernalia, Lyra had turned to the age-old pastime of picking daisies and making a chain. 'I'm wondering about the cake on Pullman's mouth and the child murdered on her birthday. Are they dead because of the birthday?'

'Maybe it's significant,' Ali replied. 'They might be intimate killings, family related. Why murder the child as well? That's vicious.'

The sun was chasing shadows across the lawn and a nipping sea breeze was blowing in.

'What's on the other side of the garden wall?' Siv led the way to the far end of the lawn. She slipped the hood down from her bodysuit, glad of the cool air on her head.

The wall was about five feet high, the dark green ivy dense and tangled. At one side was a wooden gate with a bolt near the top, drawn back.

'Either they're not worried about security, or someone undid this bolt,' Siv said. 'Go round the other side and see if you can reach over to undo it.'

She slid the bolt across when Ali had exited. His gloved hand appeared and he pulled it back.

He opened the gate. 'Easy-peasy.'

Siv stepped through to a pebbled track that ran along the backs of the houses. A couple of metres away was a path leading down to a small strip of beach called Wherry Cove.

'Our killer might have come in and exited this way,' Ali said. He'd lit a Gitane and the smoke was curling in the wind.

'Thought you'd given those up.'

'Cutting down,' he replied, on the defensive. 'Just three a day now, and I'm using those wee patch things to fend off the cravings.'

She smiled. 'No comment.' She could hardly criticise, her own crutch in life being a nightly intake of akvavit. 'Let's head inside, make sure that Steve's lot are going to check this area at the back and see if Patrick's arrived.'

* * *

DC Patrick Hill had Destiny's Child playing loudly in the car. He'd been in Brighton, attending an invigorating course in telecoms data analysis. The role of data analyst was becoming more crucial in presenting court evidence and exhibits, and Patrick reckoned that was the way he wanted his career to develop. Until recently, he'd been too concerned about his brother Noah to focus much on his own life, both personal and work. Noah had been left disabled by a stroke, and after their mother died, most of Patrick's spare time had been occupied with assisting him. But Noah was now on a more even keel with regular carers and a companion called Eden, who had been and might still be a sex worker. She made Noah happy and cooked terrific breakfasts, so Patrick wasn't asking questions. He had a steady girlfriend, Kitty, who was a warden in a local country park. Things were on the up and it was time to change gear at work.

Patrick's thoughts turned to the guv, who'd been a real support last year with Noah. He liked her well enough, even if she could be a tad scathing. Sometimes he'd deserved her telling him off. DI Drummond was a hard taskmaster, but that was OK and he admired her focus, learned from it. She'd warmed up a bit recently too. Less prickly. Ali reckoned she was starting to get over the loss of her husband, who'd been knocked off his bike in London.

Patrick listened to Ali and used him as a sounding board. There was something reassuring about his voice and relaxed manner. Polly, his wife, said he had 'easy country ways', referring to his farming family in Derry. Not that Ali was a walkover. Suspects were often taken in by his geniality, and he could turn on bad cop and wrong-foot them when it suited him.

Now that he was able to concentrate on his own life, Patrick was restless and ambitious, unlike Ali, who seemed content to stay in the guv's shadow, follow orders, battle with his diabetes and go home to Polly. When Patrick anticipated the future, he saw himself leading a team of crack analysts, maybe even leaving the police and setting up his own business.

He tapped the steering wheel and turned into Cove Parade, heading towards the crime scene. It was a long street, winding at the far end above the coastal road, where Patrick and Noah lived. Their front windows rattled when the traffic thundered past. Up here was quiet, no diesel fumes. Mainly detached houses, positioned well back from the road. The kind that had names as well as numbers, with great views and beach access. Maybe one day he'd be able to afford one.

Number eleven was called Seascape. It had a wide paved drive and a pebbled garden dotted with clumps of rosemary, thrift and sea holly. Patrick pulled in beside Ali's car. A rainbow-striped banner dotted with silver fairies flapped over the porch — *Birthday Girl Lives Here!* Not anymore.

It jarred him to walk into a house filled with joyful birthday goodies and find forensic colleagues picking their way carefully around toys and party food. Patrick studied the body lying in pooled blood in the kitchen. He recognised the watch and its bright yellow strap with a start. The man wouldn't need his smartwatch to monitor his heart rate now. This was a grim one, with a little kid gone too. He turned as the guv and Ali came through the back door.

'I know him,' Patrick said. 'He's Tom Pullman, chair of Berminster Senior Students. I went to one of their talks, about Hannibal. Do you remember, guv? That retired teacher we met earlier in the year gave it.'

Siv recalled that Patrick had revealed an interest in history when they'd interviewed the teacher during a previous case. 'You met Mr Pullman there?'

'Yeah. Nice guy, very welcoming. Seemed popular.'

'Not with someone,' Ali said.

Siv quickly brought Patrick up to speed. 'Let's crack on. I'll see Kay Turton, if she's able to talk to me. Patrick, can you organise a door knock along this road with uniform, find out if anyone saw anything suspicious this afternoon. Ali, I'd like you to visit this Meg Sterling who found the bodies, get a detailed account of what happened. Check if any similar crimes have taken place around Sussex or bordering counties, or if we have any violent offenders recently released from prison.'

Siv watched them go: Ali with his broad frame and rolling gait and skinny Patrick bobbing up and down beside him, his gelled hair teased into spikes. At times, they were like a comedy duo. Berminster's Laurel and Hardy.

She checked her phone and saw that a family liaison officer called Geordie Coleman was on his way. She headed towards the stairs, bracing herself to see Kay Turton.

CHAPTER 3

There was a hint of vomit in the bedroom, and it was stiflingly hot. Kay Turton sat on the side of the queen-size bed, her feet not touching the floor. Siv saw the physical resemblance between father and daughter, both small with slight frames and slender limbs. Kay wore smart black trousers with a cream shirt and the stunned air of the freshly grieving. Her fair hair skimmed her shoulders.

As soon as Siv entered the room and introduced herself, she asked, 'Where's Lyra?'

'Her body is being taken to the mortuary. We'll arrange for you to see her as soon as possible. Your father too.'

Kay said, as if she'd forgotten the other death, 'Dad . . . yes.'

Siv asked the constable who'd been sitting by the bed to make tea. She said to Kay, 'Are you up to answering a few questions?'

The woman raised dull, reddened eyes. 'Yes.'

'Thank you. I'll open a window first, if that's OK.'

'Go ahead. Sorry, I got sick. I hardly ever get sick.'

Siv let in a welcome breeze and sat in the chair next to the bed. 'I'm terribly sorry about your daughter and your dad.'

'Thank you,' Kay said formally. 'Lyra was born at six in the morning. She didn't have long being four, did she? Not even a full day.'

'No, sadly.'

'At least she got a bit of time with her playhouse. She was out there early this morning, making pretend breakfast for her toys.' Kay pulled a pillow towards her and placed it on her lap, fingering the scalloped edges. 'The playhouse was Lyra's main present. She was so thrilled with it. We were going to add a little sign over the door. *Lyra Lodge*. Who . . . who would do such a thing?'

'Have there been any problems or arguments within or outside of the family?'

She said tersely, 'No.'

'How about your father — had he fallen out with anyone?'

'Dad? I doubt it. He didn't say so.'

'And your mum?'

'She died a while ago.' Kay had been gazing down at the pillow, but now she turned her bleary gaze to Siv. 'Was Lyra molested?'

'We're not sure yet, but it seems unlikely.'

Kay said nothing. The constable came in with two mugs of tea on a tray and a bowl of sugar. Siv indicated with a tilt of the head that she could leave again and handed a mug to Kay, who sniffed it and then put it on the bedside table.

'It smells strange. Oily or something.' Her phone rang. She answered, listening and just saying, 'OK.' When the call ended she told Siv, 'That was Ryan, my husband. He's stuck in traffic, an accident. He'll be an hour or so.' She yawned. 'I feel as if . . . I don't . . . as if I'm outside of myself.'

'Yes. Where's your husband coming from?'

'Canterbury — somewhere around there, anyway.'

'What does he do and what time did he leave for work today?'

'He was away overnight, left yesterday morning. He's an engineer.'

23

Kay appeared unemotional about her husband's absence and delay, but perhaps that was down to shock. Siv sipped the weak, milky tea. It was revolting. The constable should have learned that you always make a strong brew in these circumstances, the kind you could stand a spoon up in. On reflection, she should have opened a window as well, to air the room and spare Kay's discomfort. Siv would have a word afterwards.

'Would your dad have had the back doors unlocked?'

'Yes, I expect he would. I mean, Lyra would have been in and out on a warm afternoon. She's always keen to run around when she gets . . . gets home from nursery . . .' Kay took a shuddering breath, rubbed her eyes and said abstractedly, 'All that food. What'll I do with it?'

'We can help with that, if you like.' The vicar at St Helen's allowed rough sleepers to stay in the church overnight and she'd make use of it. At least these awful deaths would benefit someone.

Kay said robotically, 'That's kind. You've all been kind.'

'Your garden gate has a bolt but no padlock. Do you not lock it?'

'We never have. It's always seemed so safe and quiet here, and Lyra's not tall enough to reach the bolt. We've been here nine years, never any trouble. Is that how this man got in?'

'We can't say yet.' Kay was assuming the killer was a man. 'Had anything been disturbed in your bedroom when you came in here?'

'No. One of the constables asked me about valuables, but we don't have many. I checked my jewellery and it's all there in the drawer. Not that I'd care if it had gone. Things don't matter. Whoever did this could have had everything I own if they'd only left my dad and Lyra alone.'

'Ms Turton, I won't keep you much longer. Can you just talk me through how today's party was planned?'

Kay ran a finger over her lips. 'Dad offered to start the party at four thirty, because I was at work until five, at the

Town Hall. I'd got everything ready. Dad has . . . had a key. He's always here on a Thursday anyway, brings Lyra back from nursery and stays with her until I get home.'

'What happens on other days?'

'I have a nanny. She attends college on Thursdays.'

'A live-in nanny?'

'No. Alicia shares a house in town. Dad was here from two today, so that he could let the caterers in before he fetched Lyra. I'd invited a dozen of Lyra's friends. An entertainer was due . . . oh, what happened to her?'

'We sent her away,' Siv said.

'Yes, of course. So, there we are.'

'What's your job at the Town Hall, Ms Turton?'

'I'm a deputy registrar.'

'And you were there all afternoon?'

'Yes, it was a full schedule.'

'What time did your dad collect Lyra from nursery?'

'It finishes at three.' She drooped, her shoulders sinking.

'I'll be quick,' Siv said. 'Do you have a list of the party guests?'

'Somewhere, yes.'

'That would be handy, just so we can be sure we've checked with all the parents.' It would be interesting to see if there was anyone who hadn't turned up.

'Check what?'

'In case any of them saw anything.'

'Oh.' Kay reached for her phone. 'I've got a list on here. I sent it to Dad, with the parents' contacts. In case anything went wrong . . .' Her face crumpled as she realised what she'd said.

Siv gave her a minute while she dabbed at her eyes, and then handed Kay a card with her email. 'Forward that list to me now, please.'

There was a hesitant knock on the door and a woman edged in, a hand to her mouth. 'Oh God, Kay!' She moved to the bed, stood for a moment staring down, and then slumped beside Kay, who put a hand out and patted hers.

Siv asked, 'Are you Nell Pullman?'

'Yes.'

'I'm so sorry.'

Nell made a strangled noise and put her head on Kay's shoulder. She was the same build as her sister, but a coarser version, with a fleshy nose and bushy brown hair. She was squeezed into tight red jeans and a khaki jacket, and she smelled strongly of weed.

'I can't believe this,' Nell whispered. 'I'd got Lyra's present ready to bring tonight.' She started to cry loudly.

Siv waited. 'Ms Pullman, I realise that this is a very difficult time, but your sister and her husband will have to stay somewhere until our forensics team have completed their searches. I understand that they can go with you?'

Nell sniffed and rubbed the back of her hand under her nose. 'Yeah, that's OK. We'll manage.'

'Thank you. Ms Turton, the officer who's been here with you can help you pack some things for yourself and your husband. Is that OK?'

'I suppose it has to be,' Kay murmured.

'A family liaison officer, DC Geordie Coleman, will be here shortly. He'll help you with getting to your sister's and with any questions you have, both now and in the coming days. I'll leave you now. I'll come to see you in the morning, so that I can talk to you and your husband.'

Kay stared up blankly, her slight frame supporting her sister's sagging body.

Siv closed the bedroom door and explored the rest of the upstairs rooms. Lyra's bedroom was opposite her parents' and decorated with wallpaper featuring woodland animals. It was tidy, with a white wooden cabin-type bed surrounded by integral shelves and drawers. A folded nightdress lay on the pillow, which was guarded by six teddies, three on each side. There was a well-stocked bookcase and a large toy box with a range of cloth animals sitting on top. A half-finished crayoned picture of a farmyard lay on the pale-green carpet. When Siv opened the built-in wardrobe door, she saw racks of dresses, trousers and tops. Lyra'd had more stuff to wear than most adults.

Next to Lyra's room was a spare bedroom with fitted wardrobes and a double bed, then a huge bathroom and a good-sized office, with a man's jacket on the back of the high leather chair. Siv stepped over to the desk and saw a folder labelled *Proposal for Automated Animal Feed Dispenser.*

Downstairs, Steve informed Siv that the bodies had been taken away. 'We've got Tom Pullman's car and house keys. They were in his jacket in the hall. I've sent his phone to the lab. That's his grey hatchback outside.'

'Thanks, Steve. Have you finished with the food on the kitchen table?'

'Yes, all done, and we've removed the cake and cake knife to take to the lab.'

Siv returned to the kitchen and surveyed the table. The stunning cake had left a large gap, but the rest of the food sat undisturbed beneath film covers. Siv spoke to the officer who'd sat with Kay and asked her to help the Turtons pack a few things. The young woman appeared wan and upset.

Siv asked, 'Is this your first murder?'

'Yes, guv.'

'Remember to breathe, then.' She'd leave the comments about tea strength and windows for now.

Siv beckoned another constable and asked him to call the vicar at St Helen's and bag the food from the table to take there.

In the living room, she surveyed the pretty banners and balloons. Greetings cards clustered on the mantelpiece. The furniture had been pushed back against the walls, ready for the fun that never happened. Lyra had been a cherished child. A lot of effort had gone into preparing for this birthday.

Siv heard a jovial male voice and recognised Geordie Coleman's Scouse accent. He'd recently joined the Berminster force, and this was her first time working with him. She'd heard that he was competent, with a caring manner that reassured people — desirable qualities in an FLO. She went to the living room door and beckoned to him.

'This is a shocker,' he said. He had a sallow complexion and fair hair, parted in the middle.

Siv briefed him while he gazed around the room, a worn leather bag hooked over one shoulder. He listened attentively, head tilted to one side, nodding now and again. She approved of his black jeans and grey wool jacket, an outfit that was smart enough but not too official.

'Make sure that the Turtons are sorted for tonight and remind them that I'll visit them at Nell Pullman's in the morning.'

'Sure, guv. Leave them with me.'

It was almost eight and she'd had nothing to eat. She'd pick up a takeaway and head to the station, start phoning round the parents who'd brought their children earlier. She left the house and stood on the path, taking breaths of salt air under a deepening blue, serene sky. Siv found solace in being by the sea and walking for hours in the nature reserve, along the cliff path and by the River Bere. At times she missed the buzz of London, but too many things there reminded her of her husband and all she'd lost.

As she started her car, she glanced up the coast to where DCI Will Mortimer, her boss, lived with her mother. Mutsi had moved in with him a couple of months ago and Siv felt sorry for him, now that her mother had invaded his life and was reorganising his home, fired with ambitious and expensive decorating schemes. Siv had an uneasy relationship with her mother and Mortimer, and tried to keep liaison with her boss to a minimum. She'd email him from the station, having learned that brief updates usually kept him happy and out of her hair.

On the road back to town, a car flew towards her, well over the speed limit. She glanced in her mirror, and as she saw its taillights vanish, she wondered if that was Ryan Turton.

* * *

Meg Sterling lived on a newish estate two streets away from Ali. Her house had fancy window drapes, a carriage lamp by the door and a pretty flowering pear tree in the centre of the tiny patch of front lawn.

He sat in his car outside and demolished a chocolate-covered caramel bar before he went in. He'd had no dinner, but he should have eaten the trail mix or a protein biscuit from the glove compartment. His wife Polly lovingly made the protein biscuits for him, for just such an eventuality. She appreciated that when he was immersed in an investigation, he neglected his health and went for quick fixes. He struggled to manage his diabetes and had been rushed to hospital with a hyperglycaemic attack only months back. Both Polly and the guv would disapprove if they could see him — the guv had blamed herself for his collapse at the time, and Pol had been angry with her for not noticing that he was getting sick — but he had to have some guilty pleasures. Although he'd never say it to Polly, the biscuits resembled bird food, probably tasted like it too and provided nothing near the bliss of full-cream milk chocolate with a gooey centre. Live now, pay later. He'd make up for his sins tomorrow, steer clear of the bad stuff and try to stick to Nurse Keene's rule at the diabetic clinic: DEP — diet, eating and physical exercise.

As if Polly had an invisible eye on him, he got a text from her.

Have you eaten? Make sure you don't skip proper meals x

Guiltily, he took a protein biscuit and chewed one mouthful, swallowing with an effort, then texted back.

Don't worry, just had some protein bic x

He added a thumbs-up for good measure. Well, it wasn't untrue. He badly wanted to light up a Gitane now. Chocolate followed by a cigarette was nirvana, but he'd already had his three for today. He scolded himself to have some self-control, and found a piece of chewing gum instead. He chewed for a couple of minutes, then binned the gum, tucked his escaping shirt into his trousers and headed for the Sterling house.

He sat with Meg Sterling in her kitchen, which had the exact same layout, worktops and cabinets as his own. It was a bit spooky, being in this mirror image. He half-expected to see Polly standing at the cooker, making him a healthy meal — grilled chicken with vegetables or salmon stir-fry, while he craved chips, one of his mother's steak-and-kidney pies and a hearty pudding.

Meg was tear-stained, with pools of mascara in the corners of her eyes. A large glass of red wine stood by her elbow. Ali wouldn't have minded a slug.

'My husband's upstairs with Elsie, trying to settle her,' she said. 'She's been so upset and can't understand why the party didn't happen. We told her that Lyra's having a long sleep.'

Ali wasn't sure that the euphemism was such a good idea, but he was no childcare expert. He got her to talk him through the afternoon and heard how there'd been no response at the front door.

'So, you were there about a quarter past four?'

'That's right. Early, as usual.'

'And you didn't see anyone?'

'No, just a car parked outside. I assumed that was Mr Pullman's. There was nobody until Mr Costa arrived around twenty past with his little girl, Manda. I was so annoyed with him, letting Elsie and Manda run round the back, but I suppose it wasn't his fault. He wasn't to know anything was wrong. It's just . . . I can't stop worrying because Elsie saw Lyra there . . . They were keen to see the playhouse. Lyra'd been telling them about it at nursery.' She caught a breath. 'Oh, I've only just . . . what if the killer had still been there, in the garden?'

Ali said gently, 'It's unlikely, so no need to dwell on that. It doesn't help. Has Elsie mentioned if she or Manda went into the playhouse or touched Lyra?'

Meg shuddered. 'No, and I haven't wanted to bother her with questions.'

'I understand. We'll arrange for someone to chat with her, just in case there's anything helpful she can tell us.'

Meg sat upright. 'I don't want her having to go over it and getting upset.'

'We'll do our best not to cause any distress. It will be someone with special training,' Ali said reassuringly, although there was no guarantee, no winners in this situation.

He took Meg step by step through seeing Tom Pullman and then going to the playhouse. 'Had you met Mr Pullman before?'

'Once properly, just before last Christmas, when Kay gave a little do for some of us who'd met through the nursery. I spoke to him for a couple of minutes. I've seen him at the nursery, just to smile and wave. He was a retired gentleman, a widower. That poor man, just caring for his little grand-daughter. It's the last place you'd imagine violence happening, at a child's birthday party.'

Ali nudged her drink towards her. 'Have some wine, you need it after the shock you've had. How about Kay — are you close? Had she mentioned any worries to you?'

'Not close, no. We met through the nursery and we've chatted a few times. Nice woman, very businesslike. She works for the council, so she's not a regular around the mums. She dropped Lyra off in the mornings and always seemed busy, needing to get away. She's never mentioned that anything's wrong. I don't know the family that well.'

Ali wasn't getting much. 'And her husband?'

'Ryan, yes. He was at that do at their house I mentioned, but he seemed a bit standoffish, didn't mix much.' She put her hands to her face. 'That cake around Mr Pullman's mouth. That was dreadful.'

'It was indeed. About Lyra — who usually picks her up from nursery?'

'Kay has a nanny, Alicia Ferreira, but she's on a course on Thursdays, so Mr Pullman fetches Lyra.'

'What can you tell me about Ms Ferreira?'

'She's been Lyra's nanny for about two years. Seems really nice, sensible and steady. She's at Rother College on Thursdays, taking some A levels.'

'You saw Mr Pullman collect Lyra this afternoon?'

'Yes, I saw him taking her home. Lyra was so excited about her party and putting her dress on, dancing around like a giddy goat.' She sighed and drank wine. 'How is Kay?'

'Very upset, obviously.'

'I suppose I should contact her tomorrow, because I was there, I found . . . but I'm not sure what to say.'

'Best leave it a couple of days, let Kay and her family have some space,' Ali advised. The last thing he'd want if a loved one died would be to have well-wishers piling in, although back in Derry, it was exactly what the local community would do. His brothers would joke that he was being corrupted by English ways.

Meg sagged slightly, let off the hook. Ali said he'd see himself out. As he opened the front door, he heard a child's sob from upstairs. It would be a long night in the Sterling household.

CHAPTER 4

At eight the next morning, Siv called at Gusto, the Italian café the team frequented. She bought coffees, honey brioche buns and a little vegetable frittata for Ali. As usual, the tiny café smelled heavenly. She'd fantasised about renting the flat above and having all her meals delivered from the kitchen below — she pictured a dumbwaiter arrangement, with delicious food arriving silently. The reality was that she usually chucked something in the microwave, or made the most of what she found in her fridge.

When she arrived in the team room, Patrick had started an incident board and written up basic details. She checked her emails and read one from Geordie Coleman, sent at 7 a.m.

The Turtons arrived at Ms Pullman's flat OK last night. The place is a bit of a tip. Ryan Turton didn't have much to say. Both in shock and said they just wanted to be left alone. I said I'll call them lunchtime about visiting the morgue. I'm in court this morning. GC

Siv set out the breakfast, aware of the positive energy in the room. Patrick was more purposeful these days, now that life with his brother had become easier, and he was apparently invigorated after the course he'd been on yesterday. She'd have to keep tabs, though, on the number he was attending. They seemed to come around with great regularity. Ali was back on form after a health scare. She relied on him and could trust his judgement. Eighteen months after Ed's death, she was starting to engage more with people. His memory was still as fresh, but she'd adapted to the harsh reality of living without him. Her skin was no longer so thin and sensitive, and her hair had grown back over the bald patches she'd developed in the weeks after Ed's funeral.

'Let's get started,' she said, standing in front of the board with a bun. 'We have two victims. Tom Pullman, aged seventy. Retired, a widower and grandfather to Lyra Turton. It was her fourth birthday. Kay Turton, Lyra's mother, was at work at the Town Hall, where she's a deputy registrar. Ryan, her father, had been working away overnight in Canterbury. Mr Pullman had picked Lyra up from nursery at three and taken her home. She'd got ready for her party, which was due to start at half four. Caterers provided the food, delivering it some time after two o'clock. Mr Pullman was there to let them in before he fetched Lyra. He usually looked after her on Thursdays, because the nanny was at college.'

'Her name's Alicia Ferreira. She's been the nanny for two years.' Ali was nibbling the frittata without much enthusiasm while devouring a brioche bun with his eyes.

Siv reached for her coffee. 'Sometime between three fifteen, when Mr Pullman would have got home with Lyra, and before four twenty, when Meg Sterling entered the back of the house, someone killed Mr Pullman and his granddaughter. There was no sign of a break-in, Mr Pullman's car and personal items were untouched and Ms Turton told me that her jewellery was intact, so we can rule out a burglary that got messy. Until we have confirmation from the post-mortems later today, we're assuming that Mr Pullman died from a blow to the head with an iron griddle pan and that Lyra was suffocated.' She took a gulp of her drink. 'I've had an email from Steve. His team will finish in the house this morning. They've harvested a number of fingerprints, which is to be expected. A search of the track behind the house and the path going down to the shore has been negative. Lots of people walk in that area, so there are footprints galore. Steve will have a full report for us soon. Then his team will move on to Mr Pullman's house and check it out.'

Ali asked, 'How did you get on with Kay Turton last night?'

'I had an initial talk with her. She wasn't aware of any problems connected to her father or within her family. Her sister, Nell Pullman, turned up and got emotional — more so than Kay.'

Ali talked them through his interview with Meg Sterling. 'Ms Sterling told me that Pullman was a pleasant man and Kay's a nice woman, but that Ryan Turton was standoffish.'

'I thought I picked up something around the husband when he rang Kay, but it was hard to tell,' Siv said. 'She didn't seem as upset about his absence as you'd expect.'

Patrick was licking his fingers. 'Guv, house-to-house along Cove Parade gave us almost nothing. The woman at number twenty saw the caterer's van go by at about two fifteen. That was all.'

'No similar crimes committed in the region and no offenders with records of violence released recently,' Ali told them.

'Last night I spoke to all the parents whose children were invited to the party,' Siv said. 'None of them who were dropping off their kids noticed anything unusual. Mr Costa, whose daughter Manda saw Lyra in the playhouse, was angry and upset and couldn't add anything helpful. What he told me coincided with Meg Sterling's account.' She sat down and reached for another bun. 'Why murder the child? Intergenerational killings are rare, and when they do happen, it's usually a father doing away with his children and himself.'

'Obvious. Pullman was the target, but Lyra saw the killer,' Patrick said.

Siv raised an eyebrow at him. He did have a penchant for the quick fix, which wasn't useful in a murder investigation. 'Possibly, but I'm always wary of the obvious, and so should you be. Lyra wouldn't have posed that much of a threat. She was a bit young to be a reliable witness.'

Ali unwrapped chewing gum. 'That cake in Pullman's mouth and then Lyra . . . seems to me it was about the birthday.'

'Could well be, but we won't run before we can walk,' Siv said. 'I'm going to see the Turtons this morning, at Nell Pullman's flat. Patrick, can you see if she has a record — she reeked of weed. Also, check out the caterers, find out who delivered the food and how Mr Pullman was when they arrived. Ali, I want you to talk to Alicia Ferreira, see what she can tell us about the family. She must have picked up quite a bit about them over a couple of years. Query what the techies have from Pullman's phone and arrange for interviews with Elsie and Manda — there's that specially trained psychologist we've used before, can't recall his name.'

'Lex Rani,' Patrick told her.

'That's him. I'll check in for the post-mortems. I'll want one of you to visit Mr Pullman's home with me later, when Steve's team have finished there.'

Before she left, Siv ran upstairs to give DCI Mortimer a briefing. He was standing near the window of his office, gazing into a picture of Lake Keitele that her mother had given him.

'DI Drummond, good morning to you,' he said with a strained laugh. 'Do sit down and bring me up to speed.'

Siv ran through the bullet points of the murders, noting that his hair was now honey brown and stylishly layered. Mutsi had taken charge of his appearance and he'd been ringing the changes on his shades of dye. He was a slight man with narrow, sloping shoulders. Unprepossessing, but Mutsi was doing the best she could with unpromising material, and she always set to with a will. She did like a project, although her enthusiasm usually dwindled before too long. A low boredom threshold meant that many of her relationships had petered out at the six-month mark. Mortimer's rosacea was much better these days, his skin less inflamed, so perhaps he had found some contentment with her mother. *For now*, Siv told herself.

'Dreadful, a child killing of that nature,' Mortimer said.

'It does affect people, sir. We're releasing the story to the press this morning, with the usual request for information. No details for now about how Mr Pullman or Lyra were killed. I'm heading off to interview the Turtons.'

'I won't keep you, then.' He coughed. 'Do drop by for a coffee any time. Your mother's always happy to see you. As am I, of course! She would enjoy your company more often, given that she moved here from Finland to be near you. She was worried that you'd be too much alone when she heard you'd left London and taken this job.'

The lie floored her. So that was the story Mutsi had sold him. Siv could give him an alternative version, that Mutsi had left her home town of Turku after yet another failed relationship, this time with Ernst, who'd decided to return to his wife. She'd exhausted Turku's possibilities and her friends' patience, and turned up in Berminster because she'd had nowhere else to go. But love is blind, and Siv had a tricky enough relationship already with her boss without antagonising him.

'Life has been a bit full on, sir,' she said.

'I understand, but it's open-house at Clifftop, seeing as we're . . . well . . . family now.'

The forced geniality grated. Siv had preferred him when he'd been snappy, trying to catch her out. She'd been appointed over his favoured candidate and protégé, Tommy Castles, who'd since gone to Kent.

'Very kind, sir. The picture of Lake Keitele is just slightly out of true, needs to move about two centimetres to the right.'

Mortimer checked. 'So it does. Thank you. I expect you have a good eye, with your artistic talents.'

Siv said goodbye. As always, exiting his office felt like a liberation.

* * *

Nell Pullman lived in a down-at-heel area of the town called St Luke's, or more colloquially, Luke's End. Some kindly described it as raffish. Siv parked outside and took in the weed-covered strip of front garden and peeling front door of the tall terraced house. Nell's flat was on the top floor, with a view of a small industrial estate at the back. The sisters had certainly followed divergent paths in life.

Kay Turton let her in and Siv followed her up narrow stairs. An odorous cat litter tray stood on the landing near the flat door. The rank smell made Siv wince.

Kay had made an effort with her appearance. She was pallid, with hollow eyes, but her lipstick had been carefully applied and she was immaculately turned out in grey trousers and a navy shirt. Her freshly washed, thinnish hair was drawn back in a grip. Perhaps it was her way of keeping her misery under control. She looked somewhat upmarket against the backdrop of her sister's grubby living room with its cheap furnishings. The floorboards must have been elegant when originally painted creamy yellow, but were now scuffed and marked. A window was open, not quite disguising the lingering aroma of weed. They sat opposite each other in creaking wicker armchairs. So far, no sign of the husband.

Siv took out her notepad. 'I'm sorry to have to bother you with more questions, Ms Turton. I understand that it's hard for you at a time like this, but we need background details to help us investigate.'

'Yes. It is what it is.' Kay placed her feet neatly together. 'Nell's gone to work. She didn't want to let her client down, and I told her there was no point in staying around here.' She must have noted surprise on Siv's face. 'To be honest, I couldn't deal with her grief as well as my own.'

Maybe Nell was hard going. Siv recalled the way she'd leaned heavily on her sister the night before. 'It's you and your husband I wanted to talk to for now, so if he could join us . . .'

Kay stroked her right thumb and said abruptly, 'Ryan's not here, actually.'

'Why is that?' Surely the man hadn't gone to work the day after his daughter's death.

'He . . . he booked into a hotel last night. The Dovecote.'

Siv remembered Geordie's message. 'Was that after DC Coleman left you?'

'That's right. Not long after.'

Siv was mystified. 'Did your husband decide to go to a hotel because there's not enough room here?'

Kay swallowed and sounded evasive. 'It is a bit cramped, and he's allergic to cat hair — starts itching and sneezing when he's around it.' She gestured at the open window. 'The cat's out at the moment.'

Siv tamped down annoyance. She'd wanted to interview the Turtons together. Kay was holding herself rigidly. Something wasn't right here. What kind of couple wouldn't want to stay close in these awful circumstances, despite allergies? She wanted to ask why Kay hadn't gone to the Dovecote with her husband, but the woman was so tense she decided to leave that question for now.

'Would you like tea or coffee?' Kay asked, back to her formal manner.

There was a brittleness to her that Siv imagined might be her usual disposition rather than just the expression of sadness. 'No, thanks. I'd rather get on, if that's OK with you.'

'Fine. When can I go home?'

'Later today, hopefully. I'm sure you want to be back there as soon as possible, and DC Coleman will liaise with you on that. Tell me about your father. What was his job before he retired?'

Kay folded her arms in a V shape across her chest, gripping her shoulders. 'Dad was an actuary with an insurance company. He retired five years ago, but he was an active man, very involved with Berminster Senior Students. Dad was just . . . enthusiastic. Sometimes I reckoned he had more energy than me.' She smiled faintly.

'He lived alone?'

'Yes, since Mum died seven years ago. They . . . he lived in Harfield.'

'We have keys to his home. I'll need to examine it later.'

'Oh, of course.'

Siv shifted in the hard chair, causing it to wheeze like an asthmatic. 'Did you and your sister get on with your dad?'

A longish pause followed, and then Kay said, 'I'd say so, yes. He'd nag Nell about getting a better job, having more ambition in life.'

'What does she do?'

'You'll find it hard to believe after seeing the state of this place, but she's a cleaner. She also has a jewellery stall on the market on Saturdays. She's happy with what she does, but Dad could never understand that, thought Nell was underachieving.' She added hastily, 'But it was just the usual family sparring.'

Siv got the impression it might have gone deeper than that. 'And how about your dad and your husband? Did they get on?'

Kay frowned. 'This seems a bit intrusive, Inspector. What's it got to do with my daughter and my dad being murdered?'

'I'm sorry. I realise that this is difficult. I have to get a picture of your father and his life. It's unlikely that a random stranger committed these murders.'

'There were no problems. My dad hadn't had any quarrels. What kind of maniac kills a little girl? She'd never hurt anyone.'

A large tabby cat had appeared on the window ledge and was gazing at them, sitting perfectly still. Siv stared back at it for a moment, knowing that she'd blink first. 'We'll be speaking to your nanny, Alicia Ferreira. I understand that she's been with you about two years.'

'Yes, since I went back to work. I took a long maternity break.' Kay covered her mouth for a moment, as if pressing grief in. 'I'm glad I did now. Had that time with Lyra.'

'And Alicia has been satisfactory?'

'Absolutely, a godsend. Lyra settled with her very quickly.'
Kay put a hand to her temple. 'Alicia . . . I forgot . . . I suppose
I should contact her.'

'One of my colleagues is getting in touch with her this
morning.' Siv pressed on. 'Who would have been aware that
your dad was at your house yesterday afternoon?'

'Any number of people among his circle. He doted on
Lyra. I expect he chatted about her party and the love . . .
lovely cake.'

'And I suppose you'd have mentioned the party to quite
a few people.'

'Yes. Don't ask me who. I couldn't possibly remember.
There were the parents from nursery and people at work .
. . probably some shops where I bought things. Lambkins,
where Lyra and I went to buy her dress . . . her beautiful,
beautiful dress . . .' Her control was starting to crumble. 'I
can't do any more of this for now. When can I see Lyra? I
want to see her.'

'We'll ensure that you and your husband will see her as
soon as possible.'

'Ryan . . . yes.'

Kay reacted strangely whenever her husband was mentioned, and Siv had noted that she referred to returning home
and seeing her daughter in the singular. There was no mention of *we*, and Siv wanted to probe that.

'And Ryan, I imagine he'd have told people about the
party too?'

'Yes . . . I expect so.' She placed her hands over her eyes.

Siv was unsatisfied, but she'd better ease off this woman
for now. She'd been doubly bereaved. Geordie might be able
to throw some light on the situation when he'd spent more
time with the Turtons.

'DC Coleman will be in touch later this morning about
visiting Lyra and your father,' Siv said. 'Would you like him
to take you to the mortuary?'

'No, no need.'

'Of course. Ryan will be with you.'

41

Kay didn't respond, but got up and headed to the door. 'Thank you for coming,' she said, her grip on herself tightened again.

'Are you sure you're OK here on your own for now?'

'Yes, quite sure.'

Siv stared at the closed door of the flat. What on earth was going on with this woman?

* * *

Kay Turton watched from the front window as the detective walked to her car. She had an eye for good-quality clothing and DI Drummond's dark grey suit was well cut, as was her springy hair. Kay had noted her precise manner and the way she observed the state of Nell's living room with her navy-blue eyes. Just as well she hadn't seen the kitchen or asked to use the bathroom.

Nell was such a slob. Kay could never understand it. Their mother had raised them in a well-kept home, and Kay couldn't abide mess. It was ironic, that Nell spent her working hours cleaning other people's homes and offices, and then returned to this disorder. She suffered with anxiety, had since her teens, and took medication for it. Her moods were variable and you could never predict how you might find her. Kay couldn't help feeling that she used her illness as an excuse for never taking responsibility for anything. Dad had visited Nell here now and again, but he'd always refused to eat, telling Kay he worried he'd catch gastroenteritis or something worse. Once, he'd made the mistake of tidying the kitchen when Nell had popped out for milk and she'd blown up at him, accusing him of interfering. That was the thing about Nell. Most of the time, she was easy-going, mellowed by medication and the weed she smoked — another bone of contention, although they'd stopped trying to reason with her about that ages ago — but when she blew, she blew.

When they'd got back here last night, Nell had rolled a joint as soon as DC Coleman had gone. That was when Ryan had said he couldn't stay in this muck hole and got on the phone to the Dovecote. Nell had smoked and blubbed and smoked, until Kay had slipped away to bed and left her to it.

Kay could smell the dirt in the curtain. A greasy, rancid pong. They'd been hanging there when Nell moved in and had probably been a fixture for numerous tenants. If she couldn't go home today, she'd book a hotel herself. She didn't want to spend another night here. When she got home, she'd have to wash all her things because they stank of weed. DI Drummond had no doubt clocked that distinctive smell.

Kay sat back in the horrible wicker chair and stared hopelessly at the grimy tan carpet. The questions kept tumbling through her brain. How could Lyra not be in the world? What had happened with Dad — had he known the person who did this awful thing? Did he let them into the house or had they come round the back and taken him by surprise? All night, she'd replayed various scenes. Whenever she'd closed her eyes, she'd seen a figure approaching Lyra, casting a shadow on the grass.

How could she be sitting here in this shabby, dingy flat instead of being at work? Today, she should have been overseeing birth and death registrations. Soon, she'd have to arrange for her own father's and Lyra's. There'd be no point asking Nell to do it. She'd forget to provide the correct documents or lose them. And Kay couldn't ask Ryan. Couldn't bear to.

Ryan. She'd better ring him, tell him about the DI's visit and the excuse she'd given.

Ryan. What would happen now? It would have been better if she'd never told him the truth, but the weight of what she'd discovered had finally been too much. She could have left well alone, instead of allowing her niggling anxiety to make her seek verification and then unburden herself. Trouble was, she hadn't been able to deal with the fear that, one day, Ryan might somehow find out, couldn't bear the anxiety of waiting for that day to happen. Now, something had been broken and it was unlikely to be mended.

She should call him, but it seemed an impossible task. She had no energy and he'd offer little comfort. Closing her eyes, she saw Lyra, lying like the sleeping beauty in her pretty dress. In Lambkins, Lyra had spread her arms and swayed with pleasure in front of the dressing-room mirror. She'd needed clothes for five-, sometimes six-year-olds, but luckily, they'd had the dress she longed for in a big enough size. When they'd hung it up at home, she'd attempted to count the sequins.

Lyra. Sorrow overwhelmed Kay. Tears spilled down her cheeks and turned into racking sobs.

CHAPTER 5

Patrick was in the office of Brendan Deeley, the manager at the catering company, Cavendish Treats. He tweeted while he waited to speak to him:

> @DCBerminsterPolice
> *We are seeking information about the murders of Thomas Pullman and his granddaughter, Lyra Turton, in a house on Cove Parade yesterday afternoon. If you saw anything unusual, or can provide any detail that might help us, please contact the station. We always need your help to fight crime and bring criminals to justice. #keepingberminstersafe*

Patrick's tweets were popular in the town and had produced some useful responses. He lived in hope that one day he'd get that snippet of info that broke a murder case. That would impress the guv. He scanned the news and saw that the two deaths had been widely reported. The *Berminster Herald*'s headline was *LITTLE LYRA BRUTALLY MURDERED ON HER BIRTHDAY*. There was a photo of Mr Pullman, taken from the Berminster Senior Students website. He'd hosted the evening talk that Patrick had attended. Patrick recalled a friendly handshake, and admiring Mr Pullman's outfit of a denim shirt, red woven tie and olive chinos. He'd envied his Apple Watch. When he'd commented on it, Mr Pullman had said it came in very handy for checking his blood pressure and heart rate. He'd added wryly, 'Time isn't so important as you get older — you realise it's flying — but monitoring your vital signs is crucial.'

Deeley hurried into the cluttered office. A bustling, friendly man.

'Sorry to keep you waiting, DC Hill. We had a problem with an order, but all sorted now. I'm terribly shocked by these murders. Such a young child. Dreadful. How are the family coping?'

A daft question, but the kind of thing people came out with for something to say. 'It's a distressing time for them. I'd like to speak to the person who delivered the party order while I'm here.'

'That's Drew Gifford. He's out on deliveries, but on his way back. I've asked him to come to the office as soon as he's here.'

'Thanks. In the meantime, when did Ms Turton place the order with you?'

Deeley turned to his computer. 'I have it here. She did it online, on the twentieth of March. We have a number of children's party menus and she chose menu five, which includes dairy-and-gluten-free options. She didn't need a cake. We agreed delivery for two o'clock yesterday, eighteenth of April. She paid eighty pounds. Mr Pullman, the deceased gentleman, signed to confirm delivery.'

'Thanks. Signed electronically?'

'Yes, on one of those handheld gizmos.'

'Presumably, Drew Gifford was making other calls yesterday afternoon?'

'That's right, he had about six deliveries in all.'

'And they all had to be signed for?'

'Always.'

'I'd like you to email me records of the deliveries and signatures.'

Deeley was put out. 'Why d'you want those?'

'Part of our process.'

'Well, if that's the case. Here's Drew now. Do you need me? It's just that I've plenty to see to.'

'That's fine, you can get on.' Patrick moved around to Deeley's side of the desk as he exited, leaving his chair for Drew Gifford.

'I can't believe that old guy's dead. He tipped me a fiver.' Gifford was panting slightly. He was in his early twenties, with sharp features and a green-and-blue snake tattoo at the left side of his neck. He wore jeans that drooped from his skinny backside and a white T-shirt with the logo *Cavendish Treats* in red.

Patrick watched the snake ripple as Gifford moved his head. He liked tattoos but had never plucked up the courage to have one, and Kitty abhorred them, saying they were self-harm, so his opportunity had vanished. He intended to hang on to Kitty.

He said, 'Tom Pullman was his name. That was generous of him.'

'Yeah. Ever so sad, what's happened. Poor little tot. Lyra was her name, that right? I saw a banner, sure it said Lyra.'

'Mr Gifford, what time did you deliver the food yesterday?'

'Just gone two. About five past. Mr Pullman offered to help me carry it in, but I said no, 'cos it's all part of the service. And I learned the hard way when I started here. I was delivering a load for a party of fifty and this woman started to help me. She tripped and spilled a box of goodies and then blamed me for getting in her way — asked for a refund. I was gutted. Brendan warned me not to accept help in future. Best to keep it simple. I don't always listen to him when he's droning on, but that was a handy tip.' He puffed his cheeks out and wiped his forehead. 'It's been a busy day today and it's only half eleven!'

'Were there any other vehicles there when you arrived at the house?'

Gifford crackled with energy. Patrick was sometimes accused of being restless — the guv told him off for drumming his fingers — but Gifford was dead jittery.

'Yeah, a grey car, parked in front of the garage.'

'You took the food through the front door?'

'That's right. I rang the bell and the old guy answered. He showed me where he wanted the stuff set out, on the kitchen table. Then I carried the cool boxes through and unpacked it. He said to leave the cling film on, and he'd uncover the plates just before the party was due to start. There was a gorgeous cake on the table, very classy.' He added with a grin, 'Much better than anything we provide, but don't tell Brendan I said that. One of those ones where it's a pity it's going to be cut.'

Patrick seized on that last remark. 'The cake was definitely whole?'

'Course. They'd have been cutting it for the kid, wouldn't they? Blowing out the candles and all that, making a wish. I used to love that bit when I was little. I usually wished for super powers. Fat chance!'

Patrick silently agreed that Gifford bore little resemblance to a superhero. 'Did you see anyone else there?'

'Just the old bloke.'

'How did he seem to you?'

Gifford scratched his chin. 'Fine. Tasty house, nicely dressed man, very polite. Not like some customers, who hardly smile. When he saw the food, he said something about kids' parties being an industry these days, and I told him I wasn't going to knock it, it was good for our business. He laughed at that, said something about that's how the world turns.'

'How long were you there for?'

'Ten minutes max. It wasn't a huge order. I put it on the table, the gent signed for it, gave me a fiver and I headed off.'

'Did you see anyone else around?'

'Nope. It was a quiet time of day. Did all that food go to waste?'

Patrick was surprised by the question but supposed it was reasonable enough. 'No, it was donated to charity.'

'That's good. I mean, it would be a terrible shame if it had just been chucked. Did . . . did the little kid get to have any of the cake?'

'I can't comment on that,' Patrick said.

'Oh, right. Just . . . well, it's sad. Great grub and everything. Gives me the willies, thinking that I was there and then afterwards someone killed them.'

'Did you notice if the back doors to the garden were open?'

Gifford ran a finger up and down his tattoo and squinted past Patrick. 'Oh, now you're asking. Not sure. I didn't notice that they were. Were they murdered in the garden, then?'

'Where were you for the rest of the afternoon, when you'd finished delivering to Cove Parade?'

'I had four other deliveries, two in town, one in Aldmarsh and one near Cliffdean Point. I got back here just before five with the van and signed off for the day. I was well knackered.'

'Thanks for your help, Mr Gifford. We'd like your fingerprints, as part of the investigation. Is it OK if we arrange that with you?'

'Yeah, no problem.'

Patrick watched Gifford dart away, his jeans sliding down over striped underpants. He'd asked quite a few questions of his own. Maybe he was just a nosy parker, or did it signify a weird interest in what had happened?

* * *

Siv parked at the back of the Dovecote hotel. It was near the centre of town, just off the high street and dated from the sixteenth century, when it had been a coaching inn. Her father had once bought her lunch here when she'd visited him. She'd been at police college at the time, and the prospect of a good meal had been appealing. The food had been plentiful but mediocre, with tough meat and canned vegetables. Just up her father's street, though — he'd loved plain fare and had a particular passion for tinned mushrooms. Siv recalled that they'd eaten in pleasant, traditional surroundings. Although her dad hadn't been hard up, he'd liked the Dovecote because it did a pensioner special on Mondays and Fridays — two courses for a tenner. She recalled also the brief conversation they'd had about Mutsi during the meal.

'I'm aware that your mother keeps in touch with you,' her father had said in his mild voice. 'She emailed me recently, asking me to return an oil lamp that she says belonged to her grandmother. A Finnish antique, apparently. I've no memory of it and I certainly don't have it. She was annoyed when I told her this, and appears to believe that I'm holding onto it out of spite. If that were the case, it would indeed be mean.'

Her father had worn his usual bemused expression when speaking of his ex-wife. He was the least vindictive person Siv had ever come across.

'Why does she suspect that you've got it?'

'Search me. I only told you because your mum might accuse me. She has popped up now and again, over the years, alleging some misdemeanour on my part.'

Siv had wanted to say, *That's probably when she's been bored, between men and casting around to create some interest*, but she'd bitten back the words. Her sister Rik wouldn't have hesitated.

Her father had asked, 'You or Rik haven't got it, I suppose?'

'I haven't, and I can't imagine that Rik would have taken it all the way to Auckland.' Rik was two years older than Siv. She'd moved to the far side of the world — mainly, Siv reckoned, to put thousands of miles between her and Mutsi.

After that lunch, she'd been cross. Her parents had been divorced for years, yet Mutsi still wanted to pester the man she'd left when Siv was two. She'd danced into his life (literally — she'd travelled from her home in Finland to perform in a travelling production of *Hair*) and then pirouetted away again when she'd tired of him. She'd taken Rik and Siv with her and led them into a haphazard existence, with many changes of address and men friends, until she'd lined up a Finnish baronet to marry who disliked children. Just before her nuptials, Mutsi had put her daughters on the train to their father in Berminster before legging it to Helsinki.

Siv headed through the hotel foyer. She'd phoned Ryan Turton and asked him to meet her in the coffee lounge on the ground floor. He was the only person in there and stood as he saw her walk towards him.

'DI Drummond? I got you a coffee, I hope that's OK.' He extended his hand. 'You might be one of those people who only drink herbal stuff, decaff or whatever. The biscuits are chocolate and digestives.'

'Thank you. Regular coffee is fine.' The tray was on the table, the coffee in small white cups with a jug of milk, a bowl of sugar crystals and a plate of biscuits.

'Oh, that's good. Glad to have got it right. Dietary choices can be a minefield. I had to arrange lunch for a colleague last week who's wheat, nut and lactose intolerant. That was a challenge.'

Siv studied him. Why was he going on about food when his daughter was dead? Nerves maybe, but there was no sign of a tear. He was behaving as if they were acquaintances meeting for a chat. Perhaps he was trying to control the interview by playing the host. He was in his thirties, medium height and trim, with feathery brown hair, a big jaw and a long, straight nose. Confident voice and manner. His dark business suit was pristine. The top button of his shirt was undone, his tie slightly loosened. He didn't appear sleep-deprived or distressed.

'I'm very sorry about Lyra and your father-in-law,' Siv said.

'Yes. Thank you. It's appalling, a terrible shock. I haven't really taken it in yet.'

'I need to ask you some questions. I'm aware that this is difficult for you.'

'No problem, I understand. You have a job to do, Inspector.'

'Why are you here?'

'Pardon?'

'Staying in this hotel.'

'Oh, I see. Well . . . I'm allergic to Nell's cat and it's pretty cramped at her flat. Being around any cat makes me sneeze and cough.' He shrugged. 'Nell doesn't overuse her vacuum cleaner. I expect you realised that when you were there, talking to Kay.'

Siv added milk to her coffee and sipped. Not bad. 'What time did you get home last night?'

'Just after eight. I left as soon as Kay rang me with the awful news. There was an accident and heavy traffic.' He rummaged through his hair, so that it stuck out on one side. 'I drove Kay to Nell's. The family liaison guy came along too, although we didn't need him. More of a hindrance then a help. After he'd gone I booked in here.'

'For how long?'

'Oh — two nights for now. I wasn't sure when we'd get back home.'

A waitress hovered near them. Siv frowned at her and she sidled away.

'Talk me through where you were yesterday.'

'I'd based myself in a hotel on the outskirts of Canterbury. I travelled up there early on Wednesday. I'm an agricultural engineer and I was visiting several landowners, advising them on issues such as sustainable land use. I was at the last of my appointments when Kay phoned me. I started straight back. I can barely remember the journey, I was so upset.'

How come your words don't match your manner? 'You didn't want to be around for Lyra's party?'

He spread his hands out. 'I'd have loved to be there, but I had to attend these very lucrative appointments. I'm self-employed, so I have to take the work when it comes my way.' There was a tremor in his voice now. 'I'd told Lyra that I'd have cake with her when I got back. She said we'd sit in the playhouse, but I laughed that I wasn't sure I could squeeze in there.' He sank back and bit the side of his thumb.

'Are you OK?'

'Yes. Carry on.'

'Do you travel a lot for your work?'

'Frequently. I was in Scotland last month.'

'How did you get on with Mr Pullman?'

He paused for a few beats. 'He was a kind man. Busy with his own life, but always ready to lend a hand. He'd babysit sometimes. Lyra was mad about him, and vice-versa.'

'How about Nell — did she babysit?'

Turton's pose stiffened. 'Rarely. I didn't want her spending time on her own with Lyra.' He picked up a biscuit, examined it and put it back.

'Because of her weed habit?'

'Exactly. Kay and I agreed on that. Not that Nell was rushing to offer her services, you understand.'

'Does Nell cause problems in the family?'

He sounded evasive. 'You'll have got an idea of her life-style. She's a nice enough woman, just a bit of a mess.' He ruffled his fingers through his hair again.

'She seemed very upset last night.'

'She loved her dad and Lyra, even if there were occasional differences of opinion. Families are like that, with ups and downs. Would you like more coffee?'

'No thanks. Tell me about the differences of opinion.'

'Nell can be short-tempered. She and her dad fell out sometimes when he criticised her lifestyle. Nell didn't take kindly to that.'

'Did these fallings out last for long?'

'Don't ask me. I stayed well out of it. So did Kay. She'd like Nell to make more of herself, but I reckon she gave up on trying to offer her any advice a long time ago.'

'What time are you meeting your wife?'

'Some time this afternoon.'

Siv sat forward. 'Mr Turton, it strikes me as a bit odd that Kay didn't book in here with you. Grieving parents would usually want to be together and console each other.'

Some emotion fleetingly crossed his face. Siv couldn't tell if it was annoyance or sadness.

He half-smiled. 'Of course, I get what you're saying. Nell was distraught last night when we got to her place. Couldn't stop crying. She's not the strongest of people emotionally. Kay felt she should stay with her, given the circumstances.'

'I see.' Siv put her cup on the tray. It was a peculiar choice, to stay with her sister, rather than her child's father.

'Inspector, have you any idea who could have done this? It seems as if nothing was taken from the house. Is there some lunatic roaming around?'

'I can't say, Mr Turton. I promise you that we'll do all we can to find the perpetrator. Had Mr Pullman mentioned any problems to you?'

'No. I last saw him a couple of weeks ago when he came for Sunday lunch. He didn't refer to anything worrying him.'

Turton hadn't asked if Lyra had suffered or when they could see her, Siv noted, or pressed her about when he could go home.

'DC Coleman will inform you and your wife as soon as you can visit Lyra at the mortuary, later today. Kay has asked about that several times.'

'Thank you. We understand that you have your procedures.'

Siv was trying to comprehend Turton's emotional register. Kay came across as formal and keeping herself controlled, but her suffering flooded through her defences. Her husband was oddly detached.

She watched his face and emphasised, 'It's hard to see loved ones in these circumstances, but it's important, most people find it crucial, and a comfort, even if that sounds strange.'

'I appreciate that.'

'We'll need your fingerprints, to eliminate them from those found in the house, and the details of your hotel and appointments in Canterbury.'

'No problem. I'll do whatever I can to help. This is so appalling, so shocking. Please, catch this person before they damage anyone else.'

Siv had the impression that he'd suddenly remembered to show some emotion. 'We will, Mr Turton. I'll be in touch again after the post-mortem.'

He stood and shook her hand again, then turned to his phone as she left. She had no idea what to make of him.

* * *

Ali and Alicia Ferreira were struggling to understand each other. They both spoke rapidly, she with a pronounced Spanish inflection, he with his Derry accent. After a couple of misunderstandings, they were both smiling.

'Whoa,' Ali said. 'Let's back up here and both talk more slowly.'

Alicia put her thumb up. 'OK.' She had a strong face and body, large glasses and short black hair. Her eyes were red from crying.

'Right, so, let's see now. When did you start taking care of wee Lyra?'

'I start September, two years now. Four days a week. Not Thursday, because I go to Rother College.' *Rothaire,* she pronounced it.

'Were you with Lyra morning and evening?'

'No. In mornings, her mother took her to nursery breakfast club. So I pick her up from nursery at three and take her home, stay until half five or six, when Kay came back.' Alicia twisted the pendant at her neck. 'Little Lyra. She so excited about her party. I teach her happy birthday in Spanish: *feliz cumpleaños.* Did she . . . have pain?'

'Probably not.'

'That is some small thing.'

'Were you happy, working for the Turtons?'

'Yes, happy. Kay is nice woman. I not often see Ryan — he is working, not home before I leave.'

'When you did see him, was he friendly?'

'Always polite to me, yes.'

'How did you find Lyra?'

'She is lovely, very imagination and always so busy. A clever *niña pequeña* . . . little child.'

'In Derry we say, *wee wain,*' Ali told her.

Alicia repeated this and said, 'Is like another kind of English!'

'Aye, you're right there.'

'*Wee wain*,' Alicia said again, as if storing the words.

'Was there anything different about Lyra recently, or was she her usual self?'

'She was so excited by the party, talk about it all the time.' Alicia tucked a strand of hair behind an ear. 'Lyra always . . . that expression . . . *full of beans* . . . but not quite herself around January. A bit quiet, suddenly for a couple of days. I tell Kay.'

'What did her mum say?'

'She say Lyra had a tummy thing, made her a bit tired.'

'And Lyra got better?'

'Yes. She cheered up. Her mum bought her new trike.'

'So,' Ali asked, 'you didn't notice that the Turtons had any problems?'

'No problems. They work very hard, have lovely house.'

'Did anyone come to the house recently while you were there? Anyone you found odd or suspicious?'

'Suspicious . . . ah yes, I see. No one come to house. Just a parcel last week. Lyra's party things. Only me and Lyra after school. We play and I make her a snack — fruit and nuts, maybe some cheese or yogurt.'

Ali nodded. *Sounds like the diet I should follow.* 'Did you meet Mr Pullman, Kay's father?'

'A couple of times. Nice man, and Lyra talk about him. She call him Poppa. She love him very much.'

A man opened the door and hesitated. 'Oh, hi — sorry, I didn't realise you were still in here.'

'Almost finished', Ali told him. 'And you are?'

'Vince Naish.'

'My boyfriend,' Alicia added.

'Sorry for interrupting. See you soon, then,' Naish said to Alicia and vanished.

'Do you live here together?' Ali asked.

'No, Vince has own flat. I share house with three other students at college.'

'It's the neatest student house I've ever been in.' It was clean, newly painted and well furnished, with none of the usual dirty crockery, strange smells and signs of neglect.

'My rules,' Alicia said firmly. 'I not want to live in pig home.'

'Pig *sty*,' Ali offered. He recalled Meg Sterling's and the guv's comments about Ryan Turton. 'Have you ever noticed that there were any problems in the Turton marriage?'

She seemed uneasy. 'The marriage? No — but I not often see them together as a couple. Ryan always at work.'

'You're sure?'

'I only see Kay, like I say before.'

'And how about Nell Pullman, Kay's sister?'

'I see her there sometimes. Not often. She always eating when she came round and opening wine. Kay grumbled that Nell cleared out the fridge, help herself without asking.'

'Did Nell get on with Lyra?'

'Yes. A bit . . . how you say . . . rough with her sometimes, swinging her around, throwing her in the air.'

'Did that upset Lyra?'

'No, she like it, but Kay tell Nell to stop.'

'Just to check with you — were you at Rother College yesterday afternoon?'

'Yes, I had math and English classes. The math lecture at four was cancelled, because tutor was ill, so I went to library.'

'What time were you there until?'

'About five thirty.' Alicia sighed. 'Was a wonderful job, in a beautiful house. Such a pleasure to go there. I have to get new work now.'

'Are there many opportunities for nannies around here?'

'Not so much. Maybe I have luck. Is hard. I so fond of Lyra, so fond. Hard to move to another child. She couldn't say Alicia, called me Lissy. So affectionate, always kiss me goodbye.' Alicia teared up. 'Poor Kay and Ryan. How can they bear this?'

Vince joined her as she showed Ali out. They stood at the front door, his arm around her waist, waving him goodbye, the way his parents always did on the step of their farmhouse.

CHAPTER 6

Siv accepted a barley sugar from Rey Anand when they were
seated in his office. She had worked with the pathologist for a
while and knew by now that he always offered sweets in there.
He was of the opinion that people needed sugar and comfort
in his palace of death. Siv appreciated his courteous, direct
approach to his work, and he understood that she'd rather
not watch corpses being cut open. She just needed the details.

Rey pushed his rimless glasses up his nose. 'I'll start with
Mr Pullman. He was a healthy man for his age, with the usual
signs of wear and tear, and would undoubtedly have lived a
good deal longer if permitted. The iron griddle was the weapon
used to kill him. He was standing near the cooker and died
where he fell, almost instantly. Just one blow to the head
caused an intracranial haemorrhage and extensive bleeding.'

'Did you note any signs of a struggle or other injuries
on his body?'

'No. I'd say that Mr Pullman wasn't expecting the attack
and had no time to defend himself. Turning to the little
girl, she was suffocated with the cushion her head was on,
so her murderer placed it beneath her when she was dead.
Judging by the position of her body, I'd suggest that she
died in the playhouse. The rug was slightly ruffled beneath

her, indicating that she twisted and squirmed a little. There was no sexual activity or other marks on her body, and she was well nourished. However, I did find evidence of chlorphenamine during a blood analysis. It's a sedative, found in some cold remedies and antihistamines.'

'So it's worth checking if Lyra had allergies or if she'd had a cold. Her father's allergic to cats, so maybe she suffered similarly.'

Rey inclined his head. 'You need to ask those questions.'

'No one has mentioned that she seemed sluggish, and her mother said that she was up early yesterday, playing in the garden.'

'It would depend on when she'd been given the medication. If it was a child dosage and at night, then she'd probably have been OK in the morning. That's all I have for you. Some sweets to take away with you?'

'I'll have two, I'm meeting Patrick.' Steve's team had finished at Mr Pullman's home so they were going to check it out.

'Just as well it's not Ali — you wouldn't want to tempt him with sugary treats. How is he?'

'A lot better, but waging his daily struggle with his appetite.'

'He lives to eat.' Rey smiled.

Back in her car, Siv checked Mr Pullman's address. Harfield was a small village a couple of miles from Berminster. As she started her engine, she saw a car parking outside the morgue, with Ryan Turton driving. She watched as he and Kay got out and walked to the entrance. Both were stony-faced. They didn't speak or touch. No hand-holding or reassuring gestures before they vanished inside, and no sign of Geordie Coleman.

She rang Geordie and explained that she'd just seen the Turtons at the morgue.

'I went to Ms Pullman's flat early afternoon to confirm arrangements. Ryan Turton arrived at the same time as me,' Geordie told her. 'I asked if they wanted me to accompany them to the viewings, but they said no. He was brusque, rude almost.'

'After you left them last night, he booked into the Dovecote hotel.'

'You what? He left his wife?'

'Yep. Because he's allergic to Nell's cat, apparently. There's something about the Turtons that doesn't figure. I'd like you to visit them as soon as they return home, spend some time there, see what you make of them.'

'Will do. Am I after anything in particular?'

'General impressions of the marriage and family dynamics.'

'I'll do my best.'

Siv ended the call and headed to Harfield. The country lanes were budding with hawthorn and cherry blossom. The sun was warm in the kind of sky that children draw, pure white fluffy clouds against an intense blue. Like the sky that Lyra had crayoned in the picture she'd left on her bedroom floor.

Siv opened her window, breathed in the spring scents. If she had the energy later, she'd walk by the river when she got home. And tonight, she promised herself, she wouldn't have a glass of akvavit. It was too much of an evening routine and on too many mornings she had a dull head. She didn't live to drink, as Ali lived to eat, but she was too fond of the comfort offered by the bottles with the blue fish label. The habit had developed after Ed's death, and since moving back to Berminster and this job, she'd used the spirit to ease the ache of grief and the pressures of the days. Her custom when she got home to her wagon was to light the wood burner, change into Ed's sweatshirt, pour the first glass of akvavit and microwave a meal. *Things have to change*, she told herself. *Put Ed's sweatshirt away and have a drink every other night.* She waited to hear if Ed would comment, but no response. He used to whisper back to her frequently in the first year after his death, but rarely these days. She decided she'd take his silence as consent.

Patrick was waiting when she arrived at Tom Pullman's home, a detached cottage on a quiet lane. He stood at the gate in his narrow-cut suit, thumbs flying on his phone screen. No doubt updating his Twitter feed. He resembled a teenager with his gawky, angular body and spiky hair. Some women had a sixth sense that his mum had died, and they liked to mother him and make a fuss.

Siv unlocked the front door. The stairs led up from the centre of the house, with rooms off to either side. She asked Patrick to check upstairs. 'And look in the bathroom, just in case there's a child's medication containing chlorphenamine.' She explained about the sedative in Lyra's body.

'Grandad might have been keeping her quiet?'

'It's a possibility. Lyra might have played him up and been a little madam with him.'

Turning to her left, she entered a spacious kitchen. It was homely and neat, with herbs on the window ledge and a shopping list on the pine table in a flowing hand. A boxed cheese-and-onion pie sat on the draining board. Siv guessed that Tom Pullman had taken it out to defrost for an evening meal he'd never eat. The living room was equally tidy, a vase of carnations on the coffee table beside a TV guide. Pullman had circled programmes — a Danish thriller, an antiques show, a film review. Siv had always been saddened by these little markers of a life abruptly ended, and even more so since Ed's death. She'd left his can of shaving cream in the bathroom for months after he'd gone.

'Guv! Come and see this!'

She ran upstairs and found Patrick in Pullman's study. It was lined with crammed bookshelves. A laptop stood on a handsome walnut desk, with a printer beside it.

Patrick handed Siv a sheet of paper. 'This unsigned letter was in the printer.'

She scanned it quickly:

Dear Belinda,

I have decided to write to you. I expect it will strike you as old-fashioned, but I prefer to express myself in this way.

I hope you appreciate that being the chair of BSS is a responsible, indeed occasionally onerous task, but one that I derive great satisfaction from and carry out to the best of my ability.

We are a thriving organisation with an enthusiastic membership and new groups forming all the time. It is disappointing that you choose to challenge and block so many items that I put forward at committee meetings. This has got to a point where you are embarrassing yourself and others, even though sadly, you can't see it.

I can't help but worry that your motives are personal and that you're trying to make my role difficult. I'm sorry that you need to express yourself in this fashion. Surely, as an adult, you can accept and move on from past events, as I am trying to do. I have accepted your part in those with good grace and it would be helpful if you could respond in kind. You must see that this is not the way to behave, especially when you encourage others to follow your lead. Frankly, it is immature.

I do hope that you can see sense.

With best wishes.

Tom

'Patronising or what?' Patrick said.

'And angry. I wonder if he sent a copy? Hardly the way to get this Belinda on side. A bit self-important, wasn't he?'

'Seems so. He didn't come across that way when I met him, but I suppose that was his public face.' Patrick flicked the top of the page. 'Does it mean Pullman and this Belinda had been an item?'

'Could be. We need to talk to Belinda, whoever she is. Anything else up here?'

'No, guv. I went through the filing cabinet and drawers. Just aspirin and a tube of haemorrhoid ointment in the bathroom cabinet. Nothing for kids.'

Siv placed the letter in an evidence bag. 'Pack up the laptop and we'll get it to the lab. Let's head back to the station and catch up on the day.'

On the way back to Berminster, Siv kept dwelling on the Turtons and the apparent distance between them. An idea occurred to her. She pulled in, found the number of the Dovecote hotel and spoke to reception for a couple of minutes. Then she drove on, persuaded that all was not well with that marriage.

Back in her office, Siv checked the BSS website and her emails. Steve had forwarded an initial forensics report and alerted her that his team had finished at the Turtons' house, so they could go home now. She emailed Geordie with the update and rang Kay Turton, crossing to the window, from where she had a view of the museum and theatre. The trees across the road had sprung into life, green and leafy.

'I'm sorry to bother you after you've been to see Lyra and your dad.'

'Yes. Lyra looked . . . asleep,' Kay muttered.

'You can go home now, whenever you like.'

'That's a relief.'

'I can discuss the post-mortem with you, but I'd rather do that in person. I'd like to meet you and your husband at home tomorrow morning. Together, please. I can reassure you that Lyra wasn't molested.'

There was silence and then Kay breathed, 'Thank goodness.'

'Ms Turton, did Lyra suffer with allergies?'

'No.'

'Had she had a cold recently?'

'Lyra was fine, she hadn't been unwell. Why?'

'Just a detail. I'll discuss it in the morning. Can we say ten o'clock?'

Siv stood and watched the museum closing for the night, its heavy oak panelled doors slamming shut. She was scheduled to attend the opening of an exhibition there soon. The museum manager had discovered that she was a skilled origamist, and had commissioned her to make a collection of origami sculptures of boats and ships for a new history of sailing and fishing in the town. She hoped she wouldn't have to miss the opening, even if she could make only a brief appearance.

She fetched a coffee and sat by the incident board with Ali and Patrick, where she ran through Steve's forensics report.

'There were no blood traces anywhere else in the Turtons' house, just the kitchen. The fingerprints found have matched the Turtons, Lyra, Pullman and Nell. One set unaccounted for, but I assume they'll prove to be the delivery driver's. Only Kay and Ryan Turton's were on the griddle pan, so whoever wielded it wore gloves. Nothing of note in Pullman's car. Very tidy, just a copy of the *Daily Telegraph* on the passenger seat.' Siv took a drink of coffee and gave feedback from the post-mortem. 'The placement of the cushion under Lyra's head after smothering her makes me wonder if our killer felt some regret, guilt or affection.' She filled Ali in on the chlorphenamine in Lyra's body. 'Her grandad doesn't appear to have been doping her. Kay Turton has just told me that Lyra didn't have a cold or allergies, so it's strange that she should have been medicated. I didn't pursue it further for now, but I'm seeing them in the morning. There is something peculiar about the Turtons as a couple and in his reactions to his daughter's death. I'd say more than can be attributed to shock and grief. The marriage seems at best semi-detached. Turton stayed away in Canterbury overnight for work, yet it's only an hour or so's drive from here. I checked with the Dovecote hotel. They informed me that he's stayed there before recently, for three nights in January and two at the beginning of March. So, for some reason, Turton has needed to get away from his family.'

Ali raised a finger. 'The nanny, Alicia, told me that Lyra was a bit quiet in January. Her mum said it was a tummy bug. According to Alicia, Nell Pullman freeloaded on food and wine when she visited, which annoyed Kay, and she played a bit rough with Lyra. The wee girl didn't mind, but her mum did. Otherwise, Alicia didn't mention anything of note and seemed to have been very fond of Lyra. But she wasn't quite happy when I asked her if the Turtons seemed OK together.'

'There's something going on there,' Siv said. 'I've asked Geordie to visit them and see what he can tease out.'

'Aye, I did wonder if it's the old cliché that Turton and the nanny had a thing going,' Ali commented. 'Regarding Thursday afternoon, Alicia was at Rother College, but difficult to verify that from late afternoon. I checked that her maths lecture at four was cancelled, as she said. She told me she was in the library until five thirty.'

Siv mused, 'Ryan and the nanny meeting at the hotel? Possibly, although they said it was a single booking. Double-check that, please. Anything from Pullman's phone?'

'So far, nothing of note,' Ali said. 'Phone calls and texts to family and some emails to Harry Hudson, who's the news-letter editor of Berminster Senior Students. He didn't make or receive any calls on Thursday.'

Siv showed him the letter they'd found at Pullman's house. 'The BSS website says that Belinda Hanak is the group coordinator. There was clearly a problem between her and Pullman. It's the only hint we have so far of him falling out with anyone. Patrick, how did you get on with your tasks?'

Patrick smoothed his skinny knitted tie. 'Drew Gifford was the guy who delivered the party food. He didn't see any-thing unusual. He arrived at just gone two and was there for about ten minutes. Gifford had other deliveries that after-noon, and I've requested records of those to check his where-abouts. Nell Pullman doesn't come up on our database, so her weed habit has never got her into trouble.'

Siv stretched. 'Nell seems to be the thorn in the family's side. She argued with her dad, according to Ryan Turton.'

'And she gets on Kay's nerves,' Ali added.

'These murders show every sign of being personal and they must start with Pullman,' Siv said. 'Nothing was taken from the house. Quite a few people would have heard about the party. It's hard to gauge how many would have been aware that Tom Pullman was going to be at the house at that time. We focus on the family and Pullman's network for now. Ali, we'll go and see Nell Pullman this evening and we'll visit the Turtons in the morning. Patrick, can you verify Kay and Ryan Turton's whereabouts yesterday afternoon as well as this Gifford guy? Contact Harry Hudson at BSS too, see what he has to say about Pullman.' She turned to Ali. 'Got any bananas in your stash? I need something to keep me going. And make sure you eat too — I don't want any more emergency dashes to hospital.'

* * *

Ali gestured at the clump-filled cat litter tray outside Nell Pullman's flat. 'That's minging. Did you say she's a cleaner?'

'Yes, but only for other people,' Siv said.

Nell had been eating a bowl of soup in the living room when they arrived. It smelled meaty and created quite a pungent brew with the lingering weed. A clothes airer draped with drying underwear stood by the window. Ali's wicker chair sounded as if it might collapse when he sat down and he put his hands on the sides, testing it. Nell wore tracksuit bottoms and a T-shirt with the logo *I may be wrong but it's highly unlikely*. She had a dreamy, vacant air, suggesting that she'd smoked a joint recently.

'Kay's gone home,' she said in her deep, lazy voice. 'Left me a note. I shouldn't have gone to work today, couldn't concentrate.'

'Aye, grief does that, but the weed has that effect too,' Ali told her.

Nell shrugged and sighed. 'I was wondering how quickly that would get a mention. I suffer with anxiety, see. Really bad sometimes, sort of freezes me and I get panicky. Now with Dad and Lyra gone, I've been getting the shakes. Weed takes the edge off. Lots of scientific studies prove that, you only have to google it.'

Siv decided to get this subject out of the way. 'Cannabis is a class B drug and illegal, unless prescribed by a specialist doctor. I recommend that you get rid of any that you have. However, we're here about your dad and Lyra.'

Nell rubbed her face. 'Got any suspects?'

Siv replied, 'Maybe you can help us with that.'

'Me? Not sure how. Do my best.' She took a hank of her long hair and started to plait it.

'How often did you see your father?' Siv asked.

'Wednesday mornings, when I cleaned for him. Other than that, now and again.'

'You were his paid cleaner?'

'Yeah. And Kay's. I do her place on Fridays. Reliable customers.'

Siv continued, 'So you last saw your dad on Wednesday morning?'

'Yeah. I did ten to eleven thirty, as usual. Dad was out in the garden most of the time, pottering about. Suited me. I prefer to get on with the job.'

'How was he?'

'His usual self. Mentioned Lyra's party. We didn't chat much. That was a relief.'

'Why do you say that?'

'Meant Dad didn't get a chance to nag me about improving my life, going to college, getting some qualifications instead of hoovering carpets. "Raising your sights" was one of his favourite phrases. Wish I had a tenner for every time I heard him come out with that old chestnut.'

'Parents can really annoy their children by worrying about them,' Siv said.

Nell laughed. 'I've never wanted to go to college or raise my sights. I'm happy with my life the way it is. It's ordinary and probably looks dead boring from the outside, but it's what I can cope with. I like my cleaning jobs and I like this flat — it suits me and it's my comfort zone. I make a bit of extra money on my market stall and it's fun. I don't aspire to the detached residence by the sea. Dad just couldn't get that at all. See, I was a disappointment to him, but I'm not to myself.'

That was a lot of self-justification for someone who claimed not to care. Siv raised an eyebrow at Ali.

He said, 'Sounds like there was friction between you.'

'Sometimes. I tried to tell him about the anxiety, how it's an illness, but he didn't take it seriously. Thought I was self-indulgent, lacking backbone.' She sniggered. 'Mostly, I didn't pay him much attention. He was just an old fogey, limited in his world view. Liked the sound of his own voice. Kay was willing to listen to him, unlike me. But I'd give anything to have him bore the pants off me now and wind me up. Never expected I'd say that.' Nell abandoned the plait and left it hanging. She asked Ali, 'Do you do your own cornrows? Do they take ages? I love them, so neat and sort of geometric.'

'Thanks,' he said. 'Were you planning to be at Lyra's party?'

'No, I was working until sixish. I was going to call in later with her prez. I couldn't afford that much. I got her a little birdhouse.' She welled up. 'Can't believe they've both gone. Me and Dad got on each other's nerves, but I'll miss the hassle now.'

'Aye, it's hard,' Ali said sympathetically. 'Your dad hadn't mentioned any problems, then?'

'No. Dad was one of life's ironers.'

'Meaning?'

'He ironed things out as he went along.' She made a smoothing motion.

Ali gripped the chair as he shifted. 'Do you know a woman called Belinda Hanak? She's in Berminster Senior Students.'

'No. I've only come across one of those oldies, Jill Bartoli. I clean for her on Mondays. Dad got me the gig. He did loads for BSS. He loved committees and stuff like that. Dead tedious, if you ask me.' She smiled absently.

Ali asked, 'When you were cleaning upstairs at your dad's on Wednesday, did you see a letter in the printer on his desk?'

Her response was surprisingly quick, given her general lethargy. 'I didn't do upstairs this week. I do that every other week and Dad saw to his own bedding.'

'Are your sister and her husband happy?' Siv asked.

'Seemed to be, until this crap happened. What's not to be happy about? They bought a lovely big house by the sea with a huge garden and all that. Living the middle-class dream . . .' She selected another strand of hair and plaited, humming softly.

Siv wanted to give her a shake. 'Ryan didn't stay here last night. He booked into a hotel.'

'Yeah, well . . . he's allergic to cats, or so he says. I was in a right state when we got back here, don't really remember. He's a snob, doesn't care much for my lifestyle. Expect staying here was beneath him.'

Ali gave Siv a glance that said, *She was probably too doped up to notice.* 'And Lyra — was she a happy little girl?'

'Yeah, of course.'

Siv asked, 'Did she ever seem drowsy when you saw her?'

'Come again?'

'Did Lyra ever seem sleepy?' *The way you do right now.*

'No. Only at bedtime, but that's a relief with a small kid.'

'Where were you yesterday afternoon between three and half four?'

'Cleaning a house in town. Lovely harbour views.'

'Was the owner there, or were you on your own?'

'On my own. Mr Johnstone was at work.'

'How do you get around? Do you have a car?'

'A scooter. All I can afford.'

Ali took out his notebook. 'Can you give us Mr Johnstone's details, please?'

'Sure. Would I be able to do my hair like yours? Would it take ages?'

'Just the details,' Ali said impatiently.

They left as soon as Nell had given them the employer's name and address. On the pavement outside, they both sucked in fresh air.

Ali gestured at the beat-up blue scooter padlocked by the front door. 'That's on its last legs. Suits its owner. I wouldn't want her cleaning my house. She's a manky article and probably out of her head a fair bit of the time.'

'She's not going to be a lot of help to her grieving sister,' Siv agreed. 'She's a contrast to Kay, that's for sure. Chalk and cheese. Was there a touch of spite in what she said about Kay living the dream? And there might have been deeper animosity between her and her father than she acknowledged. We need to establish if Mr Pullman had made a will, and what's in it.'

'He might have been worth a bit. That would be an easy win, somebody killing him for an inheritance.'

'Easy wins rarely happen in our game, though, so don't get too excited.' Siv unlocked her car. 'See you at the Turtons' in the morning.'

* * *

It was gone half eight by the time Siv reached home, trying to remember if there was anything much like a meal in the fridge. She recalled a slice of quiche, but she wasn't sure how long it had been there. When she climbed the steps to her wagon, she was pleased to see that Corran had left a container by the door. He and Paul were her friendly landlords and neighbours, who lived on the other side of the meadow in a converted barn. Corran was a weaver, with a loom in one of their sheds and he was also a gifted cook. He often gave her portions of the meals he made. Inside, she opened the lid to see pasta with meatballs.

It had been a warm day, but the evening was cool. She lit the wood burner, put the pasta in the microwave and stepped the few paces to her bedroom, where she threw off her suit, remembered her new resolutions and changed into jeans and a fleece. Ed's sweatshirt hung from the wardrobe handle. She buried her face in it and kissed it.

Back in the tiny kitchen, she opened the fridge door and gazed longingly at the bottle of akvavit. She could taste the caraway notes and the lovely chill that warmed her as it slipped down. She reached for a tub of parmesan and firmly closed the door again.

When she'd finished eating the rich, spicy pasta, she made a mug of tea and walked for a while by the river. The moon was high and full, casting plenty of light. The water gleamed beneath it. Why Lyra? Siv rested against the trunk of a massive oak. Maybe it was as simple as Patrick had suggested, and the child had had to die because she'd been a witness. She turned back, restless and wide awake despite the long day, wanting to see the Turtons again, have them sitting in the same room and get their measure.

In her wagon, she sat by the fire with coloured sheets of paper on a tray and spent an hour folding a blue fruit bowl, with little red apples and yellow bananas to sit in it. The concentration calmed and relaxed her. Maybe she should recommend origami to Nell Pullman for her anxiety — many people smoked as a distraction and to give themselves something to do. Then she laughed. Nell wouldn't have the attention span.

There, finished. She'd put the bowl on Ali's desk as a reminder to behave and watch his diet.

* * *

Kay drank a glass of water while she waited for the kettle to boil. At least making coffee gave her something to do. The silence from the living room was palpable. She heard DC Coleman make another comment but it was met by a grunt. Ryan had never been one to put himself out socially, and these days he didn't bother at all. Not around her, anyway.

The policeman seemed friendly and kind. Kay didn't mind the contact. Ryan had groaned when he saw him coming up the path, carrying a bunch of flowers. He'd called him a snoop earlier in the day, and told Kay she was naïve if she really believed he was there to help. Everyone knew the police planted family liaisons to gather information. Never mind Coleman's smile and helpful manner. He'd be trying to trip them up, find out their personal business. *You need to watch your step and be careful what you say, or they'll be all over us like a rash.*

Kay stuck the flowers, tulips and gerberas in a vase. They were garage bought, with the Tesco sticker still on the side, and seemed a bit over the top, as if Coleman was trying to ingratiate himself.

The policeman came into the kitchen as she was pouring boiling water onto coffee grounds. He'd probably had enough of the cold shoulder in the living room.

'Smells good. Can I give you a hand?'

She did like his Liverpudlian accent, sort of easy and soothing, somehow. A bit like John Lennon's.

'I'm fine, no need to bother. You can take the biscuits through, if you like.'

He gestured at a photo of Lyra attached to the fridge. She was bending over a lamb. 'This is a great picture. Where was it taken?'

'At a petting zoo. She loved it there. Do you have children, DC Coleman?'

'Please, call me Geordie. No, I don't. I'm single. I'd like to have a family one day. I always imagined having lots of kids in a big old Victorian house. Laughter and horseplay round the kitchen table, coming home to noise and an evening meal together.'

He sounded wistful, a tad romantic. She was touched by the emotion in his voice and the idealised picture he carried in his head. 'Hopefully you will, then.' Although she reckoned he must be in his forties, so he'd need to be getting on with it. It was different for men, though. They could father children into old age.

'We'll see,' he said. 'In the meantime, I have solitary dinners for one from the supermarket.'

'You should cook for yourself, get into practice for when you have your brood.'

'I'm sure you're right, but somehow the motivation just isn't there.' He stepped nearer. 'I hope it wasn't too tough for you at the morgue.'

'It was hard. Do you take milk?'

'Black for me.' He picked up the biscuits. 'You'll shout, won't you, if you need help with the coroner or if you have any questions? I have the impression that Ryan isn't too keen on me being around. A man thing, probably. I get it, but you should make use of me, it's what I'm here for.'

'I have my sister, too — all that's left of my family now.'

'I understand, but I get the impression that Nell's in a world of her own. Anything at all you want to chat about. You can always ring me, any time.'

She didn't care for that. A bit obvious. Her marriage was her own affair, as was her relationship with her sister, and she had no intention of confiding in *Call Me Geordie*. Maybe Ryan was right and the friendly DC was here to pry. She summoned a smile. 'Let's have our coffee. Then I must have an early night. I'm sure you want to get home too.'

CHAPTER 7

Ryan Turton was holding a black bin bag when he let in DI Drummond and DS Carlin the next morning.

'I've been clearing away all the party stuff,' he said. 'It's for the best. Just too awful, seeing it there. I told Kay to stay upstairs until I'd finished. She hardly slept last night, so take it easy, please.'

'We appreciate how tough this is,' Siv said. 'So, you returned home last night?'

'Yes. It's good to be back,' he replied — as if convincing himself.

In the living room, he and Kay sat side-by-side on a sofa. It was Saturday, but they were both smartly dressed, as if about to set off for work. Siv couldn't picture them lounging around in pyjamas. Without the party decorations, the room was revealed as carefully furnished, a pleasing mixture of modern and antique. The sun streamed through the wide windows, casting a buttery light on the pale brick fireplace and oak floor.

'Have you any idea who did this?' Kay asked.

'Not yet,' Siv said. 'Ms Turton, did your father make a will?'

'Yes, I have a copy, as does Nell. We're both executors.'

'So you know who benefits?'

'Nell and I do, equally. Why on earth are you asking that?'

'Maybe they suspect you and Nell carried out the murders to get the money,' Ryan commented. 'The evil sisters.'

Kay gasped and squeezed her hands into fists. Maybe she wanted to thump her husband. Siv wished she would.

'That's not helpful, Mr Turton,' she said. 'It's a detail we have to cover. I'd like the name of your father's solicitor.'

Kay said, with an effort, 'It's Elizabeth Nagler, in town.'

Ali placed his hands on his plump thighs. 'Mr Turton, why did you stay at the Dovecote hotel in January and March?'

Turton had been fiddling with a button on his shirt. His head shot up at the question. 'Have you been snooping around in my life?'

'Aye. Snooping, detective work — one and the same thing, I suppose.'

'I resent your attitude.'

'Understood, but it'd be helpful if you could explain.'

'If you insist. I had some hugely important, lengthy proposals to write for work contracts and I needed to concentrate. I shut myself away for a couple of days.'

'You've got an office upstairs,' Siv pointed out. 'Couldn't you have gone in there and closed the door?'

Turton sneered, 'I can tell you've never lived with a young child, or you'd realise that's impossible.'

'Lyra was so lively and irrepressible,' Kay said. 'We agreed it was best if Ryan went to the hotel. They were very lucrative contracts.' She cupped her knees with her hands. 'You said you'd tell us about the post-mortems.'

'It's been confirmed that your father was hit on the head with the iron griddle pan that was on the cooker,' Siv said. 'Lyra was smothered with a cushion from the playhouse. As I informed you, she hadn't been molested. But the pathologist found evidence of a sedative in her body.'

Kay echoed, 'A sedative?' She glanced at her husband.

That's the first time she's looked at him. Siv said, 'That's why I asked you if Lyra had had a cold or allergies. The sedative was chlorphenamine. It's found in cold remedies, travel sickness medication and antihistamines.'

'I don't understand,' Kay stammered. 'Lyra hadn't been ill and she wasn't allergic to anything.'

'She was a healthy child,' Turton added.

Ali asked, 'Had she seemed sleepy at all?'

'No,' Kay replied.

Ali continued, 'Do you have any medication of that kind in the house?'

Turton adjusted a cushion behind his back. 'I occasionally take antihistamines if I'm going to be around pets, but I've none here at present. There are some cold and flu remedies. We keep them in the bathroom cabinet.'

'There is a bottle of children's cough remedy. Lyra had a cold last winter,' Kay said. 'But she couldn't have reached any of the medication. The cabinet is high up.'

'Mind if I take a look?' Ali asked.

'Be our guest.' Turton waved a hand.

Kay was pale, her face anguished as Ali left the room.

Siv leaned towards her. 'I'm sorry that we have to ask these intrusive questions, but we need to follow up on this issue of the sedative. It's strange, if neither of you were giving Lyra any medication. We'll check with her nanny and the nursery.'

'Alicia? I'm sure she wouldn't have given Lyra anything without asking me first,' Kay said. 'That applies to the nursery too. They have strict guidelines about these things.'

'Let them check, Kay. There's probably some obvious solution,' Turton snapped. He stood, stared out of the window, straightened the slat on a blind and then resumed his seat.

Ali returned. 'There's a box of adult flu remedy caplets, almost full, and a bottle of children's cough syrup, about a quarter used. Neither contain chlorphenamine.'

'That sounds right,' Kay told them. 'Lyra needed the syrup for a couple of days last November.'

Ali asked, 'What about when she had a stomach upset in January?'

Kay stared at him. 'What stomach upset?'

'Alicia noted that Lyra was a bit quiet and you told her that she'd had a tummy problem.'

Kay put a hand to her cheek. 'Oh, yes, that's right. I'd forgotten. It was nothing serious, a passing thing. I didn't give her cough syrup for that, of course, just plenty of fluids and waited for it to settle. I'm sorry, I don't feel too good. This is so difficult.'

Ryan Turton asserted himself. 'That's enough now. I'm sure you've got what you came for. And by the way, don't send that DC Coleman here again. We don't need him or his crappy flowers. He just gets in the way and we'd rather be on our own. We don't appreciate having a stranger hanging around the house at a time like this.'

'What about you, Ms Turton?' Siv asked. 'How do you feel about the FLO visiting you? It can be very useful to have that link to the investigation, and DC Coleman can advise you about practical matters.'

Kay studied the floor. 'No, thank you. As Ryan said, we prefer to deal with things on our own. We understand where to go if we need any help. We have DC Coleman's number.'

Siv was annoyed, but no point in pushing it. 'Just one last issue,' she said. 'Neither you nor Nell can think of anything your father was troubled about? You haven't recalled any remark he might have made?'

'Nothing.' Kay sounded weary.

'He seems to have had some argument with another member of BSS, Belinda Hanak.'

'Doesn't mean anything to me, and I don't recall him mentioning a Belinda. He had lots of acquaintances through his interests. Dad could be pretty bossy and rile people sometimes. I'm going to lie down for a while now. Ryan will see you out.'

Turton closed the door on their heels with a curt goodbye.

'Someone was giving that kid a sedative,' Ali said as he drove away, 'but not from the meds in the bathroom.'

He'd pushed the seat so far back to accommodate his girth, Siv had to turn to speak to him. 'The only other people who had regular access to Lyra were the nursery and the nanny. Get hold of them to check and find out if the nursery had any concerns about Lyra or the family. Nanny first, she's the most likely to have medicated her. Maybe Lyra was too demanding for her liking and she took steps to quieten her.'

'Surely the parents would have noticed?'

'I'm not sure that Ryan Turton would have, and Kay was arriving home at a time when Lyra would be getting tired anyway. What did you make of those two? They didn't touch and barely connected with each other. People can be frozen by grief, but not to that extent. There's something sham about them. When Turton expressed any concern for his wife, it was as if he was doing it by numbers.'

'Aye, something's off there. He's a bit of a dose, I reckon. His story about staying at the hotel could be true, but why go to that expense? I didn't buy it.'

'Me neither, but what's it about, then? It's annoying that they've refused Geordie's help. I was hoping that he'd get alongside them.'

'I'd say that was Turton's decision, even if Kay went along with it.'

'Agreed. She's not scared of her husband — she comes across as self-possessed — but she's watchful around him, as if she's gauging his mood. Also, Kay was fazed when you mentioned Lyra's tummy bug. I'm sure she was lying.'

Ali tapped the dashboard. 'The nanny said that Kay bought Lyra a trike around then as well. Is that connected? It'd be an expensive consolation for an upset tummy.'

'Guilt or bribery?' Siv knew all about that. Now and again, when Mutsi had neglected her daughters because she was romancing a new man, she'd bought them little presents. Small, inexpensive items to make up for leaving them on their own in the evenings — new hairbrushes, bath bubbles, socks. Rik always used these occasions to quote from a book of Finnish sayings their mother had. She'd examine her gift and comment dryly, *The forest answers in the same way one shouts at it*, which roughly translated into, *You reap what you sow*. Siv had never been sure if Rik was referring to Mutsi's new man or her relationship with her daughters. Rik's use of proverbs always had the desired effect of irritating their mother. Mutsi hid the book eventually, but by that time Rik had memorised enough of the sayings to produce them at will.

The sun was direct and hot. Siv pulled down the passenger seat visor. She had only met the Turtons a couple of days ago, but she was already exasperated by them and the veils they were hiding behind. It was as if they were deliberately thwarting the investigation. If these murders had been close to home, they might prove hard to crack.

Her phone rang and she answered Patrick's call, putting him on speaker.

'Hi, guv. A woman who follows me on Twitter has been in touch, says she saw Tom Pullman and Lyra on Thursday, around three fifteen. He was going into St Peter's church, with Lyra holding his hand.'

'Did this woman know him?'

'No. Recognised him from his photo in the paper.'

'Go and talk to her. Show her Pullman's photo again and Lyra's, just to be sure. Then get back to me.' She turned to Ali. 'St Peter's is a Catholic church, isn't it?'

'Aye. I went to a baptism there not long ago. It's about ten minutes' drive from where the Turtons live.'

'We'd better not bother Kay Turton again with questions just now.' Siv recalled that Nell Pullman ran a market stall on Saturdays. They weren't far from the cobblestone square where the outdoor market was held. 'Let's see if Nell's on her jewellery stall today and have a word with her. Maybe she can enlighten us.'

Ali headed for the multi-storey car park nearby and after cruising around for a few minutes, finally found a space on the top floor. They headed to the exit and through the crowded market square, searching among the rows of stalls: vegetables, antiques, fabric, vintage clothing, books, comics, cheese, bread, farm produce, organic eggs — *bring your own box and we'll fill it.* Finally, Siv spotted Corran, who sold his woven throws and knitted garments on Saturdays. He was in the middle of explaining a design to a customer. She stopped, apologised for interrupting and asked if he'd heard of a jewellery stall, run by Nell Pullman. Corran suggested the far corner of the market, by the high street.

'Frantic, this place,' Ali said as they moved on. 'Great cheese at that stall over there. They sell a lovely Sperrin Blue. Real taste of home.'

Siv didn't reply, trying not to bump into jostling people. Didn't Ali *ever* stop thinking about his stomach? She turned a corner by a stall full of shoes and saw Nell at the end of the next row, still dressed in her red jeans, speaking to a customer. She seemed agitated. The customer, a young woman, was holding up a string of beads and pointing. Siv and Ali approached and stopped near the stall. Nell didn't notice them as she was now arguing loudly with the woman.

'You must have handled it roughly. It's not my responsibility if the clasp broke.'

'I only bought it last Saturday. I wore it once, that night, and it came apart when I was taking it off.' The woman was speaking quietly but assertively.

Nell, on the other hand, was getting riled. 'Maybe you or your boyfriend broke it. It's not my fault.'

'The least you could do is give me my money back or replace it.'

Nell grabbed the necklace from her and examined it. 'You probably tried to force it. Not my problem.'

'I'm not happy about this, not happy at all,' the woman said, placing hands on hips.

Nell shouted, 'Do I look as if I'm interested in your happiness? This isn't Tiffany's, it's a bloody market stall. It only cost you three quid! What do you expect, a ten-year guarantee?'

'Don't be so rude! I expect to be able to wear something more than once. I've a good mind to go to trading standards.'

'Be my guest,' Nell mocked, shoving the necklace back at her. 'Go to the United sodding Nations for all I care.'

'So you're not going to refund me?'

'No! Now piss off and stop getting in the way of me doing business.'

They stared at each other for long moments. Nell's face was beetroot and she was quivering with anger.

'It's all cheap tat,' Ali murmured, scanning the stall. 'The kind of stuff that falls apart as soon as you so much as look at it.'

'Disposable trinkets,' Siv agreed. 'Our Nell has quite a temper, blowing up over such a small problem.'

The customer was standing her ground. 'You've no right to speak to me like that. I'm surprised you do any trade, the way you carry on. I'm not leaving it. I'll definitely contact the market inspector.' She put the necklace in her bag.

'Please yourself, babes, knock yourself out,' Nell goaded.

The woman turned and saw Siv and Ali. 'I wouldn't buy anything here, it's all rubbish and this woman's a nightmare,' she called before she stomped away.

'Another satisfied customer?' Siv asked Nell.

'Hi,' Nell said, her eyes focused for once. 'What a cow! Expecting me to refund her when she clearly broke it herself. I'm no pushover for tricks like that. If I'd given her the money back, she'd have told her mates and they'd all be here, trying it on.'

'Sorry you're having a hard day,' Siv offered.

'Yeah. Anyway, I got rid of her.' Nell put her hands to her forehead and breathed in, then turned on a smile. 'Are you after something gorgeous to wear? I've got a new line of earrings in, really tasty.'

'It's police business again,' Siv told her. 'Apologies for bothering you while you're working. Was your dad a Catholic?'

Nell creased up with laughter. 'You do come up with weird questions. No!'

'Did he attend any church?'

'Dad was an atheist, so very unlikely.'

'What about Kay and Ryan?'

She neatened a tray of metal rings. 'If pushed, they might say they're C of E, but only to get a school place, something like that. None of us have the religion bug.'

'OK, thanks.'

'Sure you won't buy?' Nell turned to Ali. 'How about you, Sergeant — something for your lady love?'

'She's all jewelled up, thanks.' Ali smiled.

As they walked back through the market, Ali said, 'If I bought Pol any of that crap, she'd make ointment of me.'

'She'd be within her rights. Nell's got a very short fuse. Her mood changes quite rapidly.'

'Might be a combo of weed and medication.'

'Maybe. Why would an atheist be going into a church?'

'A sudden conversion? An interest in architecture?'

'Handy place to meet someone, more like, and out of the way, indicating a need for secrecy.' Siv linked her fingers and cracked them. This was promising, an indication that Tom Pullman had had other business apart from a party on Thursday.

Ali gestured. 'I'll just stop at the cheese stall as we're here, won't take a minute.'

Siv was in a good mood, now that they had another lead to follow. 'Fine. I'll get some of this Sperrin Blue, see what the fuss is about.'

* * *

Harry Hudson was sitting at his living room table, tapping the computer keyboard, working on the May edition of the BSS newsletter. He double-checked that he'd included all the information that members had sent him about coffee mornings, book group selections and the new 'walking cricket' team. People got very upset if their contribution was missed, as he'd learned the hard way from initial mistakes when he'd taken on the job. One woman had been tearful because he'd omitted her mawkish poem about friendship. He'd had to apologise profusely while thinking, *It was hardly poet laureate material, love.*

He read over the section he'd just typed:

Hi everyone, I hope you're all enjoying the gorgeous spring sunshine. It certainly helps to lift the mood and a fine summer is promised!

There are two general events in May.

We have a talk titled, Indian Folklore and Folk Tales, on 5 May at 2 p.m. The speaker is Sabina Singh. It's going to be an entertaining, light-hearted presentation with something for everyone, so do come along.

On 23 May, we have a picnic at Bere Marsh Nature Reserve, 12.30 to 2.30 p.m. If the forecast says rain, bring a mac, 'cos we're not cancelling. And don't forget the cakes!

Tom Pullman had grumbled that Harry's style was too vernacular, and objected to the use of *hi* rather than *hello*. He wouldn't have been keen on *light-hearted* either, with his preference for the serious and worthy. He'd have tutted over that *'cos*. It had been a case of flagrant snobbery — Harry had worked all his life as a garage mechanic, and Tom clearly believed that he brought a whiff of axle grease to the BSS table. Tom had favoured more heavyweight topics for talks, such as 'Great American Composers', 'The History of Fine Dining' and 'The Victorians and Railways'. He'd been a patronising, heavy-handed, pompous git behind his outward show of geniality, and Harry wouldn't miss him. He'd been a control freak, too — always wanted his finger in every pie. Not that Harry would say that to anyone, of course, given recent events. Tom had helped to set up BSS — to listen to him, you'd reckon on his own — and had been a driving force and a big cheese in the group for five years. There was no doubt that he'd been important to its development and success. Didn't stop him being a git, as Belinda could testify.

Belinda had been on the phone to him since the news broke about Tom, calling when Aled, her husband, was out. 'If the police come asking questions,' he'd told her, 'just keep it simple.' Of course, she was a bit of a drama queen, so she'd probably ignore his advice and make even more of a mountain out of her molehill. Still, she had quite a lot on her plate, especially now Tom was dead. When she'd told Harry about the situation, he'd been dumbfounded. It was well beyond his life experience, but he'd been gratified that she'd chosen him to unburden herself to. 'I trust you,' she'd said. 'I had to tell someone, and I can rely on your discretion. You're an amazing friend to me.'

Harry found Belinda attractive, admired her zest for life and liked the way she treated him as a confidant. He was also a bit overwhelmed that she cultivated his friendship, as she'd been to university while he was learning about exhaust pipes and wheel nuts. She was witty, especially when she made fun of Tom's precise manner and his habit of saying, 'It's as clear as day' when he was emphasising that he was in the right. Harry was a solitary, shy man, a dreamer who liked the idea of a woman in his life but realised he probably wouldn't cope with the reality. His favourite films were about doomed love: *Brief Encounter*, *Casablanca*, *Ghost*, *An Affair to Remember*. He'd wept buckets at *Titanic*.

If Belinda hadn't been married, he might have summoned the courage to ask her out. He'd tried to picture her here with him, in his pretty terraced cottage. No, it would be too modest for her, and anyway, she'd have turned him down. She was in a different social bracket to him, had an expansive personality. She needed space, and he recognised that her vitality and penchant for fuss would be hard to cope with full time. It was better to admire and cherish her from a distance.

People rarely visited his home, but Belinda popped in now and again. She'd pronounced it cute the first time she came, and urged him to host an afternoon tea in his tiny but lovingly tended garden. He'd said he'd consider it to please her, while quailing at the idea of BSS members gossiping about his cramped accommodation. Most of them were retired professionals and owned spacious houses.

Harry had always preferred to avoid politics, both national and personal. BSS was supposed to be a friendly organisation of people who wanted to stay active in their senior years, and it was in the main. But there were some powerful personalities and, unfortunately, a sprinkling of members who needed to parade their egos and pursue their own agendas. Harry had been taken aback at how peeved people could become about a comment made in a book group or at a talk about Japanese shrines. Of course, it was human nature, this need to form cliques and take sides, but Harry didn't see that it quite resonated with the BSS ethos: *Share, Learn, Flourish*. He kept out of the shenanigans that went on at the BSS committee, held his tongue and stuck to talking about the newsletter, which he derived quiet satisfaction from producing once a month.

Harry wasn't sure what he'd say if the police called on him, but there was no point in complicating matters, so he'd choose his words carefully. He was by nature cautious. Someone on the committee had once referred to him as 'a steady pair of hands'.

He typed another paragraph, taking satisfaction from the fact that Tom would have disapproved of *we've* instead of *we have*:

> *We've two new groups starting end of May: Geology and Guitar for Beginners, so if you're interested, contact the group leader via the website.*

He started on a section about Tom Pullman, deciding that he'd put a black border around it. He wasn't sure whether it should go at the start or the end of the newsletter. He'd check with other committee members. It was hard, writing about the death of someone he'd disliked, which was why he'd left it until last. It took him half a dozen attempts before he was satisfied.

Tom Pullman

We've been deeply saddened to hear of the death of our chairman, Tom Pullman, and his little granddaughter, Lyra. Our thoughts are with his family at this very difficult time.

Tom was a founder member of BSS and had been at the helm since the organisation started. His commitment and energy were always impressive.

Tom will be much missed by us all.

RIP Tom.

Harry was finishing the draft document when the doorbell rang. He answered and saw a young chap, natty suit, fashionably unkempt hair with that mousse stuff in it. Might be an estate agent. They canvassed for property sometimes when business was slow. Harry was about to say that he wasn't planning to put his home on the market when the chap held out a warrant card.

'Mr Hudson?'

'That's right.'

'I'm DC Patrick Hill from Berminster police. Can I have a quick word about Mr Pullman?'

Here we go. 'Of course, come in. Want a cuppa?' He led the detective into the living room and pointed to an armchair.

'No thanks. Have I disturbed your work?'

'I was writing May's newsletter for Berminster Senior Students.'

'That's why I'm calling, about BSS.'

'I did wonder if you'd be in touch, given my connection with Tom. I was so shocked to hear of his murder. And little Lyra.'

'Yes, it was a dreadful incident.' The detective tapped his fingers on the arm of the chair. 'Mr Pullman had sent you a couple of emails in recent weeks. Suggestions for the newsletter, mainly.'

Interfering Tom, always poking his nose in. 'That's right. Tom liked to offer his ideas and support. I produce a monthly newsletter, you see. I've just been writing a little piece about Tom, in fact.'

'Had you know him long?'

Harry's mouth was dry, his hands clammy. He was worried that his dislike of Tom would show. Police were trained to spot those signs. *Keep it factual*, he told himself. 'I met Tom when BSS started. I went along to the first meetings, when we were setting the group up.'

'He was the chair, is that right?'

'Yes, from the start. People found him a natural leader.'

'He was popular?'

'Yes. He got things done.'

The detective made a note and asked the question Harry least wanted to hear. 'Had there been any disagreements in the organisation?'

'Nothing major. Members would sometimes have different opinions about things, as they do, but we always sorted issues out.'

'People would have heard about the birthday party last Thursday. Did you?'

'I've no idea who Tom had told. He'd mentioned it at our last committee meeting, at the beginning of April. He was proud of Lyra and he described the cake he was having made. Can't say I'd remembered what day the party was, just that it was happening.'

The detective pressed his pen against his lip. 'Who was Mr Pullman closest to in BSS, would you say?'

Harry swallowed. 'I'm not sure. We all mix in various ways through groups and social events. I'm not a great socialiser myself, I stick to attending the groups I sign up for. Tom was a very gregarious man. Other members might be able to tell you more.' He was pleased with that response. It hit the right note.

'So, you hadn't noticed that Mr Pullman had been worried or upset in any way recently?'

'No, I hadn't, and he didn't say anything of that nature.'

DC Hill gazed straight at him. 'Had he had any difference of opinion with Belinda Hanak?'

Harry rubbed his fingers against his wet palms. How had the police pinpointed Belinda so quickly? 'They sometimes clashed a bit in committee over topics we should cover. Belinda's our group coordinator.'

'Angry clashes?'

'No . . . it's a committee of arthritic pensioners with a fair sprinkling of hearing aids and dodgy hips, not a group of international wheeler-dealers.' Harry gave an awkward little laugh. 'It amounted to grumbles over cups of tea and jam sponge.'

'I once had to intervene in a nasty domestic dispute which started because someone had damaged the icing on a sponge cake,' DC Hill remarked. 'Where were you on Thursday afternoon?'

Harry was rattled by the detective's comment and by the question, although he was aware that the police did routinely ask it. 'I went for a bike ride around three and got back at five.'

'Whereabouts did you go?'

'Out to Minster Beach and back.'

'Did anyone see you or talk to you?'

'No. I was minding my own business.'

'Did Tom Pullman ever express an interest in St Peter's church? It's the Catholic church on Forest Road.'

Harry had to make an effort to track the topic change. His brain was definitely slower these days. 'Tom wasn't a churchgoer. He was proud of being a non-believer, referred to reading that Richard Dawkins — his book's called *The God Delusion*. Quite a few of the BSS members do attend church. Mainly C of E and Methodist. I go to the Christmas service at St Helen's. Not sure why, just a bit of comforting ritual, I suppose.'

DC Hill thanked him and went off. Harry hurried to the kitchen, drank a glass of water and splashed his face. Then he unlocked the back door, stepped into the garden and let the fresh air wash over him. He touched the silky petals of a rose for reassurance.

Overall, he reckoned that had been OK and his comment about arthritic pensioners had defused things nicely. (Belinda would give him grief if she heard he'd offered up that awful stereotype of BSS.) If the police questioned her, it wouldn't be because of anything he'd said. He'd ring her now to reassure her.

* * *

In his car, Patrick added to his notes from the interview. *Nervous, definitely uncomfortable about something to do with BSS.*

He checked his Twitter feed but there was nothing helpful, just the usual expressions of public sympathy.

So sorry, condolences to the family.

Hope you catch the scum who did this awful crime soon.

Poor little girl. Rest in Peace.

Wishing our wonderful local police well investigating these terrible crimes.

All well and good, but what he needed was a hot tip. At least he'd had the contact from the woman who'd seen Tom Pullman at St Peter's. Time to visit her now. Maybe she'd remember some crucial details.

CHAPTER 8

Siv managed to speak to Ms Nagler, Tom Pullman's solicitor, as she was driving to Belinda Hanak's house. Elizabeth Nagler confirmed that Mr Pullman had left his estate to his daughters in a fifty-fifty split.

'Any idea how much we might be talking about?' Siv asked.

'This will was updated three years ago. My notes from that time indicate that Mr Pullman's house was worth about six hundred thousand, and he had shares and other savings to the tune of about the same amount, maybe a bit more.'

Siv thanked her. Each daughter was about to inherit a substantial amount. Definitely a motive for killing your dad if you took against him for some reason, but Lyra? She found her sunglasses and drove on through the bright streets to one of the town's outlying suburbs.

Belinda Hanak's bungalow had a handsome, gleaming silver motorhome standing in the drive. Siv couldn't resist a peek inside and was impressed by the luxurious fitments and the sleek, padded leather seats. They reminded her of the furnishings on the deck of the *USS Enterprise* from *Star Trek*. Ed had been a fan of the series and he'd always been able to find an episode playing on TV. Perhaps she should upgrade to something like this if she ever tired of her miniscule wagon. It occurred to her that then, if she saw Mutsi approaching, she could drive away. She chuckled and rang the doorbell, which played the opening bars of Beethoven's 'Ode to Joy'.

Ms Hanak answered the door and took her into a conservatory at the back of the roomy home. The décor featured a lot of hot pink and pale green. Belinda herself was in a blue linen dress with big front pockets, paired with black leggings. Her short brunette hair had one pink streak at the side, which matched the wall behind her. She was in her late sixties, a pretty, well-preserved woman with an upbeat manner to go with her 'I may be old but I'm staying funky' style.

'Now, Inspector, would you like some fresh orange juice on this warm day?'

Siv accepted and watched a man clipping a hedge at the far end of the garden while Belinda fetched the drink.

She asked, 'Is that your husband?'

'That's my Aled, yes.'

'Is he a member of BSS?'

'No. When we retired, we decided we'd do some things together and also have separate interests. Keeps a long marriage fresh. Are you married?'

'No.'

'I can recommend it. Do make time for it in this busy life.'

I did, but life snatched it from me. Siv took a sip of the tart juice. 'I've come to ask you about Tom Pullman.'

'Poor Tom and little Lyra,' Belinda said in a sober tone. 'We can't believe it. Such a tragedy.'

Belinda's nails matched her dress. Siv wondered if she changed her nail varnish each day to suit her outfit. It was the kind of thing Mutsi would do. It was possible that Belinda and her mother might have met, being of an age, although Mutsi would be unlikely to join something like BSS. She wasn't the collaborative type, preferring to paddle her own canoe.

'Were you close to Tom?' Siv asked.

91

'We'd both been on the committee of BSS since it started, and we worked together a lot.'

Not exactly an answer to the question. Siv had the impression that Belinda was choosing her words judiciously. 'Had you had any disagreements?'

Belinda's hands were more lined than her face, dotted with liver spots and linked loosely in her lap. 'We sometimes had robust discussions in committee, about who we should invite as guest speakers, things like that. Tom could be a bit old-fashioned.'

Siv smiled encouragingly. 'How do you mean?'

'Let's just say that feminism had passed him by. He never thought beyond men for speakers and group leaders, and he always favoured the same old mainstream topics, usually somewhat stale and male-centric. He had no notion of diversity. Some older men are still hard work like that. Not my Aled, thank goodness.'

'He's more enlightened?'

Belinda's smile was smug. 'I've trained him up to be, Inspector.'

Siv observed Mr Hanak's back as he trimmed a honeysuckle and wondered if he realised he'd been coached. 'It sounds as if Mr Pullman could be a bit of a wet blanket.'

Belinda nodded. 'For example, if he'd met you, he'd have been polite but ever so slightly patronising. You'd have got the subtle message that he didn't really rate female DIs, and if you'd been accompanied by a male colleague, Tom would have focused on him.'

'I have experience of just such a scenario. Mr Pullman would have got the unsubtle message that I was in charge.'

Belinda clapped. 'A woman after my own heart!'

Siv was puzzled. 'Yet Mr Pullman had one daughter with a responsible job, and was disappointed that his other daughter didn't set her sights high enough.'

'Double standards. Or, perhaps talking the talk but not walking the walk. Tom had no understanding of just having fun — one of our members wanted to start a group called

Extreme Crochet and he nearly had a fit. Luckily, I usually managed to carry opinion with me, and Tom didn't always like that. He seemed to regard me as a bra-burning feminist firebrand, which did cause me some amusement. I'm afraid I'm at an age where the fire is more of a gentle flicker, and although I did burn my bra in 1970, I definitely need one these days, given the effects of gravity!' She sniggered. 'This probably all sounds very petty to you, a group of old people and their niggles.'

'Not at all.' Despite Belinda's attempt at feminist bonding and forthcoming manner, Siv had an inkling of unreliability. The smile was a little too ready and shallow. She produced the letter from her bag. 'Mr Pullman didn't seem to find it petty, either. We found this letter to you at his home.' She handed it to Belinda, who reached for a pair of reading glasses.

Siv watched her as she read. She put a hand to her chest, tapping her breastbone. When she'd finished, she removed her glasses and shook her head. 'I didn't receive this letter. I don't understand it at all.'

'What was Mr Pullman referring to when he talked about your motives being personal, and suggesting you move on from past events?'

'Inspector, I just can't say. As I mentioned, we did have our disagreements, because of Tom's rather old-fashioned views. I've no idea why he'd want to write me something like this. I have to say, it's very much Tom's style, rather superior. Insulting too, actually.' She was angry, but attempting to conceal it behind puzzled smiles.

'It's odd then, isn't it?' Siv asked.

'I can only assume that Tom was annoyed about our last committee meeting. I suggested inviting someone to speak about reiki healing. Tom said it was mumbo-jumbo and we'd be a laughing stock and so on. I've benefited from reiki treatment when I had a bad back. I argued and we voted overwhelmingly for it. I suppose Tom was sore and he'd been dwelling on his grievance about my opinions. He did like to have the last word.' She put a hand to her mouth. 'Sorry, that sounded a little insensitive, given why you're here.'

The conservatory door opened and Aled Hanak appeared, dressed in an old twill shirt and cord trousers. Belinda introduced them.

'Sorry to barge in,' he said. 'Have you made off with the twine, darling? It's not in the shed.'

'I might have left it in the kitchen,' Belinda told him.

'Terrible news,' Hanak said when she'd gone into the house.

'Yes. Had you met Tom Pullman?'

He was a smiley man with a soft voice. 'A couple of times. I went to one of the BSS picnics last year and I did a talk for them as a guest speaker. I wasn't that keen, but someone dropped out at the last minute, so Belinda roped me in.'

'Belinda was telling me that she didn't always see eye to eye with Mr Pullman.'

Hanak made a little moue. 'This is true. Belinda's a strong woman with definite, progressive views, and Tom was a bit blinkered and illiberal, from what I gathered.'

Siv didn't enjoy causing marital disharmony, but she needed to find a murderer. 'What do you make of this letter that Mr Pullman wrote to your wife?'

Hanak removed one of his gardening gloves and was reading the letter when Belinda returned with a ball of green twine and a glass of orange juice for her husband. She saw him and glowered at Siv.

'This is a bit vicious, darling,' Hanak said. He seemed more upset than his wife. 'When did you get this? You didn't mention it.'

'I didn't receive it,' Belinda was quick to reassure him. 'The inspector brought it with her.'

'It was in Mr Pullman's house,' Siv said.

'Well . . . deeply unpleasant. You must have really riled him, Bel.'

'Much more than I realised,' his wife agreed. 'I told DI Drummond that Tom must have been saving all his gripes up and decided to get them off his chest. Sometimes people write things down to vent and that in itself makes them feel better. I like to think that Tom didn't actually plan to send it to me.'

Hanak handed the letter back to Siv. 'Pretty nasty stuff to be remembered by. No need for it. At least he didn't post it, or thought better of it. Maybe he was hoping to see you off, Bel, make you leave the committee or even BSS. He underestimated my girl.' He put a hand on Belinda's shoulder and she covered it with her own.

It was Tom Pullman who'd been seen off, not Belinda, and his letter suggested a more deep-seated rancour than being outvoted over reiki healing. He might have posted a copy and Belinda was lying. If she had shown it to her husband, they were both skilled dissemblers, and Siv couldn't detect any tension between them.

She enjoyed their discomfort when she asked them to attend at the police station to have their fingerprints taken.

'*Really?*' Belinda sniffed. 'Seems a tad over the top.'

'Routine,' Siv replied. 'Where were you both on Thursday afternoon between three and four thirty?'

Belinda swept her hair back. 'Goodness, first fingerprints, now alibis! We're not suspects, surely?'

'We ask everyone.'

'I went to a couple of garden centres for plants and compost around half two, got back about four,' Aled Hanak said.

'Which garden centres?'

'Blossom and then Drayton Fields. You were at home, weren't you, darling?'

'I was, yes,' Belinda said. 'Reading out here and pottering. You haven't finished your juice, Inspector.' She made it sound like an accusation.

Siv picked up the glass and drank the by now tepid orange. This woman was concealing something, and in a murder investigation secrets tended to detonate.

* * *

95

Siv heard Patrick before she entered the team room. He was a talented mimic and he had Mortimer's reedy tones off to perfection. '*You don't need me to tell you that we're all under the cosh where budgets are concerned, so don't expect vacancies to be filled as soon as anyone leaves. There are more cuts and economies coming down the track, so let's all prove that we're invaluable.*'

Ali gave one of his belly laughs as she coughed and came through the door. Patrick sidled to his chair and busied himself with his notes. She'd asked Geordie Coleman to attend the meeting, and he was grinning, his bag cradled on his lap.

'Thanks for coming, Geordie. OK, let's see where we are. You go first,' Siv told Patrick, enjoying his blushes.

He flipped open his notepad. 'So, I spoke to Jean Scully, who was walking her dog past St Peter's church at around three fifteen on Thursday. She saw a grey car pull up in the parking bays outside. Tom Pullman got out and went into the church with Lyra holding his hand. She said the little girl was skipping and so excited, it made her smile. She was definite when I showed her the photos.'

Siv said, 'So, depending on how long they were in the church, that narrows down the time of the murders. Even if they were there for just five minutes, they can't have got back to Seascape until about half three, so a forty-five-minute window until Meg Sterling arrived. Pullman wasn't religious, so why visit a church?'

'Maybe Lyra was interested in it,' Geordie suggested.

Siv hadn't considered that. 'Possibly, although surely all her attention was focused on her party.'

'He could have been making a donation to charity,' Ali said. 'St Peter's runs various appeals.'

'As an atheist?' Siv shook her head. 'Surely he'd have selected non-religious causes.'

Patrick continued, 'Regarding Ryan Turton, no one at the Dovecote could recall seeing him with anyone else when he stayed there, although that doesn't mean he wasn't meeting someone. I rang Turton's work appointments last Thursday. The morning checks out, and I'm waiting to hear back from the farmer he was with in the afternoon. Kay Turton was in a management meeting from three until five. I timed Drew Gifford's deliveries. He was in the area and could just about have doubled back to Cove Parade at some time between half three and four.'

'How about Harry Hudson?' Siv asked.

'He told me that there were some tensions at BSS, but nothing major and no particular rows between Pullman and Belinda Hanak. Painted a picture of creaky pensioners niggling at each other over tea and cake. He was chary, though. I'm sure there was stuff he wasn't saying. He told me he was riding his bike to Minster Beach and back on Thursday afternoon.'

'Belinda Hanak is no creaky pensioner,' Siv told them. 'She claimed that she didn't receive Pullman's letter and she described him as a throwback with old-fashioned ideas, whereas she flies the banners for diversity and equality in BSS. She admitted that they did have disagreements, but it didn't add up to what he expressed in that letter. Her husband was there. Seemed a quiet, inoffensive guy.'

'Often the ones to watch,' Ali observed.

'He was out at garden centres on Thursday afternoon and Belinda was home alone,' Siv added. 'Geordie, I gather the Turtons have iced you out. Did you glean anything?'

Geordie held his hands out. 'Not really. They swerved attempts at conversation. I spent an hour or so there with them when they went back home. Kay did the hostess thing, making coffee. She chatted a bit in the kitchen, inconsequential stuff. Ryan was monosyllabic. I did note that they moved around each other without really connecting. Any attempt I made to engage them was rebuffed — politely by Kay, Ryan less charming. He told me they didn't want my services and asked me to leave them alone. I was really frustrated by them.'

'Me too,' Siv told him.

'Sorry, guv, I did my best but they were intent on thwarting me.'

'You can only try.'

'I phoned Kay again earlier on, to see if I might divide and conquer. Ryan answered her phone, said thanks but no thanks, and rang off.'

'People do refuse an FLO sometimes, but the refusal in itself can speak volumes,' Siv commented.

'Yeah, Ryan kept giving me suspicious glances. They've something to hide, all right. Want me to try again in a couple of days?'

Siv pondered that. 'No, it could be counterproductive. We'll try digging in other ways.' A comment Ryan Turton had made came back to her. 'Did you buy the Turtons flowers?'

'Yeah, just a small bunch, a gesture.'

'Probably a bridge too far and hardly necessary.'

He seemed taken aback. 'I thought it would smooth my way in.'

'Not in this case and I wouldn't generally recommend it. Thanks, Geordie, you can head off now if you like.'

'Righto. Just shout if there's anything I can do.' He hoisted his bag and left them.

Ali drained his coffee like a man who hadn't seen a hot drink for weeks. 'I spoke to Alicia Ferreira again. She hadn't noticed Lyra being sleepy or sluggish, and she said she'd never given her any medication. The nursery isn't open now until Monday.'

'We need to prioritise speaking to them,' Siv said. 'I got hold of Pullman's solicitor. She confirmed that his estate is divided equally between the sisters and they're both in line for at least six hundred k each.'

Patrick formed a silent whistle. 'Tasty.'

'Very,' Siv agreed. 'Nell Pullman does a good line in vagueness, but she can't earn much from cleaning jobs and flogging jewellery on a stall. She's clearly the bargain basement family member. She made a few remarks about Kay being better off than her, and her dad criticising her lifestyle. But it's a long way from a bit of sibling envy and irritation with your dad to bashing his head in and smothering your niece, and there are no signs of any real antagonism in the family.'

'I tried to contact the guy Nell cleans for Thursday after-noons,' Ali said. 'No reply from his mobile, so I left a message.'

'Right. Who doesn't have a verified alibi?' Siv went to the incident board and started a list.

Ryan Turton — in Canterbury
Drew Gifford — driving van
Aled Hanak — garden centre shopping
Belinda Hanak — at home
Nell Pullman — at cleaning job
Alicia Ferreira — college library
Harry Hudson — out cycling

'Always good to have a wide field,' she said with heavy irony and checked her notes. 'They all have means of trans-port, so any of them could have been at Cove Parade. Between you, can you get the reg numbers and pictures of the types of vehicles they drive, and ask around the neighbours again. It's hard to believe that someone didn't notice something. And check CCTV as far as possible — at the garden centres, Rother College library and the route to Minster Beach.'

'We need to find out what Pullman was doing in the church,' Ali said.

Siv made a note. 'I'll get on to that. We haven't spoken to Dotty Debbie yet. Also, we have to talk to the other com-mittee members at BSS — can you two sort that. You might find someone else who didn't approve of extreme crochet.'

'Come again?' Ali asked.

'It's the latest craze, didn't you know?' Siv laughed, van-ishing to her office.

* * *

Father Murray, the parish priest at St Peter's, said that he could meet Siv at the presbytery after evening confession, at seven thirty. When she finished the call to him, she saw that she'd had a text from Bartel Nowak.

I'm fishing by Bere Leas, if you fancy a chat. Got coffee, but wouldn't say no to something sweet.

She knew the spot he'd be at, sitting on his camping stool, solid and still. They'd met during her first case after she'd moved back to Berminster, and had become good friends. The River Bere formed a flowing backdrop to their friendship, because that case had involved a wild swimmer and a fisherman. Siv had no interest in fishing, but she enjoyed the peaceful monotony of sitting by Bartel on the riverbank, observing the rippling water and the wildlife. She supposed it was her therapy.

Gusto was just closing as she left the station, but they paused to sell her a small box of *aragostine* with lemon cream. Bere Leas was a stretch of river near the nature reserve, about three miles out of town. Siv parked alongside a handful of cars, and walked to the spot near a tall wych elm where she'd find Bartel. The evening was cloudy and warm, the river smooth and silky in the dimming light. Tiny flies danced over the surface. Drifts of bluebells with pointed buds were opening under the beech trees.

There he was, sitting with feet planted apart, a finger stroking his pointed, reddish beard. With his barrel chest and imposing bulk, he resembled a Norse god, albeit a bald one. She couldn't help smiling when she saw him. He was salt of the earth, the only close male friend she'd ever had, apart from Ed.

'*Madame!*' he called. 'How are you this fine evening? I see you're in your smart work suit, so you must be on duty.' He took a rug from his rucksack and laid it on the ground beside him.

'In the middle of two murders.' She sat cross-legged on the rug.

'I read about it. Savage. Any suspects?'

'Plenty, in the sense that there are plenty of fish in the river. I brought goodies from Gusto.'

'Then I'll pour coffee.'

Bartel bought his coffee at Polska, the Polish centre in town. It was robust and bracing. A bit like him. They shared the pastries and drank in silence. That was one of the things she liked so much about him. You didn't have to talk. He'd mentioned a new friend a while back, a woman called Astrella, and Siv had caught a glimpse of them in town. Astrella was tall and wide-hipped, with black hair in a plait. Bartel was vague and non-committal about her, saying only that she worked in a Brighton hotel. Siv understood that she was visiting family in Estonia at the moment.

She sipped coffee and brushed a smear of lemon cream from her trousers. They were due for the dry-cleaner at the weekend. She had her work uniform of four suits — two grey, one navy and one black — which she rotated and teamed with bright T-shirts. Ed had called them her armour.

'Delicious flavour,' Bartel said, running his massive fingers through his beard to dislodge any crumbs. 'Almost as good as my mother's lemon *babka*. Your boss emailed me, asking if I could fix his guttering.'

Bartel was a roofer, and when he'd accompanied Siv to a lunch arranged by Mutsi at Mortimer's house, he'd pointed out that the guttering was damaged. Siv heard a question in his voice. He was well aware of her fractious relationship with her mother.

'Are you interested in doing it?'

'It's work, wouldn't take long. I could fit it in.'

'You don't need my permission, as long as you're up to Mutsi pumping you for information, or giving you details of her style blog.' Her mother wrote a blog called *60Chic*. It offered tips about diet, fashion, exercise and make-up for the mature woman and had a substantial following.

'I believe I can withstand her interrogation. Just in case, I'll keep my cyanide pill in my shoe.'

Siv snorted and watched him twitch his line in the water. 'Er, Bartel?'

'Yes, *Madame*?'

'This man has asked me out for a drink. Well . . . three times, actually. I've said I was busy.'

'Yes?' Bartel continued gazing at the river. A late ray of sun caught his beard in a fiery glow.

'His name's Fabian Draper.' She'd encountered him at some flats where she was searching for a suspect. He was attractive and persistent.

'You're unsure?'

'I suppose.'

'You like him?'

'Um, yes.'

Bartel turned to her and smiled. 'You worry Ed will mind?'

'It's not that. I'm hesitant, really.'

Bartel watched the river again. 'It's not such a big thing, a drink. If it doesn't go well, you haven't lost anything.'

Two adult swans sailed past in slow procession, with six cygnets in tow.

After a few minutes she said, 'Maybe I will, then.'

'In Poland, we have a saying: *What is supposed to hang, won't drown.* In other words, what is supposed to happen, will happen.'

The Poles and the Finns seemed to share a predilection for obscure maxims. 'That sounds profound and wise, but I'm not sure it's helpful.'

'Sleep on it. Shh! I believe I spy a fat carp.'

* * *

The presbytery was a small, detached house to the side of the church, surrounded by high hedges which afforded it meagre light. Father Murray was young and uncomfortably bony, with a posh accent and nervous mannerisms. His dim living room was a cramped mixture of seating, dining table, filing cabinets, books and a desk full of folders and pamphlets. He offered tea, which Siv declined. Behind him was a painting of a robed Jesus walking on water under a dishwater-coloured sky, his open-mouthed apostles in a wooden boat beside him.

'How can I help you, Inspector? You said it was concerning that poor man, Mr Pullman, but I didn't know him and he wasn't a parishioner. Even so, I'll say a mass for him and his little granddaughter next week.'

Siv explained that a witness had seen Pullman entering the church on Thursday afternoon with Lyra. 'This was at about a quarter past three. It's important, because they were murdered after that, between the time they reached home and four fifteen, when the first party guest arrived. Is the church usually open?'

The priest linked his long, skinny fingers and spoke earnestly. 'It never used to be, but when I took over the parish, I wanted it to be more accessible. People worried that there might be thefts or vandalism, but I took the view that God would protect his house, and He has. We've had no incidents. The church is open daily between ten and five, and when there are services, of course.'

'Were there any services on Thursday afternoon?'

'No, there are none on that day.'

'Then why would Mr Pullman have stopped on his journey home with Lyra and called in? He wasn't a Catholic and appeared to have held no religious beliefs.'

Father Murray turned his pious expression on her. 'Perhaps Mr Pullman was moved to pop in. People are sometimes, for no reason they're aware of. God might have beckoned him, stirred his spirit, touched his soul. It does happen. The unseen realm can call to any of us.'

Siv had quite enough on her plate dealing with an all-too-human murderer, without an invisible deity getting involved. 'Would anyone have been in the church at that time? Were you?'

'I wasn't, Inspector. I was here, trying to sort out the parish accounts. There might have been someone from the general maintenance rota in the church. Parishioners volunteer to clean and freshen flowers, and so on. Luckily, there are enough of them to help me to balance the budget. I have to attend to the material as well as the spiritual. At times, I could do with a miracle.' He gestured towards the painting behind him. 'I wish *I* could walk on water, as it were.' He smiled at his own wit.

Siv asked impatiently, 'Do you have a copy of the rota?'

'There is one online that I can access if you want me to.'

'Please.'

Siv waited while he fetched a laptop and scrolled. He fiddled around, muttering to himself while she tapped her foot.

'Yes, here we are. Marina Desmond was down for last Thursday, three to four.'

Siv handed him her card. 'Can you email me a copy of that rota and Marina Desmond's contact details, please.'

'Marina's in her seventies and a bit timid, so go easy with her.'

She decided to try him with a list of names from this investigation so far, and ran through them. 'Are any of these people parishioners or familiar to you?'

'I don't claim to have met every member of my flock, but no, I don't recognise them.'

'You'll be conducting masses tomorrow, I presume, Father?'

'That's correct. Masses at eight a.m. and ten thirty on Sundays.'

She took out printed photos of Pullman and Lyra. 'I'd like you to put these photos up in the foyer and make an announcement, asking anyone who was in the church on Thursday afternoon, or who saw Mr Pullman there, to contact me urgently.'

He clutched the laptop. 'I will, certainly. Anyone — not necessarily a parishioner or a Catholic — could have been in the church on Thursday, just calling in to say a prayer or light a candle, taking a moment from the busy day to quieten their mind.'

Siv stood. 'Yes, Father, but my concern is, was there someone with murder, rather than God, on their mind?'

The priest crossed himself, as if she'd invoked demons. He struck her as a man who lacked the steel and vigour to run a church and a parish. Maybe he excelled at the spiritual, while his band of volunteers provided the corporeal backbone.

* * *

Debbie Wilford, aka Dotty Debbie, reminded Ali of those gymnasts you saw rolling, jumping and balancing on TV. The sight of them always made him feel lumpen. She was compact and wore shorts and a sleeveless T-shirt, showing well-muscled arms and calves. Her hair was pulled tight on top of her head. She sat opposite him on a black balance ball while he took the only armchair, removing an iron and putting it on the floor.

'I moved in two weeks ago, hence the chaos,' she explained. 'Just haven't had time to unpack yet. A lot of kids round here having birthdays this month, so I've been busy with parties — not that I'm complaining.'

Cardboard boxes were stacked against the walls, some open. The windows of the ground-floor flat were still curtainless, so that passing car lights swept the room.

Ali couldn't see any tools of her trade. He'd always been a sucker for magicians on the telly, loving all the bits of business and show. 'Where do you keep your magic stuff?'

'My van's in a lock-up nearby.' She had a loud, jolly voice.

'How did you get into doing magic for a living?'

'My mum bought me a magic set when I was a kid. I'd always been fascinated by it and I fancied being my own boss.'

'Sounds good, making a living out of doing what you love.'

'Scraping a living most of the time.' Debbie bounced on her ball. 'I'm not sure why you're here. I can't tell you anything about what happened on Thursday. I never got inside the house.'

'Let's run through it,' Ali said. 'Did Ms Turton engage you for the party?'

'That's right. She emailed me mid-March. I asked for a few details — number of kids, size of room, stuff like that. I was going to do half an hour of suitable magic tricks for four-year-olds.'

'What would they be?'

'Spoon bending, disappearing coins, levitating cards, stuff like that. I was going to get Lyra to join in with a simple trick called "walking through paper". I always get the birthday kid to do one with me . . . but not this time, sadly.'

'Had you been to the house before?'

'No. I got there, saw the police and parked on the road. I waited outside until a constable took my details and said I could go.'

'So you never met Mr Pullman or Lyra.'

'I'd met Mr Pullman, yeah. Not for ages, though.'

'How come?'

'I went to school with Nell. Used to call by her house sometimes. There's a stables near there where I rode as a teenager. Her mum was lovely. There was always home-made cake. Her coffee and walnut was to die for. She always gave me a wedge to take home as well.' Debbie smiled at the memory. 'And I'd always do a bit of magic for her mum as a thank you.'

'Are you still friends with Nell?'

'Not friends. If I'm honest, I was never that keen on her.'

Ali guessed, 'But you liked her mum's cake?'

Debbie nodded guiltily. 'Her house was a handy pit stop and I was always ravenous after a hack. I've stopped by her stall now and again and picked up a bit of jewellery. It's cheap and handy for tricks. We did that thing about "must have a drink sometime", but it's never happened.' She didn't sound bothered.

'What was Nell like at school?'

'She caused trouble in class and she'd pick arguments with teachers over the smallest thing. I'd say she was bored. Pushing boundaries. She was into weed at an early age. I reckon she was stoned half the time.'

'Did you know Kay back then?'

'Only to see. She was at home sometimes when I called by. She was at college, a studious type.'

'And Tom Pullman?'

'Yeah, he was often there, because I'd ride on Saturdays. He was always busy, in the garden or doing stuff to the house. A bossy sort of man, always pronouncing on things in the news. He was quite short with Nell — he'd be telling her off for not cleaning her room or doing homework. Saying things like, why couldn't she be more like her sister? I always reckoned he could do with some lessons in basic psychology. I mean, that's a guaranteed way of riling a teenager.'

'And how did Nell's mum react to that?'

'She'd never say anything, but I'd see her wince. She chatted when we were on our own, but once her husband was around she clammed up. She comfort ate — she was quite weighty and she'd tuck into lots of her own cake.'

Ali could identify with that. 'Would you say Nell has a problem with her temper?'

Debbie stood and stretched upwards. 'Can't say I've noticed, but weed can make you grumpy, can't it?' She said tentatively, 'D'you . . . it's a bit difficult this, in the circumstances, but I do have to make ends meet . . . d'you reckon Kay will pay my cancellation fee? I don't like to ask her at the moment.'

'Leave it until after the funeral, and send an email,' Ali suggested.

'Hope I don't sound uncaring.'

'Life goes on, bills have to be paid.'

'Thanks.' She stepped near him. 'There's something in your hair.' She made a flourish with her right hand and produced a coin from his ear.

He laughed. 'How did you do that?'

'Secrets of the magic circle. I can't possibly divulge.' At the door, she relented. 'You can google it, astound your colleagues.'

CHAPTER 9

Siv phoned Marina Desmond just after nine on Sunday morning. Her phone went to voicemail. Maybe she was at early mass. Siv left a message, asking Ms Desmond to contact her.

She had a heavy head this morning, courtesy of akvavit the previous evening. *There's no point in having nights off if you drink extra the next time,* she scolded herself. She swallowed a couple of paracetamol and was brewing coffee when there was a tap at her door and a voice chirped, 'Sivvi, cooee!'

Mutsi. Her mother had been here just once before and had never been invited. She briefly considered not answering. Her headache was still hovering and she wanted to drink coffee and take a hot shower before she faced anyone. But her car was outside and Mutsi was capable of sitting on the steps until she appeared. Bite the bullet.

'Hello, what brings you here?'

Mutsi was straight through the door and standing by the wood burner. *'Hello, Mum, how nice to see you,'* she said mockingly. 'Still in your dressing gown, Sivvi?'

'It's Sunday. I haven't showered yet.'

'So I gather. I was seeing Corran about curtains he's making for our living room. I brought him fabric swatches and we agreed on a lovely deep apricot with a gold stripe.

He's so talented and charming — handsome too. Pity he's gay; he's clearly fond of you.'

'You're not supposed to say things like that about people's sexual orientation. It's offensive.'

'Oh? Will you arrest me?' Mutsi laughed and held her wrists out. 'Put the handcuffs on! Let's face it, Corran's easier on the eye than that hulking Bartel with his hands like shovels. That coffee smells good! I'll have a small one, black.'

She sat down on the window seat, crossing her legs and unwinding her silk scarf. She wore an orange-and-black shirt with little bows at the cuffs, paired with tight-fitting orange trousers and dangling silver earrings. Her silver-blonde hair shone and a floral fragrance surrounded her.

Siv poured coffee, feeling grubby, still stale from bed.

'This is excellent,' her mother said, sipping. 'You learned one thing from me, anyway. So, Sivvi, I haven't seen you since you came to lunch, which is now two months ago, and I have left you a couple of messages. How are things?'

'Fine, thanks. Busy.' Siv stood with her back to the cupboard door. A pain throbbed in her temple.

'Tommy Castles was disappointed that you had to disappear after our lunch. I'd say he's got his eye on you. He's attractive, isn't he?'

'If you like his quasi-military, SAS style.' Mutsi had invited Castles for coffee after the lunch, clearly with a view to playing Cupid, a move which Siv had stymied by taking Bartel with her.

'Tommy's fit, looks after himself. He runs every day and he's such a laugh.'

Siv grinned. 'It sounds as if you fancy him.'

'Oh, don't be so silly,' her mother said impatiently.

'You are keen to pair me up with someone — Corran, Tommy. I can shift for myself, thanks.'

'Oh, you're impossible. Have you heard from Rik?'

'Not recently.'

Mutsi made a hopeless gesture. 'I might as well not be alive, as far as your sister's concerned. Never a peep from her.'

She can't stand you. 'She's not the greatest communicator.'

'You're not much better. Will was surprised that neither of you sent me a Mother's Day card.'

For a moment, Siv couldn't recall who Will was. 'We've never celebrated Mother's Day and you never encouraged it.' *I'm not sure you saw yourself as a mother.* 'And let's face it, it would have been hard to keep up with the addresses to send cards to.'

Mutsi chose to ignore that. 'Will's asked your bruiser of a friend to fix the guttering. I hope he's good.'

'I'm sure he is. He's doing a great job on the house he bought.'

'Oh yes, that poky terraced place. Those Victorian streets are so huddled and depressing, especially when it's raining. Quintessentially shabby and British.'

'They've lasted. They're well built, according to Bartel. His will be lovely when he's finished renovating it.'

Mutsi's habit if someone disagreed with her was not to reply or change the subject. She ran a finger along the window ledge and examined it. 'Have you any plans to move from here to somewhere more *suitable*? You must be able to afford it. People will think you're an eco-warrior type, living in a wagon.'

'What people? You're the only person who dislikes it.'

Mutsi put her mug down and smoothed her trousers. 'You've grown snappy since Ed died. You want to watch that. It's off-putting in a woman. You were always kinder than your sister. She was a thorn in my side pretty much from the day she was born, never slept through a night until she was three.'

'I don't expect she kept you awake on purpose. Now, I do have to shower and get dressed. Work to do.'

'On the sabbath?'

'That's right. Criminals don't rest, and neither do I.'

Mutsi tied her scarf around her neck. 'Will and I are taking the boat out for a day trip next Saturday, not sure where yet. Do come. The sea air would do you good, put some colour in your cheeks. You're still rather wan. You can't stay widow pale forever.'

'I doubt I'll have the time next weekend.'

She sighed and tilted her head, scrutinising Siv. 'Very well. Have you tried a facial? It would liven up your complexion. There's a clay mineral one I recommend on my blog. Really brightens and tones the skin.'

'I'll consider it.' *Make an effort to be nice*, Bartel had said to her recently. *You only have one mother and she's getting older. Maybe she's trying, in her own weird way, to repair the damage.* It was all a bit late for Siv. Just because Mutsi wanted to play the concerned mother in this phase of her life didn't mean she had to join the game. She found it hard to forgive the chaotic years of childhood, the random neglect, the traipsing around rented flats, the constant changes of schools, the merry-go-round of men introduced into her life. But there were new lines around Mutsi's eyes and mouth and a kindly word cost her nothing.

'That's a nice scent,' she offered as her mother opened the door.

'Oh, really? I'm not sure about it. Reminds me of one your father once bought me, so I was going to give it away. Would you like it?'

Siv was speechless for a moment. She rallied. 'No, I'll pass on that.'

She made sure her mother had gone, took a few deep breaths and scrubbed the dishes harder than was necessary. Her phone rang as she was drying her hands.

'Hello? Is that Inspector Drummond?' A tiny, trembling voice.

'Yes. Ms Desmond?'

'That's right. I heard your message. Father Murray made an announcement at mass about Mr Pullman and the police. What on earth is the world coming to?'

Siv said gently, 'Were you in the church on Thursday afternoon?'

'I was. I was polishing and I took fresh flowers from my garden, tulips and cherry blossom.'

'Did you see an older man and a little girl?'

'I did see them, just for a few moments. They were the people in those photos Father had pinned up. I was in and out of the kitchen, changing water in the vases, you see. They were at the back of the church, by the confessionals.'

'Was Mr Pullman talking to anyone?'

'It's hard to say. He was a bit hidden. The little girl was interested in the cards we sell — there's a stand near the door. Oh dear . . . to think they were murdered . . .'

Siv could hear that she was crying. 'I'm sorry, Ms Desmond. Take your time. This has been a shock.'

'Thank you. Sorry, I'm being silly.'

'Not at all, and I really appreciate your response. How long was Mr Pullman there for?'

'It's hard to say . . . probably just a few minutes, but I can't be sure.'

'Did you see anyone else in the church? You were there for an hour?'

She blew her nose. 'Yes, from three until almost four. I didn't notice anyone, but I was popping out to the cleaning cupboard and the sink. I spent a bit of time in the side altar, so I wouldn't have seen if someone had just nipped in.'

'Had you ever seen Mr Pullman in the church before?'

'No.' She sounded firmer. 'He wasn't of the parish, I can tell you that. I was baptised in St Peter's, so I know all the regulars. It's a much smaller congregation these days and we're lucky even to have a priest to ourselves. Some parishes have to share one.'

Siv saw that she had a call waiting, so said goodbye to Ms Desmond. Patrick came on the line, speaking fast.

'Guv, I heard from June Fletcher. She owns the farm outside Canterbury that Turton visited Thursday p.m. He wasn't there all the time.'

'Why has it taken her till now to tell us?'

'She had hospital tests on Friday and she's been out of it. She did apologise.'

'OK. Go on.'

'Turton arrived on time at one thirty. They had a discussion and then he took off around two o'clock to survey various parts of the farm. Something about irrigation systems.

He was back at the house at four thirty. Thing is, Ms Fletcher saw him driving away from the farm about half two. She assumed he'd forgotten something.'

'Did she mention it to him?'

'No. She was busy, he reappeared on schedule and they spent an hour or so going through his proposals. I asked if he seemed agitated, but Ms Fletcher said he was fine. Then he got the call from Kay and left immediately. Guv, that farm is to the south of Canterbury. If Turton drove fast, he could have got back to commit the murders. It would have been a stretch, time-wise, but just about doable if the traffic was on his side.'

Siv glanced at her watch. 'Ring Turton and tell him he needs to come to the station at eleven a.m. to help us. Can you get in for then? Ali's got BSS committee members to track today. And get an ANPR check on Turton's car for those times.'

'On it right now,' Patrick said, fired up.

She felt that way herself. This could be a major break. She emailed Ali to update him and hurried to have a shower.

At least her head was better.

* * *

Patrick reported that Ryan Turton had been truculent about attending the station. He now sat opposite Siv and Patrick in the interview room, arms folded. His cotton shirt smelled of fabric softener.

Siv started off easily. 'Thanks for coming in.'

'I didn't have much choice. Kay's very upset about it. We need to talk about the funerals today, get a plan in place, so not great timing.'

'I'm sorry about that. We urgently need to check some information with you, and this was the quickest way to do it.'

Turton's expression was impassive. 'Get on with it, then.'

'Thank you,' she said, aware that her politeness would annoy him. 'You informed us that on Thursday afternoon, you were at June Fletcher's farm near Canterbury from one thirty until approximately five thirty, when your wife rang to inform you of the deaths.'

'Yes. And?'

'DC Hill will explain.'

Patrick informed Turton about his conversation with Ms Fletcher. 'Where were you driving to at two thirty, Mr Turton?'

Turton rolled his tongue inside his cheek. 'She's mistaken. I was out in the fields, doing my job.'

'She was quite sure about seeing your cherry-coloured Renault,' Patrick said.

'It's a common enough car. I can't account for her error.'

Siv pulled her ear lobe. 'Thing is, Mr Turton, we're running a check on your car's number plate and the traffic on Thursday afternoon. Your car will undoubtedly show up, with times and locations. I'm sure you're aware how the system works. It would be easier for us all if you tell us the truth. Much easier for your wife, because you can get home to her and talk about funerals.'

Turton ran both his hands through his hair, massaging the crown of his head.

'Did you return to Berminster that afternoon?' Siv asked.

'Absolutely not!'

'Then tell us where you went,' Patrick told him, 'and we can all go and have our Sunday lunch.'

Turton scowled at him. 'I don't want Kay to hear about this just yet. It's a deeply personal, delicate matter. You'll understand when I tell you.'

'We're all ears,' Siv said. She'd sat through this kind of scene a number of times and could never guess what the confession was going to be. The certainty was that it would involve sex, money or relationships and possibly all three.

'Well, then, I can see that there's no way round this. I popped into a solicitor in Canterbury, an old friend. I was consulting him. I'd told him I was going to be working in the area. He rang me and said he had an hour or so spare because of a cancellation, so I took the opportunity.'

Siv asked, 'What time was this?'

'I met him just before three, left again about half an hour later and went back to the farm. I wasn't in town, murdering my daughter and my father-in-law.'

'What were you consulting this solicitor about?'

'It's got nothing to do with your inquiries.' Turton set his jaw.

Siv told him, 'That's for me to decide.'

Turton pushed up his sleeves, revealing coarse, dark hairs. 'I want a divorce. I was scoping the territory. My friend specialises in that field and was going through my options and financial matters. Kay has no idea, and obviously, I'm not going to raise the subject right now, given the circumstances.'

Siv gazed at him. What a charmer. It could explain the stiffness between the couple. 'Are you sure your wife doesn't realise?'

'Of course I am! I haven't broached the subject.'

'Mr Turton, you and your wife hardly seem fond or close. Are you seeking a divorce because the marriage has broken down?'

'That really is none of your business. I don't suppose a man who believes he has a healthy, viable marriage considers divorce, does he?'

'True,' Siv said, 'but going behind Kay's back strikes me as pretty nasty.'

'What goes around, comes around, as they say,' Turton sneered. 'I'm not having you sitting in judgement on me. Now, I'll give you the details of my solicitor friend so you can check what I've told you with him. Then I'd like to get home.'

When he'd given them the solicitor's name and phone number, he stood and shoved his chair in. 'By the way, something has been stolen from our house. I noticed last night. A valuable jug, a rare William Moorcroft. It stood on top of a corner cupboard in the kitchen. It was an ugly green thing, decorated with mushrooms, but worth a couple of thousand.'

Siv asked, 'When did you last see it there?'

'Neither of us can remember. An aunt of mine gave it to us as a wedding present. We both disliked the thing, and Kay put it up high so we wouldn't have to look at it. Kay phoned Nell, but she couldn't say when she last dusted it.' He added snarkily, 'Probably never.'

'It could have vanished before Thursday, then,' Patrick said.

'Of course it could, but you've been asking if anything was stolen, so I'm telling you. I can't imagine why anyone would want it, unless there's a market for revolting pottery. I've a photo of it for you. We took one as it's a valuable item.'

They let him go when he'd sent over the photo and went upstairs to Siv's office. She phoned the solicitor, who confirmed Turton's story.

'We can cross him off our list,' she told Patrick, 'but check the ANPR record just as belt and braces.'

'It's a bit strange, isn't it, guv? Not talking to your partner about wanting a divorce, just getting on with it. And especially when a kid's involved.'

'It's not unknown, but it is mean and underhand.'

'I wonder what he'll tell her about why we wanted to speak to him?'

'I'm sure he'll have no trouble making up a lie. Turton's story checks out, but there's still something about that couple. He talks about his wife being upset by us questioning him, but he's acted very coldly towards her. What did he mean by that remark, "What goes around, comes around"?'

Patrick spun his pen on the table. 'And who was sedating Lyra, and why?'

* * *

Ali was sitting in Jill Bartoli's living room, waiting while she made coffee. She was the last of the BSS committee members on his list and he hoped talking to her would prove more productive than to the others, who'd sung Tom Pullman's praises and wittered on about fundraising teas and countryside rambles until his brain was numb. He anticipated biscuits with the coffee. Polly had promised a roast chicken dinner this evening, but that seemed a long time away.

He checked the new smartwatch Polly had presented him with last night, wishing now that Patrick had never mentioned the one Tom Pullman had been wearing. Patrick had called into Nutmeg, the café where Polly was the chef, and had commented that Pullman used his watch to check his blood pressure. Polly had taken inspiration and bought one for Ali, saying that she'd checked with Nurse Keene at the diabetic clinic, who'd agreed it was an excellent idea, 'given his job and challenges'. The watch incorporated a continuous glucose monitor which would track his blood sugar 24/7. The leaflet informed him that the timepiece would be his 'daily diabetes friend', but right this minute he felt like it was spying on him. He'd exclaimed at the cost, but Pol had told him he was beyond price. That was a guilt trip — he was grateful for her care and kindness, but would have preferred to take the decision to wear the monitor for himself. Also, he didn't like her ganging up with Nurse Keene, and he was aware that 'challenges' was a euphemism for his greed and lack of self-discipline.

Sometimes he managed to forget that he had diabetes, but now, with this constant reminder, he could say goodbye to those treasured moments of oblivion.

He glanced at the screen, trying to visualise the watch as his friend. The readings were in vivid orange and blue. Unmissable. At the moment, they were within his healthy target range. He'd eaten a banana and some walnuts between visits to BSS members, so something sweet would be permissible.

Ms Bartoli brought in a tray with a tin of assorted biscuits, newly opened. The lid featured puppies gambolling in a cornfield. 'I won these in a raffle. They're posh, so dig in.'

Ali took one while she poured coffee. Ms Bartoli had a weathered complexion topped by severely cut grey hair, and wore a striped blue shirt with white collar and white trousers teamed with white-and-blue trainers. She might be about to umpire a tennis match. Her no-nonsense manner went with her sporty apparel, so he decided to abandon the niceties.

'Did you like Tom Pullman?'

She stopped pouring milk into her coffee. 'Not particularly. He wasn't a friend, but I admired his commitment and energy. We'll miss him at BSS: he was an efficient ship's captain.'

Ali caught a biscuit crumb in his hand. 'What didn't you like about him?'

Ms Bartoli raised a thumb, followed by index and middle fingers. 'A, his pomposity, B, his narrow views and C, his philandering. Oh, and—' she raised a fourth finger — 'D, he was very anti-religion, quite vocally so at times, and in a way some of us found offensive.'

'I've heard about A and B already,' Ali said. 'Tell me about C.'

She rubbed her little finger along her top lip, where she had a faint moustache. 'This is just my own suspicion, possibly way off the mark, you understand.'

'Fine.'

She was flat-chested, but folded her arms where her bosom should have been. 'Tom was the kind of man some women find sexy. Not particularly good-looking but well-spoken and peppy.'

Ali chewed the last bite of his custard cream. He liked a gossipy interview. You could never tell what nuggets you might mine. 'You didn't find him attractive?'

'Not at all. He was the kind of man who preferred a woman to be quiet while he aired his opinions. His wife was a mute sort of person, probably because she was used to never getting a word in edgeways.'

'I can see why he and Belinda Hanak crossed swords then,' Ali prompted.

Ms Bartoli smiled. 'Ah, you've heard about their wrangling. Some of the committee meetings did get heated.'

'Getting back to the philandering . . .'

'I've no proof, but I'd say that Tom and Belinda had something going on, or had been involved at some point.' She picked up the pot. 'More coffee?'

'Please. What makes you think that?'

'I saw them about six months ago, sitting in his car at Ambourne Water. Belinda's car was parked nearby. I was coming back from a walk around there and I spotted them. They didn't see me, because they were talking very intensely, heads close. Now, I can only imagine one reason why two people would be meeting in a car park in that way. I'm fairly sure it wasn't to discuss committee business.'

She had a gleam in her eye. Ali was sure that Ms Bartoli had been relishing the moment of parting with this information.

'So this was around last November?'

'That's right. A chilly, dank kind of day, I remember. They seemed quite *cosy* in the car.'

'Did you mention this to either of them or anyone else?'

'No. Nothing to do with me, I accept that adults make their own choices. Tom was a free agent and if Belinda wanted to deceive her husband, that was up to her. It didn't surprise me about her. I thought I should tell you now, because of what's happened. It did make a kind of sense, when I considered the way they went on sometimes in meetings.'

'How do you mean?'

'Oh — irritating the hell out of each other as a kind of flirting, or as a cover for fancying each other. Like Benedict and Beatrice in *Much Ado about Nothing*. I prefer a more straightforward approach myself, but each to their own.'

Ali had never read or seen any Shakespeare and he couldn't imagine arguing with someone as a come-on. He and Pol rarely fell out, both having peaceable dispositions. It helped make sense of Pullman's letter, though, indicating that there might have been a cooling off between lovers. But on whose side?

'Why weren't you surprised about Belinda?'

Jill Bartoli crossed her legs, patting the crisp cotton of her trousers. 'She's a flirt, or likes to see herself as one. She talks like a feminist but she's always coming on to men — flicking their ties, smoothing their sweaters, patting their hands, asking them about their hobbies. She gets poor old Harry Hudson hot under the collar. It's a power thing — almost automatic with her, I'd say. She likes to be the centre of male attention. Her husband doesn't seem to notice, but then he worships the ground she treads on, gives her everything she wants.' Ms Bartoli's mouth tightened disapprovingly. 'Spoiled women like that always reckon they can do whatever they like. They expect a smooth path through life.'

Ali detected sour grapes. Jill Bartoli gave an impression of brisk self-sufficiency but there was a hint of loneliness to her. He imagined she filled her days with timetabled activities and busyness. She'd probably like to be the centre of someone's attention.

She asked, 'Anything else? I've a bowls match at two thirty, so I'd like to get going.'

Ali left her clearing away and lit his second Gitane of the day outside. He rang Siv, but her phone went to voicemail so he left a message with an update, saying he might have uncovered a BSS love nest.

* * *

That evening, Siv was in a wine bar by the harbour with Fabian Draper. As soon as they'd ordered their drinks, he told her that he was divorced, no kids, and that his ex had remarried.

'Best to get this stuff out there.' He smiled. 'So, I have a clean sheet. How about you?'

She was taken aback at this slew of information. She'd expected some small talk, not caring for that 'clean sheet'. Who had one of those? 'I was widowed.'

He drew back a little. 'I'm so sorry, clumsy of me. That must have been awful for you.'

'It was.'

'Was it an illness, or . . .?'

'No, not an illness. I'd rather not go there, if you don't mind.' She'd only just met this man and wasn't prepared to lay out her life details like a menu.

'Sorry, of course. Delicate subject.'

His voice was louder than she remembered. 'What do you do, Fabian?'

He was attractive, with his dark eyes and lively expression. She listened to him talking about his work as a town planning consultant, her mind drifting to Ali's feedback about Tom Pullman and Belinda Hanak's meeting at Ambourne Water. They seemed an unlikely pairing, but as Ali had pointed out, a failed affair would explain the rancour and disagreement. She forced herself to pay attention.

'It involves a fair amount of travel,' Fabian was saying. 'I get to meet lots of fascinating people, although I've never met a detective before, certainly not one so beautiful.'

She'd never liked flattery. That contrived remark had put a smudge on his clean sheet. 'You've obviously kept out of trouble, then.'

'Absolutely. Unlike my neighbour, who seems to have been knee-deep in it. We'd never had the police at our flats before, or had one of the residents arrested. It kept us going for weeks. Still, her bad luck, my gain. Meant I met you.'

Siv couldn't work out if he was superficial or nervous. She sipped her delicious pinot and gazed out of the window at the anchored boats. The harbour lights winked in the dusk. Mortimer's boat, *Quicksilver*, was moored further along, out of sight. He and Mutsi might be on board with gin and tonics and snacks. Life was weird. She'd never have imagined that she'd be living back in Berminster without Ed and with Mutsi just up the road.

Fabian talked on about loving the town. 'It's compact but offers a cinema and theatre, and the coast is amazing. I rent my flat, but I might buy here. Whereabouts do you live?'

'I rent too, for now. It gives time to pause and breathe. I needed that.'

'I'm sure.' He discussed the area and the walks he enjoyed. 'Listen to me going on about myself! I understand that you're very talented at origami.'

'I love doing it. How did you find out?'

'Saw a bit about you in the museum. You're contributing to their display about the town's maritime history. Do you work to bought patterns, or your own designs?'

'Bit of both. I mainly design my own.'

He grinned. 'I suppose that means you have a problem-solving brain, which is handy in a detective. I read about those murders. I suppose you're working on them.'

'I am, but I can't discuss them.'

'I get it. But I know Ryan Turton, I've played tennis with him a couple of times at our sports club. It must be terrible for him.'

Now he had her full attention. 'He's a friend of yours?'

'I wouldn't say that. Good player, but doesn't tend to socialise after a match. His wife and daughter came to watch a couple of times last summer. The little girl loved clapping for her dad.'

Siv finished her drink. 'A happy family, would you say?'

'Seemed so. They were all hugging and laughing after the match, and he had the girl on his shoulders, his arm around his wife.' Fabian smiled. 'I remember feeling a bit jealous of their happiness, because I was there on my own, nobody to go home to.'

The honesty made her warm to him. 'Living on your own can strike like that at times.' There'd been occasions when Ali and Patrick had referred to their domestic bliss and she'd got miffed at them.

He finished his martini and gestured at her glass. 'Another drink?'

'Thanks, Fabian, but I really need to head off. I still have work to do and an early start tomorrow.'

'Oh.' He pulled a face. 'You're a hard woman to pin down, and when I finally manage to meet up, you have to rush away.' It sounded like a complaint, covered with a little laugh.

'That's detectives for you, I'm afraid, especially when they're investigating murders.'

'I'll ring you, shall I?'

'Yes, fine. Take care.' She stood and held her hand out, not wanting to invite a kiss on the cheek.

She drove home, deciding that the jury was out where Fabian was concerned. Or maybe her judgement was. Had he been insincere or just tense? It was so long since she'd been on anything resembling a date, she was rusty, de-skilled. She asked Ed, *What do you make of him?* No reply. If there was a spirit world, maybe the dead moved on after a while, became interested in other things, rather than hanging around waiting for the living to ask their opinions. That could be tiring and a bit of a drag. Just as well, if that was the case. Ed might have joined a celestial cycling club and found himself far too busy to comment on her humdrum, earth-bound life. She hoped so. The idea cheered her.

Still, the meeting with Fabian hadn't been too difficult, there'd been no awkward pauses or misunderstandings. And she had to admit, it felt nice to have an attractive man seeking out her company. Would she agree to meet again? Probably. And the drink had been extremely useful regarding the Turtons. The family Fabian had described was a far cry from the couple she'd been observing, with one of them covertly considering divorce. What had changed so drastically since last summer?

CHAPTER 10

Lex Rani, the psychologist, could see straight away that Elsie Sterling was quite different to her friend Manda. He'd talked to Manda first that morning. She'd been shy, fretful, clinging to her anxious mother, who'd sat in the corner, gripping her hands together tightly and sighing. Sometimes, the parents sabotaged any attempts at engagement. Manda had resisted his invitations to engage with the toys and find the one she liked best. When he'd said Lyra's name, she'd buried her face in her mother's lap and shaken her head. After only a few minutes, she'd been tearful. Lex had cut the session short.

Now here was Elsie, chatting to him and confidently moving around the room, which was set up as a play space, with toys, artwork and soft floor cushions. Her mother was more composed, smiling at her daughter. Elsie immediately picked up a teddy and made it do somersaults. Excellent. Lex gave her a few minutes to investigate the toys, while he laid a doll down on the table and sat two others nearby. Elsie noticed and came over.

'Here's Lyra doll,' Lex said. 'She was lying down in her playhouse when you saw her.'

'Sleeping,' Elsie said.

Lex took one of the other dolls and handed one to Elsie, who held it by its hair. 'My doll is Manda and your doll is you. That OK?'

Elsie gave a dubious nod.

'Let's run to Lyra, the way you did in the garden when you went to her party.'

'Didn't have a party.'

'That was a shame. You went to see Lyra in her play-house. Shall we run, like this?' Lex hopped his doll along the table, to the Lyra doll.

Elsie glanced at her mother, who gave a thumbs-up. She laughed and bounced her doll to his.

'What did Elsie doll do now?'

Elsie poked her tongue through her lips, called 'Lyra!' and then pushed her doll's foot against the Lyra doll.

'You nudged Lyra like that with your foot?'

'See if she wake up.'

'Fine. Did you do anything else?'

'Went to find my mummy.'

'Did you see anyone else in the garden?'

Elsie shrugged, put the doll down and turned away to a wooden house which was like a much smaller version of Lyra's birthday present. Her mother shifted in her chair, and Lex mouthed, *Not much longer.*

Elsie knelt and started to rearrange furniture in the house.

'Lyra was your friend at nursery,' Lex said, sitting on the floor next to her.

'I liked her. Her daddy shouted sometimes.'

'Oh dear. Did that frighten her?'

'She liked singing with me.'

'That's good. Do you have a favourite song?'

Elsie concentrated on shifting a tiny sofa to her satisfaction. '"Five Little Monkeys."'

'I've not heard that one. Can you sing it for me?'

Elsie grouped a couple of chairs around the sofa and then sang breathily.

Five little monkeys jumping on the bed,
One fell off and bumped his head,
Mama called the doctor and the doctor said,
No more monkeys jumping on the bed!

'That's terrific. Did Lyra sing that with you?'

'We sang carols in God's house at Christmas.'

'That must have been fun.'

Elsie turned to a wooden train set and picked up an engine. 'Lyra went to God's house with Poppa. He met a big man there.'

'Did she say anything else about that?'

'They went up the steps. It smelled funny.' Elsie snickered. 'She needed a poo and Poppa said wait.'

'Oh dear. I hope she did wait. Who was the man her poppa met?'

'Dunno.'

'Did Lyra go to the church once, twice, three times?'

'I want to go home now. Can I have this?' Elsie picked up a kaleidoscope, raising it to the light. She ran to her mother with it.

'You can't just ask for things in other people's places, Elsie, I've told you about that.' Ms Sterling gave Lex an apologetic smile.

'That's OK, you have it, Elsie.' It was a cheap toy. He'd replace it. Elsie had earned it and she'd been a dream compared to some of the kids he saw.

* * *

Patrick was having a good start to the week. He'd woken next to Kitty's warm body and lay inhaling the sweet scent of her tangled hair until she had to leave for her early shift at Halse Woods. In the kitchen, he'd found Eden making pancakes with maple syrup and sat eating his breakfast, chatting with her and Noah. The room was warm, redolent with aromas of coffee and warm sugar. This life bore little resemblance to the hard times when he was Noah's sole support. Then, his heart would sink as he returned to the mucky, drab house and found his brother sitting in the gloom, reading or staring at the TV. These days, Eden had the place gleaming, and Noah was invigorated, going out regularly.

Patrick poured a second cup of coffee and ran over the investigation so far while he listened to Noah and Eden's banter. His mind focused on Drew Gifford, the man's slipperiness and his questions about the murders. He decided to examine Gifford's background a bit further when he got to the station.

Half an hour later, at his desk, he did a few searches around the information he'd gathered on the man. Gifford didn't have any offences on record, but Patrick broke into a grin when he came across some details linked to his address. When he rang Cavendish Treats, Brendan Deeley told him that Gifford had called in sick that morning.

'Something about a cold,' he said tetchily. 'He's having too many days off for my liking and leaving me in the lurch. And here's a surprise — they're usually Mondays and Fridays. He'd better watch his step or he won't have a job to come back to.'

The guv had gone to see Belinda Hanak again and Ali was at the nursery. Patrick sent Siv a text and waited impatiently for her response.

* * *

Siv arrived at the Hanak house at 8.30 a.m. They were both still in their dressing gowns, listening to the radio in the conservatory while they had coffee and croissants. Belinda's age showed without the veneer of make-up, the skin below her eyes puckered and blueish. Siv noted a little tear in the fabric of her floral dressing gown.

'Goodness, you're an early bird, Inspector,' Aled Hanak said as he led her in. 'Coffee?'

'No thanks. I need to talk to you in private, Ms Hanak.'

'Gosh! That sounds ominous!' Belinda pulled a face at her mystified husband.

'Can we go to the living room?'

'What's this about?' Hanak asked.

'I'd rather speak to your wife alone for now. There's information regarding BSS that I need to review.'

'Can I get dressed first?' Belinda smiled up at Siv, her voice coaxing. 'I'm at a disadvantage with you so smart and efficient in your suit and me in my silly old jimjams and not even a smidge of war paint.'

That's just fine with me. 'I don't have time to wait, I'm afraid, unless you want to come to the station.'

'Oh, I see. It's like that.' Belinda rose and slipped a foot more securely into a mule. She said in a grand drawl, 'Let us withdraw, then,' blew her husband a kiss and whispered conspiratorially, 'Make sure you've got the file ready in the cake for me, darling, in case DI Drummond bangs me up!'

The living room was spacious, decorated in a poppy print wallpaper with a few generic landscape paintings. Numerous photos of the Hanaks were dotted around.

'What's this BSS information then?' Belinda asked, pushing back a strand of uncombed hair. 'Has someone been fiddling the tea fund?'

'I'm surprised at your light-hearted manner, Ms Hanak,' Siv snapped. 'This is a serious business. I'm investigating two deaths. Is there anything you want to add to what you've told me about Tom Pullman?'

Belinda wasn't used to being reprimanded. She bridled, her shoulders lifting. 'There's no need to use that tone with me. Civility costs nothing, even with the police. I've told you what I can about Tom.'

Siv appreciated that Belinda was a bright, forceful woman. She'd listened to Ali's report of her alleged flirtatiousness and expectation of getting what she wanted, with his proviso that Jill Bartoli might be jealous of her. She took out her notebook, a move which often bothered people. Siv usually protected information sources but right now, she was so fed up with Belinda's attitude she decided to muddy the BSS waters.

'Do you get on with Jill Bartoli?'

Belinda was thrown. 'Yes, she's a nice enough woman. A bit dry and humourless, maybe. Why are you asking about Jill?'

Siv clicked her pen officiously. 'Putting it another way, does she like you?'

'I suppose. She hasn't indicated that she doesn't. What are you getting at?' Belinda was disconcerted now, linking her fingers and cracking them.

Siv doodled, pretending to make notes. At last she asked, 'Why were you meeting Tom Pullman at Ambourne Water?'

'Sorry?' Belinda shifted in her chair.

'You were with him in his car a while ago — last November, deep in conversation.'

Belinda took a breath. 'Who told you that? Jill?'

'Just answer the question.' Siv clipped her pen to her notepad and sat back. She could tell that Belinda was preparing to lie from the way her eyes darted. It might be interesting or not. Whatever she made up, it would be difficult to catch her out in the fib, given that the other party to the meeting was dead.

Belinda gave a little laugh. 'I suggested that we meet up outside of the committee to see if we could agree to disagree over BSS without unpleasantness. We got coffee at Ambourne and drank it in Tom's car. It was a perfectly innocent meeting.'

'Was it successful?'

'No, sadly. Tom was so intransigent. He just wanted to have his say and not listen. I suppose that's what Jill saw when she was snooping.'

'Did you meet up again outside of BSS?'

'No. I didn't wish to repeat the experience.'

'And your husband — did you tell him about the get-together?'

Belinda tucked her hands under her legs. 'No.'

'Oh? Why not?'

'He'd have tried to dissuade me. In hindsight, he'd have been right. It was a waste of time.'

Siv sighed and said quietly, 'I don't believe you. You were meeting Tom Pullman for some other reason, and I'll find out why.'

'Oh, for goodness sake! You come barging in here before we're dressed, making insinuations . . . I've been honest with you.' Belinda's colour was high — fight, not flight. 'If you choose to listen to Jill, you'll be barking up the wrong tree. She can't find a man, probably because she looks like one herself, so she spreads gossip.'

Ouch. Siv decided that she'd leave it there, with Belinda well and truly rattled. She had one last parting shot at the door. 'Do you visit St Peter's church?'

'No. I'm not even sure where it is. We're not church-goers.' Belinda added spitefully, 'Did Jill tell you she'd seen me in there as well? She's got a more vivid imagination than I gave her credit for.'

In her car, Siv read a message from Patrick and rang him straight away. 'I saw your info. Well done on finding that. Is Ali back?'

'Not yet.'

'And Gifford's probably at home, given that he called in sick. He must have been sweating since last Thursday. I'll meet you there in fifteen minutes. Could be interesting.'

* * *

Drew Gifford lived in a house near the train station. A section of road outside had been dug up and a group of men in orange tabards were drilling. A tang of sewage hung in the air. Gifford opened the door wearing just check boxer shorts and holding a half-eaten bacon sandwich.

'DC Hill and DI Drummond,' Patrick said. 'Your cold's better, then.'

'Eh?'

'You called in sick to work.'

'Oh, yeah. I wasn't too good earlier.' He wrinkled his blade-like nose, which boasted a large yellowish pimple.

'That pong's awful, wouldn't be surprised if it's making me ill. They've been digging out here for days now.'

Siv said, 'We'll come in and get away from the smell. It doesn't mix well with the bacon.'

Gifford hesitated and then led them in, saying, 'Is it about those murders? I can't tell you nothing else.'

He was bandy-legged, his gait wonky as they followed him in. They sat in a living room with a brick fireplace flanked by alcoves with built-in cupboards and mock-leather armchairs. It was tidy, but reeked of cigarette smoke. Gifford finished his sandwich, licked his fingers and then wiped them absent-mindedly on his boxers.

Siv asked, 'Is your dad in — Brian Gifford?'

'Nah. He visits me nan in Hove on Mondays. Does a bit of shopping for her, stuff like that.' His glance flicked to the cupboard on the right of the fireplace. 'Why d'you ask?'

'He's got quite a record, your dad, at least as long as my arm,' Siv replied. 'Breaking and entering, theft, receiving stolen goods. A career that's kept my colleagues busy over the years.'

Gifford ran a nail between his teeth, extracted a sliver of bacon rind and swallowed it. 'So? He don't do that stuff no more, not for a while.'

Siv smiled. 'He hasn't been *caught* doing it. Which is surprising, because he's not exactly a criminal mastermind.'

'Yeah, whatever. Anyway, like I said, he's not here.' Gifford added cockily. 'So if you want to talk to him, you'll have to make an appointment.'

'Have you ever helped your dad out?' Patrick asked.

'Meaning?'

'Like father, like son. Helped him with his crimes.'

Gifford shook his head vigorously. 'No way. You got nothing on me, you can check.'

'I have. Doesn't mean you're squeaky clean.'

'That's slander, innit? Or is it libel? Anyway, you're not allowed to make allegations like that.' He fingered his pimple and winced. 'And like I said, Dad's going straight now.' He checked out the cupboard again.

Siv caught Patrick's eye, saw that he'd noticed Gifford's nervous glances. She coughed and rubbed her throat. 'Could I have a glass of water?'

'OK.'

As soon as Gifford had left the room, she slipped gloves on, went to the cupboard and tried the door. They were so stupid they hadn't even bothered to lock it. It was stacked with watches, jewellery, silver and china items. On the bottom shelf stood a tall green jug, decorated with mushrooms. Siv brought it over and placed it on the coffee table by her chair. She took out her phone, found the photo of the Turtons' Moorcroft jug and showed it to Patrick.

He raised a thumb, murmuring, 'He wouldn't have killed them both for that, surely?'

'Let's ask him.'

Gifford returned with a glass of water, which he handed to Siv and sat back down. He'd put on a vest with an image of a huge tarantula on the front. He didn't notice the jug until Siv pointed.

'Tell us about this, Mr Gifford.'

He half-jumped in his seat. 'You've been in our cupboard!'

'That's correct.'

'You've no right doing that. You should have a search warrant.'

Siv sighed. 'Mr Gifford, this valuable jug was stolen from the Turtons' house. We can sit here and argue, but it will only complicate matters for you and your dad.'

He blinked. 'I don't know nothing about it.'

'I bet we'll find prints on this jug,' Patrick said. 'Yours, your dad's or maybe both. You don't seem careful types.'

Gifford dug down the side of his chair for a tin of roll-ups, found a lighter and lit up. He stared up at the ceiling as if it fascinated him.

'To be honest, Mr Gifford,' Siv commented, 'I don't care much about the jug being nicked. It's an ugly thing — even its owners dislike it. I can't even get worked up about the other stuff in the cupboard. What interests me is whether the person who stole this also murdered two people.'

That snagged his attention. He choked on a long wisp of smoke. 'No way! Come on, you don't think that!'

'Then tell me how you came to have this in your possession. If you don't, I'll have to arrest you. I'm afraid it doesn't look good for you.'

'Did you steal it and when?' Patrick demanded.

Gifford took a long drag on his roll-up and picked a shred of tobacco from his bottom lip. 'I saw it in the kitchen last Thursday when I delivered the party stuff to the old guy. It was on top of a cupboard. I mentioned it, and he said it was worth a lot but no one actually liked it. I didn't nick it, though.'

'So you're telling us your dad did,' Siv said.

Gifford winced.

'You might as well tell us. If both of you are involved in theft rather than murder, best to just clear the decks.'

Gifford slumped, his reserves of bravado exhausted. 'I rang and told Dad about it. The old guy, Pullman, said he was glad I was on time, 'cos he had to fetch his granddaughter from nursery at three. Dad went round there and took it while Pullman was out, said it was like an invitation 'cos he'd left the back doors unlocked. He never killed anyone for it.'

'What time did you ring him?' Siv asked.

'About twenty past two.'

'I suppose you keep an eye open during your other deliveries as well, and tip your dad off if you see anything worth stealing. I expect we'll find that a lot of people you've taken party food to have had stuff nicked.' Siv watched his face crumple. 'The dots should add up nicely.'

'I'm not saying nothing more.' Gifford sucked the last gasp from his cigarette.

Siv told him, 'You don't need to for now. I'm arresting you on suspicion of aiding and abetting a crime.'

Gifford closed his eyes and groaned. Siv placed the jug in an evidence bag while Patrick got him to part with his dad's mobile number.

* * *

133

Back at the station, Patrick handed Drew Gifford over to custody colleagues while Siv contacted Brian Gifford. She told him she was making general enquiries about stolen goods, and to her surprise, he agreed to attend a voluntary interview at four o'clock. Maybe he'd been half-expecting a call and was relieved that he wasn't being arrested. He'd probably try contacting his son, unaware that Drew was currently deprived of his phone.

Ali arrived soon after, accompanied by Lex Rani. 'My head's throbbing,' he groaned. 'The noise at that nursery! God save and defend me from groups of screeching toddlers.'

'It's not your blood sugar, is it?' Siv asked anxiously.

'Nope, that's OK at the moment.' Ali held out his arm. 'Polly bought me this new watch. It monitors it for me.'

'That's great. I could see she was interested when I described the health functions on Tom Pullman's smart-watch,' Patrick said. 'It'll be a big help, won't it?'

'Hmm. You definitely gave Pol food for thought, so thanks for that,' Ali muttered, with a hint of tartness that went over Patrick's head.

Siv noted it. Patrick was an evangelist about all technology and believed it offered answers to many of life's problems. If he could have afforded it, he'd be living in a smart home where gadgets organised his life for him. Maybe Ali felt ganged up on, which was never easy, even if people meant well. Ed had been diabetic and he'd talked to her about the occasional depression and frustration he'd suffered. Ali masked his feelings with humour, but occasionally, she sensed distress below the show of buoyancy.

Lex Rani was tapping his own watch. Siv took the hint. 'How did you get on with the children, Lex?'

He was a hefty, bearded man in his fifties with heavy black glasses. He liked working with the police and had a weakness for studied pauses.

'I saw them this morning. Elsie was more forthcoming than Manda, who's a less confident girl. They've both been told that Lyra's in heaven, playing with the angels. Not sure what either of them make of that.'

'What should you tell a four-year-old?' Patrick asked.

Lex adjusted an arm of his glasses. 'Not that kind of nonsense. Best to explain death in simple terms of physical functions stopping. For example, "Lyra's body stopped working." Then answer questions from there. It takes time. Not too much information at once.'

'Easier said than done,' Siv observed.

'Oh, absolutely,' Lex agreed. 'It's never easy. I've given the parents some useful information and steered them to a couple of websites. Elsie was quite taken with the interview and chatted about Lyra and her party. There was an element of annoyance that it didn't happen.' He smiled. 'Elsie's one of life's pragmatists. Manda's more emotional. She got weepy and wouldn't engage with me at all, so I kept it brief with her. I didn't get much that you don't already have about that afternoon in the garden, I'm afraid. Elsie said she nudged Lyra's foot with her shoe, and she called Lyra's name. They thought she was asleep and they ran down to Meg Sterling. I asked Elsie if she saw anyone else in the garden and she didn't respond. We can take that as a negative.'

'Thanks for checking that out, Lex,' Siv said. 'We'll push on now with other matters.'

He held up a finger. 'Ah, but I haven't finished. They didn't have anything to add about last Thursday in the garden, but Elsie reported other things that Lyra had said. She has good recall for her age. You might find them interesting.' He raised his eyebrows, a little smile on his lips.

'Go on,' Siv urged, irked by his grandstanding manner.

'Here are the extra nuggets for you, then. Lyra told Elsie that her grandad met a "big man" in "God's house". She went with him to a place with steps up to the door and it smelled funny.'

'St Peter's!' Ali said.

'I assumed Lyra meant a church,' Lex agreed. 'I tried to tease out if Lyra'd said anything else about that, but drew a blank.'

Siv leaned forward. 'Did Elsie indicate if this was more than one meeting?'

'I tried to establish that, but Elsie had had enough by then. The other comment Elsie made was that Lyra had said her daddy shouted sometimes. Again, that was all I could get. Maybe that information is of some help?'

'The shouting comes as no surprise,' Siv said, 'but it's useful to know that Tom Pullman was meeting a man. Thanks so much, Lex, that's extremely useful. We'll buy you a drink when this investigation's over.'

'I'll hold you to that,' he said, sounding satisfied and putting his notes away. 'Good luck with it, anyway.'

He left the door swinging after him. Patrick got up to close it, saying, 'So Pullman was meeting a man, but how do we identify him?'

They were all silent for a few moments, digesting the information.

Siv asked Ali, 'How did you get on at the nursery?'

'There was nothing much to help us. They checked their records and showed them to me. There are two children who are given medication during the day. They'd never given Lyra anything and they confirmed that they'd never administer medication without a doctor's guidance.'

'Had she ever seemed tired?'

'That was the one thing that was mentioned and it coincided with what Alicia told me. The notes for the sixteenth of January said that Lyra had been sluggish, not her usual self and she said she had tummy pains. They'd contacted her mother and she fetched her early, at two thirty. She was back at nursery and fine the next day.'

'Could mean something or nothing,' Siv said. 'She might have heard her parents arguing, her dad shouting. On the other hand, kids do get random aches and upsets.' She recalled how her stomach used to knot when Mutsi had spoken disparagingly of her father, or mentioned another new 'uncle'.

'That was the only time any tiredness was recorded,' Ali said, glancing at his watch.

'I got nowhere with Belinda Hanak,' Siv told them. 'She admitted meeting Pullman at Ambourne Water. She claimed she suggested it, to try and sort out their differences over BSS. She was lying, but she's gutsy and I couldn't get past her defences.'

'An affair, then?' Patrick asked.

'Possibly. They hardly seem suited, from what we've heard about their personalities. I can't see Belinda wanting to sit and listen to a pompous man air his opinions. She claimed that Ambourne Water was the only get-together, and from Elsie's comment, Pullman wasn't meeting her in St Peter's. Anything more from the neighbours around Cove Parade?'

'No one recognised any of the vehicles we showed them,' Patrick reported. 'I've been checking CCTV regarding Harry Hudson, Aled Hanak and Alicia Ferreira. Nothing on Hudson, but when I asked him, he told me he cycled side roads to Minster Beach and back. Alicia's on camera entering the library at three forty and exiting at five twenty-three. Hanak was in and out of Blossom garden centre between two forty and three o'clock. There's no CCTV at Drayton Fields, so he's a question mark for the hour when the murders happened.'

Siv became absorbed with winding thread around a loose button on her jacket. 'I was talking to a guy called Fabian Draper. He told me he used to play tennis now and again last summer with Ryan Turton. He saw Turton with Kay and Lyra and described a close, happy family with laughs and cuddles. I'd like to understand what's changed since last year. Quite a contrast to the picture that couple presents now.'

Ali stopped fiddling with his watch. 'Draper — isn't he the guy we met when we were at Yaz Ferris's flat in January?'

'That's right,' Siv said.

'Did he contact you with the information?'

'I spoke to him, yes. We'll talk to Nell Pullman about her family again. I've no idea how much she takes in if she's in a dope haze a lot of the time, but she might have noticed something even if she doesn't realise it. She's our closest link to the clam-like Turtons, so might as well try.'

'I got a bit from Debbie Wilford about Nell,' Ali reported. 'Seems she's always been truculent, to put it mildly, and she's been into weed for years. Otherwise, Debbie couldn't tell me much. She magicked a coin from behind my ear, which was impressive.'

'Maybe you can learn the trick and try it on DCI Mortimer, help him forget his budget troubles.' Siv stood and rolled her head. 'Ali, I want you to interview Brian Gifford with me. Patrick, you talk to the son again in case there's anything he's not told us. Going by his record, it's unlikely that Gifford senior is our killer, but if he was in the house last Thursday afternoon, he may have useful information.'

When Siv had gone to her office, Ali turned eagerly to Patrick.

'Was she on a date with this Fabian Draper?'

'Maybe. She got shifty and blushed a bit when you asked her about him. What's he like?'

'Nice face. Fit. I could see she'd noticed him.'

'That'd be good, wouldn't it, if she's seeing him. Means she's getting out, being sociable.'

'Hope so. Yeah, it's time she started to have some good things in her life again.'

CHAPTER 11

On Monday afternoons between two and five, Belinda Hanak did a complex jigsaw while Aled was at judo classes. She enjoyed the problem-solving aspect of them and had read that they improved visual-spatial reasoning. Anything to keep her brain ticking over. She borrowed the jigsaws from the hobbies supply at BSS and set them out on the wide dining table.

Today's was a thousand-piece puzzle of the wine regions of Italy, and she was searching for pale-green shapes to complete Reggio Calabria. Usually, she found the task absorbing but she couldn't concentrate, feeling rattled by DI Drummond's visit. There was no doubt that the detective was a smart woman in every sense of the word, albeit a bit on the skinny side. And there was something not quite right about her eyes, as if she was under strain. Belinda was confident that no one would be able to challenge her version of the meeting with Tom, but the questions had left her uneasy. She'd told Aled that the inspector had wanted more detail about the working of the BSS committee, and he'd made little comment. But she'd noted him glancing at her a couple of times, as if about to ask something. And she really, really didn't need Aled to start quizzing her right now. She had enough to contend with.

She went through the green pieces again. They seemed particularly fiddly, and one she needed, with two indentations, was elusive. Maybe it was missing. Whoever received donations for the BSS hobby library was supposed to check that items were intact, but there were slip-ups. She was frustrated at the idea that she might be searching for a piece that wasn't even there, and she couldn't be bothered counting them all now. That in itself was unlike her. She was out of sorts.

She gave up on the puzzle and stared out at the back garden. The weather had turned, with a thin mizzle seeping from puffy grey clouds. When she was little, she'd say, *The clouds are crying*. She stood and walked around the table, running her finger along the raised edge. It was no good, the jigsaw wasn't doing it for her today.

On a whim, she ran upstairs, sprayed herself with scent, dashed on lipstick, grabbed a mac and drove to Harry's, hoping he'd be in. It took him a while to answer the door and when he did, he was scratching his ruffled hair.

'I was having forty winks.'

'Sorry to have disturbed your beauty sleep,' Belinda lied. She didn't approve of older people napping during the day. Aled might have his little quirks — eating shredded wheat with warm milk for supper and refusing ever to wear his shirt outside his jeans — but he never dozed off in his chair.

Harry straightened his sweater. 'Come on in, I'll put the kettle on. Cuppa?'

'Please.' He bought lapsang souchong just for her, a tea he'd never encountered until she'd told him she preferred it. She skipped down the three steps into his kitchen. She always felt girlish in Harry's company, as if the years fell away. If only they would. She peered through the raindrops on the window. 'Your camellias are lovely. What's that one on the left called?'

'It's a "Les Jury". Beautiful red, isn't it?'

'Gorgeous.' Belinda wasn't much interested in flowers, but Harry was proud of his teeny garden, so she liked to encourage him. And it was always gratifying to see him smile when she complimented him. Like giving a puppy a treat. She'd never lived alone. It must be strange, not having anyone to admire your handiwork.

Harry made her tea in a little white china pot that he kept specially for her. 'Want to sit in here or go through?'

'Let's sit here. It's cosy.'

'Biccy?'

'Not for me, but you go ahead.'

'I'll save it for later. My rheumatism's been playing up today, so I haven't had much exercise.' He patted his midriff. 'Calories consumed mustn't exceed calories expended.'

Belinda smiled at him. He was a nondescript man, but kind and sensitive. She admired the way he ran his days with efficiency and enjoyed intuiting that he was in thrall to her. He was always dewy-eyed during these visits.

'Hang on,' he said as he put sugar in his mug, 'it's Monday. What's happened to your jigsaw?'

Harry remembered every little detail about her weekly schedule, and it always gave her a flutter of pleasure when he provided evidence of his attention to her life.

'Couldn't concentrate. DI Drummond was back this morning, sniffing around.'

'Ah. Why was that?'

Belinda explained. 'I'm sure it was bloody Jill who told her.'

'I did say to you that meeting Tom like that might not be a good idea.'

'I had to meet him, didn't I? Once he found out about . . . what we've discussed. It's not the kind of thing you can talk about on the phone, for heaven's sake!'

'What did you tell the inspector?'

'That it was an attempt at reconciliation over our committee disagreements and it failed.'

'Did she believe you?'

Belinda pulled a sour expression and sipped her tea. 'She told me I was a liar.'

'Oh.' Harry turned his mug around, weighing his words. 'Belinda, it might be an idea to tell her what's happened, just to set the record straight. Covering things up when there's been these murders . . .'

She had wondered about this herself. After all, Tom was dead and she didn't owe him anything, so why was she keeping his secret when it no longer mattered to him? The problem was that she hadn't told the truth to start with, and then there were his daughters. As far as she was aware, Tom hadn't told them before he died, and right now they were mourning. And what about Aled — she'd concealed things from him. Belinda's marriage was sweet and tranquil, and she wanted to keep it that way.

She made an impatient noise. 'How can I do that? Aled would find out and I'd have a lot of explaining to do. Anyway, I'm sure that what happened isn't relevant to Tom's death, and I don't want it all brought into public view for the gossips to rake over. BSS can be such a rumour mill. Imagine Jill's pinched lips if she could openly disapprove of me for my role in what happened. There'd be wholesale character assassination.'

'It's a conundrum. What about the man in question — he should be informed about Tom's death. Pity Tom never told you his name.'

'I'd imagine he's already heard. It's been in the papers and on the news. I never dreamed that this would come back to bite me, Harry.'

'Why would you have? What you did was for the best at the time. I worry so for you, trying to cope with all of this. It doesn't seem fair. I wish I could do more to help.'

She put a hand briefly on his. His skin was roughened from years of honest toil with wrenches and exhaust pipes, or whatever it was he'd done in a garage. 'Thanks, Harry, but you needn't worry.' She meant the opposite, and understood that he realised that. 'I haven't done anything wrong. I see myself as a victim of circumstance. You've no idea how much it means, coming here and talking like this, being able to rely on you.'

He smiled his slow, sweet smile. 'Always, Belinda. Always.'

She savoured the smoky flavour of her tea, a niggling worry recurring in her head. What had happened years ago really couldn't have anything to do with Tom's death, could it?

* * *

Brian Gifford was a burly, short man, squeezed into a constricting jacket. He took up a lot of space in the interview room. His gingery hair was receding, exposing pink scalp, and his huge hands had stubby fingers. Siv stared at them. They were clumsy, unlikely hands for a burglar. Maybe that was why Gifford had been caught so often. They hadn't told him his son was enjoying their hospitality. She'd asked Ali to lead on the interview.

'Mr Gifford,' Ali said politely, 'you're quite sure you don't want a solicitor?'

'What's the point? They've never done me no good, just lined their pockets through my misfortune.'

'Fair enough. Where were you last Thursday afternoon, the eighteenth of April?'

Gifford ran a finger inside his shirt collar and said gruffly, 'Home, I reckon. Yeah, I was.'

'Between half three and half four?'

'Feet up, watching some rubbish on telly.'

'And your son?'

'Out working, driving his van. Taking expensive treats to people with more money than sense.'

Ali scratched his head between two cornrows. There were more wisps of grey in his hair these days, giving him two-tone braids. He pushed a photo of the Moorcroft jug across to the man. 'Recognise this?'

'Where'd you . . ?' Gifford twitched his neck.

'I reckon you do.'

'No comment.'

'That won't do,' Siv said. 'This jug was stolen from a house on Cove Parade where two people were murdered last

Thursday. You must have heard about the deaths — your son would have mentioned them and they've been in the news.'

Gifford cleared his throat. 'Yeah, he did. Only 'cos he was delivering stuff there.'

'Drew told us you went to the house last Thursday afternoon and stole the jug. He saw it when he made his delivery and phoned you. He's in custody right now.'

The man gave a wheezing cough and thumped his chest. 'This isn't fair.'

'Seems fair enough to me,' Siv remarked. 'There's a cupboard full of stolen stuff in your house. As I pointed out to Drew, better to be charged with theft than murder. At the moment, you're a major suspect. Don't you agree, Sergeant Carlin?'

'Oh aye. That classic, a robbery gone wrong. We could have this wrapped up today.'

Gifford shoved his chair back. 'No way! I wouldn't kill a kid. Why would I have done that? I didn't know her or the old guy from Adam, never met them. I took the jug, yeah. But there was nobody home. The back door was unlocked. I walked in, grabbed the jug and legged it, didn't even bother with nothing else.'

'Why was that?' Siv asked. 'Expensive house, might have had other stuff worth taking.'

'It was ten past three when I got there. I didn't want the old guy walking in on me.'

Ali poured water for Gifford, playing good cop now that the man was talking. 'Did you drive there?'

'I'm not that stupid. I left my car at the layby near Wherry Cove. Then I walked along and up to that track at the back of the houses. It only took a couple of minutes. The gate to the Turtons' place wasn't locked. They were asking for trouble.'

'They got it,' Siv snapped.

'I didn't mean — oh, go on, twist everything I say.'

Siv watched him drain the paper cup of water. 'The house was empty?'

'Yeah. The kitchen was all laid out for the party. I just took the jug and left. I was only in there for two minutes max.'

'Did you see anyone on the track or at Wherry Cove?'

'I was in a hurry, not hanging about, like.' He helped himself to another cup of water, more relaxed now. He'd have been in an interview room like this one so many times it must almost seem like a second home.

'Take your time,' Ali said.

'Well . . . There was someone at the far end of the cove, sitting on some rocks. A bloke.'

'Anything else you can tell us about him? How was he dressed?'

'Dark coat with the hood pulled up. His head was down.'

'Young?'

'Not a clue. He was in the distance, I hardly noticed him.'

'What about the layby?' Siv prompted. 'Any other cars there?'

'Two, I reckon. Don't ask me makes or nothing. I was moving fast.'

'Anyone in them?'

'Not sure.'

'Were they both there when you arrived and returned?'

Gifford hesitated. 'I reckon, yeah. One was silvery.' He pointed at Ali's head. 'Same sort of colour as your grey. I've helped you, haven't I? Drew has too. Can't you do a deal for us?'

Siv stood. 'We'll see. We'll be organising a forensics team to search your house. You can get a solicitor while that's happening.'

'You do believe me, though? I'd never harm a tot — on my own life, I wouldn't.'

She believed him. His history fitted with the information he'd given. 'We'll see,' she said again. Let him and his son fret about it.

* * *

145

Siv had decided to see Nell Pullman on her own, away from the confines of her depressing flat. The woman might be easier to talk to one-to-one. They'd agreed to meet in the Horizon café at Minster Beach at 6 p.m. Nell texted at six to say she was running late.

Soz. Be there in twenty.

Siv ordered a portion of chips and ate them sitting at one of the tables outside. it was a tranquil, temperate evening with thin clouds like white sheets. A couple of small boats tacked the gentle waves, twisting with the breeze. Dipping the chips into salt first, then ketchup, she was almost contented. Ed had always dipped the opposite way — ketchup first, then salt. She smiled at the memory. Her phone pinged with an email from Fabian Draper.

Really enjoyed our evening. Would love to see you again soon, hopefully when you're not so busy.

Unsure about what to say, she put the phone away. It was hard to work out what she made of him. Time had passed easily enough in his company, but was that enough reason to see him again? On the other hand, it had gone pretty well for a first meeting. Don't overthink it. Leave it for now.

She'd ordered a pot of tea when Nell arrived, parking her scooter with a squeal of brakes.

'Sorry again,' she panted. 'Last old biddy I was cleaning for said I hadn't done the shower properly. Jill Bartoli. She told me one of your lot had been to see her. All puffed up with it, as if a chat with the cops is something to be proud of.'

'Oddly enough, some people quite like having contact with us, makes them feel like useful citizens.'

'Sad saps.'

'Did Ms Bartoli say anything to you about our visit?'

'Nah.' Nell tapped the side of her nose. 'Said it was confidential. She's so up herself, that one.'

'Have you ordered anything?'

'Yeah, a lemonade on the way in. It's good here, freshly squeezed.'

She still wore the red jeans, but she smelled fresher, perhaps from the cleaning products she'd been using. Siv waited until her lemonade had arrived in a frosted glass with a tall spoon and sugar crystals around the rim.

'I want to ask you again about your sister's marriage. I get the impression it's been strained for a while.'

'News to me. Wow, that's good, got a real bite.' Nell offered the glass. 'Want to try some?'

'No thanks, I'll stick with my tea. We've discovered that Ryan spent some nights away at a hotel.'

'Yeah? Lucky him, being able to afford it.'

'You're not aware of any rows?'

'Nope. I assume they have them, as they're married. Goes with the territory. Me and Kay don't talk about stuff like that. The way she harks on, her marriage is perfect. We've never been sisterly sisters, if you get my drift. Kay's a perfectionist and I'm . . .' She chuckled. 'Well, I'm very obviously not one of those.'

Siv could see she was going to get nowhere regarding the couple. 'Do you remember Lyra having a stomach upset around the middle of January?'

'Did she? No idea. Kids do, don't they? I chucked up a lot as a kid. Mum used to say I had a cold in my tum. Lovely sunset now.'

They watched the sun dip below the horizon, turning the sea bronze.

'It seems that your father was meeting a man in St Peter's church. He took Lyra in there on the way home from nursery, the afternoon they were murdered. That still doesn't mean anything to you?'

'Weird. Not a clue. What about Kay — have you asked her?'

'Not yet. I'm going to ring her and Ryan this evening.'

'I popped in to see her earlier. Ryan wasn't around. Some guy I'd never seen before was there. I could tell Kay didn't want me to hang about — she didn't even offer me a cuppa.'

'Did you get his name?'

'She did mention it, but I can't remember. He didn't say much, kept checking his phone. Probably an undertaker.' Nell finished her lemonade. 'I miss Lyra. She always gave me a hug. Miss her more than I realised I would. Funny, isn't it?'

Siv agreed that it was. The last sliver of sun vanished and she called for her bill, telling Nell she'd get hers too.

CHAPTER 12

At six thirty on Tuesday morning, Siv woke with a start from a dream she'd now had several times. Ed had turned up at their flat in Greenwich, wheeling his bike in, asking crossly what she'd done with all his things. *Where's my iPad, my clothes, my books? What have you done with them all, Sivster?* Shocked, she'd opened her mouth to explain that she'd believed he was dead, and at that point she woke. He'd been so real, so *alive*. It took her a while to stop trembling and get into the shower.

Her head was still full of him when she drank coffee standing by the open door to her wagon. It was a cool, bright morning. Corran's goats, called Judy, Ella, Nina and Barbra, were bleating in an out-of-tune, ragged chorus. Corran claimed that he could distinguish and interpret their *maah*s. He chatted to them lovingly as if they were his children, fussing and petting them, catering to their individual tastes. Siv supposed that they were child substitutes, and they probably had better lives than some of the humans she'd come across in her career.

When she checked her email she saw one from her sister, Rik. It was lengthy and informative, compared to her usual efforts.

How's things with crime, and are the goats still waking you up early? And how about the young lovers up the road from you? I expect

149

Mutsi's still hanging on in there. She's the cat with nine lives, but even she must be running out of road by now. Speaking of which, I'm a bit jaded with Auckland these days. I might consider moving on, finding other opportunities. Keep you posted x

If Siv took after her mother in lacking an interest in cooking, Rik had inherited her restlessness. She'd lived in a number of places before settling in Auckland. Her communications were usually so scant Siv wasn't even sure what she did for a living. Aromatherapy had been mentioned. It was no good replying with any questions. Rik never answered direct queries and went quiet if she was cornered. Siv pictured the relationship with her sister as a stretched piece of elastic that could split at any moment. She composed a delicately bland response.

Mutsi still giving Mortimer a makeover. She popped in here not long ago on an information-seeking mission and to dispense some casual offence. The goats are in good voice. I'm up to my neck in murder. Keep in touch about what you decide x.

She read it through. Best not to mention Mutsi's comment that Rik had been a difficult baby. Rik might laugh or brood about it. She sent the reply and got ready for work.

At eight o'clock, Siv called into the museum to check that her origami display was set up to her satisfaction. She wasn't keen on the title of the exhibition — *Heave Ho!* — but it wasn't her call and she supposed it was catchy, with a humorous touch. Her work was set against a handsome photo backdrop of the coast off Minster Beach: a square-rigged ship with tall masts, a trio of fishing boats, a nineteenth-century steam yacht, a coracle and a cargo boat. There were labels beneath each piece and the information board beside the collection was succinct.

These beautiful origami pieces have been designed and made by Siv Drummond. They represent the types of sailing vessels that would have been seen on our waters over the centuries.

Siv has been folding for many years and has exhibited in a number of places. She accepts commissions and can be contacted through our front desk.

Siv made a few tweaks to the positioning of the coracle, and by eight twenty she was sitting in Mortimer's office.

She gave him an update about the Giffords while he neatened his cuticles with the stainless-steel pusher he'd taken from the manicure set on his desk. His hands were girlish and narrow. Not sexy at all. Siv liked men who had strong hands — Bartel did, and Ed's had been broad and competent. In her dream, he'd gripped the handlebars of his bike with gel-padded cycling mitts. What were Fabian Draper's hands like? She hadn't noticed. Maybe that told her something. Mortimer was gazing at her enquiringly. She marshalled her thoughts and continued.

'I don't see either of the Giffords as suspects. Drew Gifford could have had time to nip back to the Turtons' house, but it would have been a squeeze and he has no motive. He'd done his job, giving Brian Gifford word about the jug. His dad's prints are on the jug but nowhere in the house — he's admitted he wore gloves.'

Mortimer twirled the cuticle pusher. 'Best to keep an open mind on them both, even if they don't seem likely.'

'Of course, but we need to try and narrow the focus. We've put out an appeal for information from anyone who was parked in the layby that afternoon, or who was at Wherry Cove, or saw anyone there. Given the ease with which Brian Gifford accessed the Turtons' house, it may be that the killer also came through the back gate.'

'The lack of security at that house astonishes me,' Mortimer said. 'Leaving gates and doors unlocked. Just asking for trouble.'

'It's always been a low crime area. People get lulled into a false sense of security.'

'So,' Mortimer asked, sitting back, 'who *is* a suspect?'

'The Hanaks' and Harry Hudson's whereabouts are unconfirmed for the time when the murders happened. The Turtons have alibis but they're holding back. I contacted them again last night about Mr Pullman visiting St Peter's, but they said they had no idea why he'd have gone there. I've asked Ali and Patrick to check pharmacies in the area, to see if either of the Turtons bought children's medication with chlorphenamine. Someone was medicating Lyra, and I want to find out who.'

'Hasn't Geordie been digging around with them? He's usually excellent at that liaison work.'

'I'm sure he did his best, but they've refused him access, don't want him there.'

'Something to hide,' Mortimer said sagely.

'Hmm. Belinda Hanak is lying, I'm sure, but at the moment, it's hard to pin her down.'

Mortimer tidied his manicure set. 'Crack on, then. I have to present crime figures to regional command later this month. Two murders solved quickly would be an excellent outcome.'

* * *

Ali was slogging unsuccessfully around pharmacies on the south side of town, showing chemists photos of Ryan and Kay Turton, asking if either of them had bought medication for a child. Every shop he entered had a huge variety of tempting sweet snacks for sale. It was pure hell. In the fourth, he succumbed and bought a biscuit-sized bar of dark chocolate — not his favourite, lacking the sweet silkiness of the milk variety. But the flavonols could help lower blood sugar, and Nurse Keene — *Keene by name, keen by nature*, as she liked to boast — had said it was a reasonable option for an occasional small treat.

He was sitting in his car, making the most of the tiny chocolate boost, when Alicia Ferreira rang him.

'Is very difficult,' she said. 'I am not sure if I should say this, but I'm very worried.'

Ali swallowed. 'Take it slow. It's usually best to say if something's worrying you.'

'Is problem, very hard.'

'A problem to do with our investigation?'

'Maybe.'

152

'Is it about Lyra? About medication?'

'No, not medicine. Not Lyra. But . . . I not sure, really.'

'About the Turtons?' Ali could purr like a cat when needed. 'Something to do with them?'

'Is . . . well . . . is to do with Vince.'

'Your boyfriend? Vince Naish?'

'Yes. You meet him when you come to house.'

'That's right. Is he in trouble?'

'No, but he might be angry with me for calling.'

'OK.' Ali popped a Gitane from the packet and lit up. 'Alicia, is this to do with the murders?'

'Could be.'

'Then you do have to tell me. Shall I come and see you? Where are you?'

'I'm home, but not on my own. No, don't come here.'

'Vince is there?' Was she frightened of her boyfriend? She seemed a robust, no-nonsense woman, but that didn't mean she wasn't being abused.

'No, not Vince, but my friends are. I don't want them listening.' Her voice dropped. 'Vince, he is a therapist. He tell me that Kay saw him a little while now. She very troubled, talk about big family problem. He very worried by this, because of the murders.'

Ali opened the window and flicked ash out. 'Did Vince tell you anything about this problem?

'No. He, you understand, have to be confidential. He say he shouldn't really even tell me Kay see him, is not right. But he is so fretting and I keep asking him why. He had to say something. Not sleeping. I worry for him.'

'Alicia, you've done the right thing, telling me.'

'Yes?' She sounded dubious.

'Really, you have. Serious crimes like these, you have to tell the police anything that might help.'

'That is what I tell myself. Little Lyra — it might help find who kill her. You talk to Vince now?'

'Yes, we'll have to. We'll make sure he understands that you were right to contact us.'

'Yes. But he will be cross.'

'He'll get over it. Does he do his therapy in town?'

'Yes, at the Raven Health Centre.'

'Thanks for this information. Take it easy now.'

He finished the call, phoned Siv and told her. 'I suppose Kay might have been seeking therapy because her marriage was rocky.'

'It must be more than that for Naish to be so worried,' Siv said. 'Kay has to have told him something that rings alarm bells for him after the murders.'

'Shall I talk to him, guv?' Ali had his fingers crossed that she'd say yes, so that he could get away from this tedious round of chemists.

'No, you carry on with the pharmacy trawl. I'll find him.'

'He might play the confidentiality card.'

'He can try,' she commented. 'It won't get him far.'

* * *

Vince Naish put up a good attempt at fending Siv off. He had the use of a small room in a busy GP hub. It smelled vaguely of antiseptic and had information posters about spotting the symptoms of meningitis, TB and breast cancer. Naish was self-assured and articulate, with an air of offence at Siv's visit, or maybe he was more riled by the information that his girl-friend had dobbed him in.

'I do wish Alicia hadn't done that. It undermines me. She should have consulted me.'

It's not about you, though, when it comes down to it. 'She's worried — about you and for you. I need to clarify if Kay Turton has told you things that could have a bearing on two murders.'

'I understand where you're coming from, Inspector, but I'm bound by an ethical code. People come to see me trusting that I'll keep their confidence. The therapeutic relationship has to be based on trust. The only time when there's an onus on the therapist to break that confidence is when the Terrorism

Act is involved. As far as I'm aware, none of my clients is a terrorist.' He smirked. 'I doubt that there are any in Berminster.'

She'd sat back and let him have his say. It was fair enough, she'd no doubt do the same in his position, and she'd expected the response. Professional people needed to maintain their dignity in such situations, and some far more than others. Before seeing him, though, she'd checked a few things online. His last remark needled her.

'I wouldn't assume anything about terrorism, Mr Naish. And it seems to me that you've already transgressed your ethical code by telling Alicia that Kay Turton sought therapy with you.'

He flushed at that and knotted his fingers together. 'I admit that was a slip I shouldn't have made.'

'You're only human. You must have been very upset when you heard about the murders. And of course, you'll have been dealing with Alicia's distress too. She was very fond of Lyra. Two years is a long time to spend with a child — she'd become part of the family. Did Ms Turton realise that you were Alicia's partner when she consulted you?'

'Yes. Alicia had mentioned my job to her. Also, I made sure that she was aware of the fact.'

'Is Ms Turton still seeing you?'

'Again, that's confidential information. I simply can't divulge these things to you.'

Siv decided he'd had enough leeway. 'I have to disagree with you. The gist of it is this: a patient doesn't have an absolute right to confidentiality and there are circumstances that allow you to disclose information to the police. It's defensible to breach confidence in good faith in order to assist detection of a serious crime. I'd say that's exactly the situation you're in.'

He altered the angle of his plastic chair a little and scratched his forearm.

Siv continued, 'The Turtons have marital problems and they seem to have developed since last summer, when they were happy bunnies. I'd guess you discovered what lies behind them. Now, you can faff around getting advice and make me go away and pursue you through magistrates, but I can assure you that I'll get what I want in the end. In the meantime, there's a murderer who killed Kay Turton's child and father, and you're obstructing my investigation. I could decide to be unpleasant about that and charge you.'

Naish was frightened. He could only be in his late twenties, so probably hadn't been practising as a therapist for that long. 'You wouldn't do that, surely. I'm only trying to keep to my code.'

'Try me,' Siv challenged. 'I don't care about your code right now. I only care about two dead people. You're going to have to talk to me. I'm not after a sweet-shop robber.'

'Oh dear! This is awful,' Naish murmured. 'What if it gets out? None of my clients will trust me. It could ruin my practice, my livelihood.'

'I understand your worries. I won't name you as an informant. If your identity should get out, I'll report that I insisted you divulge information on the permissible basis that serious crimes are being investigated. There'll be no comeback.'

'Oh dear!' Naish said again, biting a nail.

He sounded like the white rabbit in *Alice in Wonderland*. Siv unbuttoned her jacket and gave him a reassuring smile. 'Tell me what was worrying Kay so much that she needed a therapist.'

A baby started bawling out in the corridor — high, enraged wails. It was ear-splitting, even through the door.

Naish grimaced. 'Vaccination clinic.' He waited until the crying receded. It would be hard to run a counselling session with that racket going on. 'Ms Turton came to see me because she needed to tell her husband something, and she was trying to work out a way to do it, to find her way to making a decision.'

'When was this?'

Naish rose, unlocked a filing cabinet, extracted an orange folder and sat back down. Siv guessed that he already knew the answer, but was taking his time, making her wait. He'd lost the battle, but could still try to maintain some foothold on his territory.

'It was last December. She came for three sessions in total, over three weeks. Then she said she didn't need any further counselling.'

'So, what was this decision?'

Naish clutched the folder to his chest as if guarding the secret within one last time before he divulged it. 'Lyra wasn't Ryan Turton's daughter. Kay had entertained doubts for a while. It had been playing on her mind, causing her great worry. She decided to get a DNA test done last autumn. It confirmed that Ryan wasn't the father.'

This was dynamite, enough to tear a family apart. 'Who was the father?'

'It's not that simple. In fact, it's one of the most delicate, tangled issues I've had to listen to as a therapist. This is a very complex matter and Kay should explain it to you fully. It has caused her huge distress, and I assume she's consulting a solicitor.'

A solicitor? Siv grappled with what he'd told her. She could see from the man's anguished expression that he was hurting. 'And had Ms Turton decided to tell her husband?'

'I believe so. Certainly she wanted to, and our sessions appeared to allow her to go ahead with that.'

'When was the last time you had contact with her?'

Naish opened the folder again. 'The twentieth of December.'

Siv turned this over. 'Let me get this straight. Did Kay not know who Lyra's natural father was?'

'She certainly didn't last December.'

'Had she talked to anyone else about this?'

'She said not. She found the therapy a relief, because the issue had been weighing her down. I'd go as far as to say she was traumatised by it.'

Siv stood. 'Thank you. This is crucial information. Go easy on Alicia, by the way. She was absolutely right to contact us. You should have done so yourself, so I'd say you should be thanking rather than blaming her.'

Naish just nodded and rubbed his forehead. He could probably do with some therapy himself now.

CHAPTER 13

Siv was hungry when she left the Raven Health Centre. She bought a cheese salad roll and a coffee at a garage near the river, then parked by the Bere and sat on the grassy bank. The moist air held a hint of rain and the reeds stirred in the breeze. Tiredness ran through her like an ache, the emotions stirred by her dream of Ed still lingering. She wolfed her roll. It was tasteless, but she had more energy once she'd eaten.

She went over the murders as she ate. Kay and Ryan had alibis for Thursday afternoon, but there was now a third person, Lyra's natural father, who had entered the picture. This could be a vital piece of information. How come Kay hadn't known who he was and why hadn't she revealed this during interviews? Had she been sleeping around, so that there were a number of candidates and embarrassment had made her clam up? She didn't strike Siv as a thrill-seeker, but people were always full of surprises.

Siv was more sure than ever that the motive for the killings was personal. Especially that cake in Pullman's mouth — signalling anger, maybe disgust. Kay Turton would need to be approached carefully. She might not have told her husband about Lyra's paternity yet. The woman was on compassionate leave from work and still grieving, but she had to be questioned on her own, with no possibility of Ryan Turton intruding.

Siv monitored the progress of a group of ducks bobbing along the current. The rippling water gave her an idea about a good location to talk to Kay.

She sipped coffee, took out her phone and made some notes about outstanding questions.

1. *Who is Lyra's father and is he aware?*
2. *Who was medicating Lyra?*
3. *Who was the man visiting Kay when Nell called in?*
4. *Who was the man Tom Pullman met in St Peter's?*

The answer to one might be the answer to three. She rang Ali and updated him with Vince Naish's information.

'Now we're going great guns,' he said. 'We need to speak to Kay.'

'I've been considering that. I don't want to freak her out by asking her to the station and I don't want to talk to her at home, where Ryan might come in, or at Nell's squalid flat. A public space is out, given the nature of the conversation. Somewhere neutral but pleasant and handy to get to, with no family connections. I thought of Mortimer's boat.'

Ali whistled. 'Yeah, it'd be private, right enough. Will he agree?'

'I'll call him now. Any luck with chemists?'

'Nothing. I just spoke to Patrick and he's got nowhere. We're going to try further afield, surrounding villages.'

Siv phoned Mortimer next, updated him and outlined her idea.

'Most unusual. I'm not sure,' he said, sounding put out.

'It's a lovely quiet space. Being on the water is so soothing. Also, there's an element of surprise, in a good way. That might help Kay relax and open up.'

'Yes, I see. And of course, Lyra's natural father might now be a suspect.'

'Exactly. So the sooner we establish his identity, the better. I could meet Kay there this afternoon, if the boat is free.'

'Hmm. Very well. Just this once, though. I don't want *Quicksilver* becoming a place to take emotional or stubborn witnesses. It is my haven on the water — and your mother's too now, of course.'

Siv couldn't help teasing him. 'I've no intention of turning it into an extra interview room, although it would be a fine alternative to our dingy accommodation.'

A silence indicated that he was nonplussed by this. Then he said, 'The harbour office holds a key. I'll phone to tell them you'll be collecting it. When you lock up, just hand the key back in there. Help yourself to tea and coffee.'

'Thanks, sir. Much appreciated.'

'Oh — and I'll see you this evening.'

'Sorry?'

'At *Heave Ho!* — the opening of the exhibition at the museum. Your mother and I are looking forward to it.'

'Right, yes, see you.'

Siv gave a mental shrug as she ended the call. It was inevitable that Mutsi would have spotted the exhibition and want to muscle in on it.

She finished her coffee and called Kay, hoping that Ryan would be true to form and out somewhere. Kay answered, her voice faint and nasal. When Siv said she needed to discuss something confidential and in private, she agreed listlessly to meet at the harbour at half three.

* * *

Kay had a vacant expression, as if she might have been using some of her sister's weed. The afternoon had grown showery and windy. She wore a smart dark red raincoat and carried an umbrella. When Siv told her they were meeting on a colleague's boat, she expressed no surprise, just followed along to *Quicksilver*.

In the warm cabin, Siv took Kay's coat and hung it up. 'Tea or coffee?'

'Coffee, please. What's this about?'

160

'Just let me make the drinks, I won't be a minute.'

In the oak-fitted galley kitchen, Siv immediately noted Mutsi's Finnish-themed touches: a set of rectangular wooden serving boards etched with birch trees, pale blue enamel mugs and little glass bowls with candles. A Finnish calendar on the wall showed a beautiful photo of Nuuksio National Park. The coffee was Finnish too, the Paulig brand. Siv had never visited Finland. It had been one of the places she and Ed had put on their list, with Siv stipulating that the holiday should be nowhere near Mutsi's home town.

When she brought the coffee through, Kay was sitting on one of the grey leather seats in the cabin, gazing out at the harbour.

'This is a lovely boat. You must have a wealthy colleague.'

'He's pretty well set up, yes.'

'Those cupboards are beautiful. Is that wood walnut?'

Siv poured the coffee. 'Yes. It's handsome, suits the boat. This is a secluded place to talk with no interruptions.'

Kay took a mug of coffee, adding a splash of milk. She gestured out at the water. 'We had a little day cruise from the harbour last summer. Lyra loved it. She claimed to have seen a shark. She had such a vivid imagination.'

The boat lifted as a shower blew through and water slapped its sides. Siv switched a corner lamp on, creating a cosy glow and sat at a right angle to Kay.

'It's Lyra I wanted to talk to you about. This is difficult and I understand that you wish to guard your privacy, but I can't allow that in a murder enquiry. It's regarding Lyra's paternity. I'm aware that Ryan isn't her natural father.'

Kay took a sip of coffee and put the mug down. She said in a resigned tone, 'How did you find out?'

'That's not for discussion. You should have told us.'

'It's a very sensitive matter.'

'Agreed, but important. Does Ryan know?'

'I told him in January.'

'When Lyra had the stomach upset and Ryan stayed at the Dovecote. There must have been great tension at home.'

'Ryan didn't take it well.' Kay bit her lip. 'He was very angry.'

'Towards Lyra?'

'No. With me, because I hadn't told him as soon as I had doubts. He said I'd gone behind his back, betrayed him by hiding crucial information. I made the mistake of telling him I'd seen a counsellor, and he was furious that I'd gone to a stranger before talking to him. That's why he stayed at that hotel sometimes. But he became cool towards Lyra from then on. I'd see him watching her oddly and not playing with her as much.' She moved the coaster under her coffee a fraction. 'Ryan's not the kind of man who can accept and get over such a thing. He's very proud and slow to forgive. I was aware of that when I told him. He became distant, didn't want to mix with my family.'

The engine started on the boat next to them and it began to reverse out, causing a slight swell. The cabin creaked and rocked. Siv waited until the boat had puttered away.

'Who is Lyra's father?'

Kay sighed. 'I couldn't tell you. I'd consulted a solicitor to try and find out, but there doesn't seem much point now.' She took out a tissue and dabbed her eyes.

Siv felt as lost as if *Quicksilver* had drifted out to sea. 'Kay, you need to explain this to me.'

Kay held a hand up, blew her nose and took a gulp of coffee. 'We wanted children, but I had trouble getting pregnant. I have some fallopian tube damage. Lyra was conceived through IVF at Fairlawns, a private clinic in Berminster. Ryan knows Glen Belanger, a consultant there, so we had a personal link. We were thrilled, because we were successful at the first attempt. More than thrilled — overjoyed. The pregnancy went well and Lyra's birth was straightforward.'

Siv poured more coffee for them both. 'In your own time, Kay.'

'I suppose I started to wonder when Lyra was around one year old. She had my hair colour and texture and my nose, but she didn't resemble Ryan at all. She was so sturdy.

Stocky and heavy to pick up. And tall for her age. Ryan didn't notice, but a couple of people remarked on it. Dad said she must take after a distant relative. It puzzled me every now and again, but then I'd reason that the genetic soup is unpredictable and I'd tuck the worries away. They'd come back, though. It was hard to put my finger on it, just something I sensed. Something wasn't right.'

'It sounds as if you were troubled. You didn't discuss it with Ryan?'

'I didn't want to because it was such a vague concern, and it seemed wrong to make him anxious when it might just be my own daft ideas. Then . . . then about a year ago, I read a story online one day, about a woman in New York who'd had a child via IVF. She'd discovered that the wrong donor sperm had been used at her insemination. She and her husband were keeping the child, but they were suing the clinic. It started me wondering again. Obsessing, you could say.'

'I'm so sorry. You must have been distraught,' Siv said.

'Tormented. I started to search online and I found more similar stories, some in the UK. I thought about little else for months. Last October, I got a DNA test done and it proved that Ryan wasn't Lyra's dad.' She pulled at the collar of her sweater. 'I wanted to tell Ryan, but I couldn't find the words. I realised he'd be devastated. He doted on Lyra. We'd decided to stop at the one child because of my health and now she wasn't even his. Eventually, I found a counsellor to talk it through.'

Siv hurried her on, not wanting Kay to dwell on that and identify the probable source of her information. 'You waited a while before you told Ryan?'

'I hesitated. It was so hard because his world was going to fall apart. Then it was Christmas and I didn't want to spoil that. I plucked up the courage in January. I told Ryan that we could sue the clinic. He said what was the point — the damage was done.' She flinched. 'Those were his exact words. He acted as though it was somehow *my* fault. He's been distant to me ever since, acting as if he's written the marriage off.

163

And now Lyra's gone and I've barely seen him. Everything's fallen apart.' She gave a bitter laugh. 'I'd have done better to do nothing, say nothing, keep my doubts to myself. So much for "honesty pays"!'

And now her husband, who had no qualms about dishonesty, was covertly arranging a divorce. Turton didn't care that his wife was overwhelmed by what had happened and might need his support. A bit of tenderness. It seemed to Siv that Kay would be better off without such a callous partner. This poor woman, struggling with an avalanche of misfortune. Listening to her had upset Siv. This case was turning into a maze of personal grief.

'Did you take legal advice?'

'Yes. Despite what Ryan said, I decided to contact a solicitor. I was angry, and I had to do something. It wasn't even about compensation, more to try and make sure no one else suffered the same error. My solicitor wrote to the clinic in March and they referred it to their governance and their legal team. At the moment, they're not admitting any error. Well, they wouldn't. But I can't see any point in following it through now. It would just prolong the misery.'

Siv chanced a guess. 'Was this solicitor visiting you at home when Nell called in?'

Kay stared and said crossly, 'Are you watching me? How did you find that out?'

'I spoke to Nell. She said a man was with you when she visited.'

'Oh, Nell. Blabbermouth. She never could keep anything to herself. Yes, he called to give his condolences. I told him I probably wouldn't continue with my complaint now. He's very kind, said to think things over in my own time, not make any hasty decisions and get in touch when I've decided.'

'Sounds like good advice. Did you tell your dad or Nell about this suspected IVF error?'

'No. I wanted to wait until we'd got somewhere legally and Ryan wasn't keen on them knowing. He made me promise not to talk to them about it. It was such a blow for him.'

'Hardly a picnic for you, Kay.'

Kay was weeping silently, a hand shielding her eyes. Rain slanted down more steadily now, dimpling the cloudy grey water. Siv tracked seagulls dipping and wheeling over the boats, which shifted restlessly in their moorings. This interview had been enlightening but in some ways an apparent dead end. There was an unidentified biological father. Still, it would be worth a visit to the fertility clinic to see what they had to say about a serious, life-changing mistake.

She waited until Kay was more composed and fetched her coat, handing it to her. 'I'll have to speak to Fairlawns. They might be able to trace who Lyra's natural father is.'

Kay buttoned her coat slowly. 'But that's nothing to do with what happened to her and my dad.'

Siv wasn't making that assumption. 'I have to check everything.'

She walked to the harbour gate with Kay, telling her she'd be in touch soon. Patrick phoned as Siv was handing the key back in at the office. She stood under the awning outside, turning her face away from the rain.

'I got a result from a chemist on the Brighton road, guv. The woman on the pharmacy counter confirmed that Ryan Turton had bought children's cold medication a couple of months ago. It's called Lemazin and it contains chlorphenamine.'

'Good work. In the meantime, I've established that Lyra wasn't Ryan Turton's daughter.' She explained the DNA test result. 'I want you and Ali to get hold of Turton, question him about the Lemazin and the DNA result and also check his connection with Glen Belanger, the consultant at Fairlawns. I've got to show my face at the museum this evening for the opening of this exhibition. Then I'll be back for a briefing.'

* * *

Ryan Turton was in high temper. His wife had told him that the police had details about the IVF error. He sat gripping the table in the interview room, his fingertips white. A vein pulsed at his right temple. Ali poured him a beaker of water, but he shoved it aside so that it slopped on to the Formica table top.

'You lot can never stop. Getting at Kay behind my back, wanting to rake over our personal life. That has nothing to do with what's happened!'

Patrick asked, 'Why did you buy Lemazin?'

'Pardon?'

'You bought Lemazin recently, at Dexter's pharmacy on the Brighton road.'

Sweat slicked Turton's upper lip. 'Who says I did?'

'The counter assistant. She confirmed it was you by your photo. Lemazin is a children's cold and cough medication, a strawberry-flavoured liquid, and it contains chlorphenamine.'

Turton took a drink of water. 'Yes, I did give Lyra some of it now and again. I kept it in my briefcase, in my study. Lyra'd been a bit difficult at times since January, not getting to sleep, up and down after bedtime. I recognised that she was picking up on tension between me and Kay over the IVF thing. I didn't intend to harm her; I just gave her some of this syrup at bedtime now and again, to calm her down and get a bit of peace when I needed to work late.'

'Where is it now?' Patrick demanded.

'I chucked the bottle in a bin by the river when you started asking questions. Kay had no idea, and I didn't tell you because I didn't want her to hear about it. She has enough on her plate.'

Ali eyed him. 'So, we have information about the IVF and the DNA test that Kay had done. That must have upset you.'

'Of course it bloody did! I was gutted, still am. My world caved in. I haven't been able to think straight since Kay told me.'

Any fleeting sympathy Ali might have felt vanished. *You've been thinking straight enough to chat to your solicitor friend about a divorce and leave your wife carrying the burden.* 'Did you talk to anyone else about the DNA discovery?'

'No.'

'Talk us through how you arranged the IVF with Dr Belanger,' Ali said.

Turton's temper had settled. His tone was almost meek now. 'I met Glen Belanger playing squash. We got talking in the bar one day and he told me about his work at the clinic. I explained that Kay and I weren't having any luck with starting a family. He was very helpful and sent me some literature. Kay met us next time in the bar and we talked to him a bit more. He invited us for an appointment, we had various tests, and six months later we had IVF at Fairlawns. It was successful, or that's what we believed. Clearly, there was a monumental cock-up.'

'Kay contacted a solicitor,' Ali said.

'I don't see the point now. I've no stomach for pursuing a legal claim that's only going to cost money. Lyra's dead and I was never her dad. End of.'

'It might help Kay.' *Selfish bastard*, thought Ali. To Lyra, he'd been her dad. Did that mean nothing to him?

'Sure. That's up to her now.' Turton sagged in his chair.

Ali and Patrick exchanged glances. Patrick mouthed, *The jug?* Ali nodded.

'By the way,' Patrick said, 'we found your Moorcroft jug. It's part of another crime investigation at present, but we'll make sure it's returned to you.'

'Give it to charity for all I care,' Turton said wearily.

Ali couldn't see any point in keeping him there. 'We'll let you get away home to your wife, Mr Turton. I expect you've lots to talk about.'

Turton rose, mumbling, 'I can assure you there's little conversation in our house these days.'

* * *

Siv had hoped to get home and change before the opening of the *Heave Ho!* exhibition, but in the end there wasn't time. She nipped into the loo at the station, brushed her teeth, combed her hair, straightened her jacket and checked herself in the mirror. Bit pallid, but maybe that was the strip lighting. She crossed the road and entered the museum just as Cava was being poured in the warm, thronged foyer. Perfumes and aftershaves battled it out as the ten-pounds-a-ticket guests mingled and sipped their bubbles. Not sure what the rest of the evening might entail at work, she accepted an orange juice.

Siv was greeting Janis, the museum manager, when she saw her mother at the other side of the room, waving to her. Mutsi was splendidly attired in a gold shimmering dress with a jade necklace and earrings. Siv waved back and saw that Janis was amused.

'I've met your mum. She arrived early. She's very proud of your folding skills.'

Siv smiled vaguely. This was news to her. In the past, Mutsi had taken no interest in her folding, dismissing her 'lonely little hobby' as an old-fashioned kind of interest. *Spinsterish*, was the implication.

'You have a good crowd,' she said to Janis.

'I'm really pleased and so glad you could make it. Lots of money for the museum's coffers! The mayor's arrived, so time to go through and get started.'

'I can't stay for more than half an hour, unfortunately, I have to get back to work. How long will the mayor's speech take?'

'A few minutes. I've been strict about that. Please disappear whenever you want once he's finished.'

Janis clapped her hands and called for everyone to bring their glasses through to the main gallery. Siv took her position near the back and was keeping half an eye on Mutsi, who was chatting to one of the museum curators, when a vast bunch of flowers appeared under her nose.

'Congratulations!' Fabian Draper was beaming down at her. 'A bouquet for a very special artist.'

Siv gaped at the ostentatious mixed blossoms: red and peach roses, pink orchids, hellebores, scarlet peonies and brilliant orange chrysanthemums. When she took them, they weighed as much as a couple of bricks. She was embarrassed and not a little annoyed. She didn't like being put on the spot like this.

'I didn't realise you were coming tonight.' *And I didn't invite you.*

'Wouldn't have missed your big night.'

'I'm just a small part of it. Lots of other people have contributed.'

'No need to be so modest. You're allowed to blow your own trumpet when you have a talent.'

Fabian wore a beautiful, fine wool suit in forest green. He had an amused smile and she could tell that he'd enjoyed surprising her. Siv could see that Mutsi had clocked him and was edging towards them around the side of the room. Several other people were glancing at her. She didn't want to stand there clutching a bouquet like a diva throughout the mayor's speech.

'Well, thank you. I'll just put these down for now.' She placed the flowers on the floor beside her.

'Be careful,' he said. 'I spent a lot of time sourcing them, finally went to a shop in Hove. I wanted something expensive and bold, a real statement for you.'

She was bewildered. They'd been out for one drink — he barely knew her. Also, she didn't care for cut flowers, preferring woodland blooms in their natural habitat.

Luckily, Janis tinged her glass and everyone fell silent as she thanked them for coming and introduced the mayor. He was a small man, barely visible from the back of the gallery and dwarfed by his chain of office.

'I'm delighted to open *Heave Ho!*, this wonderful exhibition about our town's sailing and fishing tradition. Berminster was a major trading port up to the middle ages, when the town grew worried about getting its feet wet and retreated from the sea . . .'

He paused for laughter and then continued with a potted history of Berminster's seafaring past. As soon as he'd finished and the applause had ended, Mutsi materialised beside Siv in a cloud of vetiver perfume.

'Hello, darling, how lovely to see you. Aren't you going to introduce me to your companion?'

'This is Fabian Draper. Fabian, this is my mother.'

They shook hands and Mutsi smiled coquettishly, saying, 'I'm Crista.'

'It's hard to believe you can be Siv's mother. An older sister, maybe.' Fabian laughed.

Oh please, not that old chestnut. Siv tried to keep a straight face.

Mutsi trilled, 'How did you two meet?'

'During a murder enquiry,' Siv said repressively.

Fabian added, 'I hasten to add I wasn't a suspect.'

'I should hope not — you're not a bit suspicious. These are lovely flowers!' Mutsi bent and picked up the bouquet. 'I saw you give them to Siv. Careful with them, Sivvi, they're so beautiful and delicate.' She buried her nose in them, inhaled with a loud *aah* and thrust them at her daughter.

'Sivvi suits you,' Fabian said. 'Softer than Siv, somehow.'

'It was my childhood name for her, wasn't it, Sivvi?'

'That's right. What have you done with your partner?'

'Will? Oh, he got hijacked by some councillor who wanted to discuss parking. I meant to say — I hope you locked the yacht up safely.'

'Yes, all secure.'

'You own a yacht?' Fabian asked Mutsi, sounding impressed.

'It's a boat,' Siv said.

Mutsi tutted at her. 'Yes, Fabian, Will and I do own a *yacht*. She's called *Quicksilver*. We moor her here in the harbour.'

Siv guessed that Mutsi was about to issue an invitation to tea on board or a cruise. She made a show of checking her watch. 'I have to get back to the station.'

Fabian pulled a little boy face. 'But your exhibits — I was hoping you'd talk me through them. I have made an effort to be here.' He made it sound as if she'd insisted on his attendance and was now bailing out on him.

170

She couldn't conceal her impatience. 'There's not much to say: they tell their own story and there's a description just by them.'

Mutsi gave one of her tinkling laughs and touched Fabian's sleeve lightly. 'Always rushing away, always a busy little bee — that's my daughter.'

'Afraid so, and I have to buzz away now. Enjoy the exhibition.'

Siv pushed her way from the gallery, cradling the flowers awkwardly. What kind of man made sure to explain that the gift he'd bought you had cost a lot? She imagined the comments she'd get in the station when she walked in with them.

Was it always going to be like this now? Was she doomed to be shadowed through town by her mother, who had undoubtedly started quizzing Fabian as soon as she'd left. Right now, she'd be spilling the beans on her difficult daughter. *Always quite shy as a child, and of course since Ed's death she's been in her shell. Lives in a funny little wagon at the back of beyond. Very hard to get her to engage, but she mustn't grieve forever. Maybe you'd both like to come for a drink on the yacht one evening?*

'Madame!' Bartel was hurrying towards her, covering the pavement in huge strides, his boots ringing on the concrete. 'Sorry I'm late. I had to finish a job and I couldn't come without a shower and a change of clothes.' He stopped. 'Have you just got married? And you didn't invite me?'

'Married?'

He grinned. 'The bouquet.'

'Oh, right. Fabian — the guy I mentioned to you. I had a drink with him, and he turned up tonight with these.'

'Ah, he's keen.'

'Seems like it.'

'You're not?'

'Difficult question, for another day.'

Bartel loomed over her in the purplish dusk. He smelled good — of limes and sawed wood. He reached out with a huge hand and touched the flowers. 'Not really you, are they?'

'No. They're vulgar, showy.'

'You prefer bluebells, anemones.'

'You're right. How did you know?'

'I notice things.' He smiled at her. 'Are you leaving?'

'I have to. Work. There'll be Cava left if you want some. Bit warm by now.'

'You're pleased with the exhibition?'

'Very.' She smiled into his broad Viking face. There was something so heartening about him. 'Sorry I'm going just as you arrive. Haven't seen you much lately.'

'No need for sorry, Madame. We are ships that pass in the night, but our voyages will cross again.'

'They will,' she promised. 'But be very afraid, Mutsi's in there, so you might be about to navigate stormy waters.'

Bartel laughed, a low rumbling. 'From the rain, straight under the drainpipe.'

Siv computed that. 'I'd say that translates to, *out of the frying pan, into the fire.*'

He tugged his beard. 'You're becoming more Polish day by day. I'm a bad influence.'

'I have to go. See you soon.'

When Bartel had gone into the museum, Siv changed the flowers to her other arm and eyed a bin, but she couldn't bring herself to throw them away. She didn't want to waste a bouquet that someone would take pleasure from. Then she saw a woman walking towards her, carrying a shopping bag, a little downcast. She stopped her.

'Would you like these flowers? I've just been given them but I've nothing to put them in at home.'

The woman's jaw dropped. 'But they're lovely. Must have been ever so expensive.'

'Yes, it's such a shame. You'd be doing me a favour if you took them. I'm on my way to work, and I'd hate to have to chuck them.'

'Well . . . if you're sure . . .'

'Absolutely.' Siv pressed them into her keeping. 'Enjoy them, please.'

She hurried across the road, glad to be heading back to the station, aware of Mutsi's vetiver mist clinging to her jacket.

CHAPTER 14

Ali and Patrick were eating chips and drinking cans of sparkling apple juice when Siv arrived. They put some chips on a plate for her while she kicked her shoes off and opened a can of juice.

'You two look pleased with yourselves. These chips are great, loads of salt and vinegar.' She was delighted to see them after the strain of the exhibition. In some ways, they were like a family of siblings. They bickered and annoyed each other, but there was a special bond and they had each other's backs.

'Patrick bought them.' Ali was quick to point out that he wasn't responsible for a deep-fried indulgence.

'I'm glad he did, I'm hungry. So, what have you got for me?'

Ali filled her in on the interview with Turton. 'I could understand that giving Lyra the medicine bought him a bit of peace.'

Siv licked her fingers and swigged apple juice. She'd swear she could feel it neutralising the chip fat. 'Sounds plausible, given what Turton had found out. People used to add some brandy to children's milk for the same reason before medicines were so handy.'

'Aye, my granny used to do that to us, but with whisky,' Ali said. 'I don't much like the guy, but I suppose he's been pretty stressed out, discovering Lyra wasn't his wain.'

Siv agreed. 'We can knock Turton's actions on the head, I reckon. I'm sure plenty of parents have done the same and he's got enough to contend with.' It crossed her mind that Mutsi might have sedated Rik when she wouldn't sleep. She ate her last chip, realising she'd been ravenous. 'What did he say about the IVF?'

Ali replied, 'He confirmed that he met Belanger through playing squash. Kay was introduced and they discussed IVF. Everything had gone well until the DNA bombshell dropped.'

'Turton has a solid alibi, we've no reason to pursue him further,' Siv said. 'We'll check Fairlawns out tomorrow. Maybe someone there was alarmed by the solicitor's letter and the damage an investigation would cause.'

'Maybe so, but why would they murder Tom Pullman and Lyra?' Patrick collected up their plates and chip papers.

Siv's email pinged with a message from Steve. She read it, raising her eyebrows. 'Interesting news, team. Forensics have found Belinda Hanak's fingerprints at Pullman's house, on the coffee table in the living room. Thank goodness Nell is a sloppy cleaner.'

'No fingerprints in the bedroom?' Patrick asked.

Siv grinned. 'No, but you can have sex on a sofa, Patrick. As I recall, there was a comfy one by that table.'

'Aye, hasn't anyone ever told you that?' Ali teased him.

Patrick smirked and hid behind his can of drink.

'Right. Patrick, you're with me visiting Fairlawns in the morning. Ali, you take Belinda Hanak and grill her. Now we have Pullman's letter to her, the cosy car meeting she failed to tell us about and her presence in his home. Do your bad cop act.'

Ali rubbed his hands, glanced at the display on his watch and seemed relieved. 'Chips in my belly, a juicy interview tomorrow *and* my blood sugar's OK. Life's sweet.'

* * *

It was Wednesday morning and raining heavily. Ali couldn't raise Belinda Hanak on her phone. He tried her husband, who told him that Belinda was at the BSS centre, attending a painting class.

'Anything I can help you with? You do seem to be quizzing her rather regularly. We're both finding it quite an imposition.'

'Just a general enquiry, sir.'

'Another stock phrase. The police must have a book of them.'

BSS had the use of two rooms and an office above the library, on the top floor. Ali ran up the two wide flights of oak stairs, puffing a little as he reached the top. There were two rooms with glass-paned doors on either side of the landing, with the office straight ahead. Ali looked through the door on the left and saw a group of older people sitting in a semi-circle, some with walking sticks resting between their legs. A tall man wearing a cape who reminded him of Dracula stood in front of them. He swept a hand through the air and the choir launched into song: 'Bonkers' by Dizzee Rascal. Ali was captivated by their enthusiasm and stood, tapping his foot. He then reminded himself why he was here and turned to the room on his right. Inside were half a dozen people sitting at easels. He recognised Belinda from her photo. She was near the front, gesticulating with her paint brush and talking animatedly to the tutor.

Ali knocked loudly and walked in. Everyone turned to stare at him and he became self-conscious, aware that his trousers needed hitching up after his effort on the stairs. The air was redolent with oil paint and turpentine.

'DS Ali Carlin, Berminster police. I need to speak to Ms Hanak.'

Belinda wasn't pleased. She tossed her head. 'May I finish my class? There's half an hour to go.'

'Sorry, it's urgent. I'll wait on the landing while you pack up.'

'For goodness' sake! Is this really necessary?'

'Yes.'

Several of the students exchanged glances. Belinda shrugged.

'Right. I'll be a couple of minutes.'

Ali checked that the office was empty. It was stuffy, so he opened the window, nudging it back a notch when rain blew in. There was a laminated notice beside it: LAST PERSON OUT, MAKE SURE YOU CLOSE WINDOW & CHECK ANSWER PHONE ON. He left the door ajar and waited by it, listening to repeat efforts at 'Bonkers', which occasionally dissolved into hysterical laughter. Not a bad way to spend your retirement.

His thoughts roamed to his parents, who were in their late sixties. They'd never retire. Farmers didn't, at least not where they lived. They were up at six in the mornings and outside by six thirty. They'd laugh at the concept of BSS and older people needing to keep busy, at painting classes and choirs. Ali's father maintained that he wanted to die in a field with his boots on, and as far as he was concerned, the crows could pick his bones. His mother said she'd be happy if she keeled over while feeding her hens. His brothers, who'd built their own houses on the family land, would sometimes urge their parents to slacken the pace, but their pleas fell on deaf ears.

Belinda emerged from her class with a pained expression, carrying a large shoulder bag and paint box.

'We'll talk in here,' Ali said.

She walked straight past him and sat down. She wore an arty outfit — yellow smock over dark jeans, huge blue beads around her neck, a rainbow-striped bandana around her hair and a fair bit of make-up. She resembled Siv's mother, what with the well-kept figure and the effort she'd made with her clothes. It crossed Ali's mind that this might be why the guv hadn't taken to Belinda.

He swung a chair round and sat with his legs stretched out so that his feet were near hers. She shifted hers to one side.

'You've been to Tom Pullman's house recently,' he said.

She scratched her neck. 'What on earth makes you say that?'

'Fingerprints.'

'Ah.'

'Aye, exactly. The magic of those little dabs. When and why were you there, and how come you haven't already told us?'

Belinda tweaked her bandana. 'People are allowed to visit each other's houses. It's not against the law.'

'Aye, and there are fairies at the bottom of my garden.'

She threw her eyes up. 'This is just so difficult, because it's not really my story.'

'The obvious story is that you and Tom Pullman were having an affair.'

'You're way off the mark with that, as was your DI. Why have the police got such parochial minds?'

'Then help me out.'

'Who will get to hear about it?'

Ali rapped his hand down on the desk beside him. 'Stop right there. You could be in very serious trouble over this, very serious indeed. You need to tell me the truth, otherwise I might have to arrest you. That wouldn't play well with BSS, not to mention your husband.'

Belinda's eyes widened. 'I'm cornered, aren't I? It's an unusual feeling.'

Ali took out a piece of gum, popped it in his mouth and cupped a hand behind his ear. *I'm listening.*

She folded her arms. 'Here goes. I did go to Tom's house, just the once, last month. We'd known each other a long time. We met at Rother College as mature students in the early eighties. We were both single, both late to the marriage market. You needn't look like that — there was never anything between us. Tom wasn't my type. We weren't close, but we'd have lunch together and chat about lectures and so on. We rarely saw each other after we finished our college courses, but our paths crossed again when BSS was formed.' She stopped and yawned nervously.

Ali prompted, 'So did Tom invite you to his house last month?'

'He asked me to go and see him, yes, but that meeting we had in the car at Ambourne Water was the start of it, so I'll begin there. Tom phoned me in January and he was in quite a state. He'd been contacted by a man who informed him that he was Tom's son. The man's mother was dead, but she'd been at college with us, although she was younger.'

'You were what, in your thirties?'

'Correct. Cathy Newall, the mother, was a postgrad student, early twenties.'

Ali moved his gum to the other cheek. 'So this Cathy had had a thing with Tom?'

'Yes. They were together for a while, but she found him rather pedantic and controlling.' Belinda grimaced. 'He hadn't changed over the years. He was far keener on her than she was on him. She broke it off. After they split up, Cathy discovered that she was pregnant. She didn't want to tell Tom, because she was convinced he'd kick up a huge fuss, use it as leverage to get her back. She didn't want to involve her dad, who was a widower, so she turned to me. I suppose I was a bit of a mother figure, being older.'

Belinda didn't strike Ali as the maternal type. 'Go on — she decided to have the baby?'

'Yes. She was reluctant to have an abortion and by the time she discovered the pregnancy, it was too late anyway. I talked it all through with her and got information and she decided to go for adoption. Cathy was very single-minded. She was almost five months gone but hardly showing when the summer vacation started, so she laid low in her flat. The baby was premature, born in early September, and everything was done and dusted when she returned just a little bit late for the autumn term.'

'Any idea who adopted the child or where he went?'

'No, Cathy never shared any information and I'm not sure she asked questions anyway. It's a long time ago and adoption was more of a clean break then.'

'And Tom Pullman never suspected? Maybe he'd have taken the child and raised him.'

Belinda sounded sceptical. 'Hardly. It's not the kind of thing single men tend to do, and especially forty years ago. No, he'd have tried to pressure Cathy into marrying him, and she didn't want that. For what it's worth, I didn't agree with her refusal to tell him, but I couldn't go against her wishes. It wasn't my place.'

'What happened to her after the baby was adopted?'

'She was from Hull and she went back there when she finished her studies. We didn't keep in touch much — just Christmas cards. I heard that she died four years ago.'

The choir in the next room were now belting out 'London Calling'.

Belinda shuddered. 'I love their enthusiasm, but what a racket! Tom, of course, hated their music selection. He wanted them to do light opera or classics.'

Ali was getting his head around all of this. 'So who is this son who appeared and presumably gave Tom a terrible shock?'

'Tom wouldn't say. He didn't give me any details. But of course, when the man informed him that Cathy had been his mother, Tom took a trip down memory lane and put his dates together. He recalled that she and I had been good friends at college and he contacted me. I was alarmed during that meeting in the car. I'd never seen him so rattled. I had to tell him then, about what had happened. It would have been cruel not to. He was agonising over what to do. I did sympathise with him, even if he was a difficult sod. His life had been turned topsy-turvy.'

'Presumably, Tom was angry with you — you were aware he had a son but you'd never said anything.'

'He wasn't best pleased. I told him there was no point in being cross with me, it hadn't been my decision to make. Not my call at all.' She raised her beads with a finger, then settled them again on her neck. 'To be honest, I'd pretty much forgotten about it until I met Tom again and I was hardly going to say anything all these years later. Chances were that the adopted child would never get in touch. I've read that most don't.'

'Did father and son meet?'

'Once, as far as I'm aware. Tom hadn't been at all sure that he wanted to, but in the end, it would be hard not to. Curiosity would get the better of you.'

Ali nodded. 'Does he look like me, walk like me, sound like me?'

'Exactly. I've not had kids, but it must be a tremendous pull. Tom asked me to visit him at home last month just to go over everything again. He wanted to tell me he'd met his son and have another rant at me about deceiving him back in the day. He seemed to have decided that I should agree with him about everything at committee meetings in the future as a kind of payback.' She shook her head. 'I had to tell him that wasn't going to happen. I suppose that's why he wrote me that nasty letter you found. Just another way of getting his own back. I could see that he was struggling to get the whole situation sorted in his head. And I do believe that once he'd had time to absorb the news, he would have been a bit chuffed to find he had a son.'

'And you have no clue as to this man's identity?'

'Sorry. All I can tell you is that he's forty years old.'

'Does he live around here?'

She raised her hands. 'Honestly, Tom didn't give anything away. I did ask him that, and whether he was planning to pursue things with his son, but he clammed up. He was clearly awash with conflict about the whole subject. He hadn't told his daughters, because he wasn't sure what he was going to do.' She smiled at Ali and wrinkled her nose. 'He made me promise not to breathe a word, of course, and I didn't. Until now.'

'You should have told us this straight away. It might have a crucial bearing on the murders.'

'*Please* don't tell me off. It's hard to break a confidence when you've kept it for so many years.' She hesitated and said, as if reassuring herself, 'Anyway, you're hardly likely to murder your dad and your niece as soon as you've met him, are you?'

They'd need to double-check, but Ali was sure there'd been nothing in Pullman's phone or digital history to suggest contact with a long-lost son. 'Is your husband aware of this?'

'No. Tom didn't want me to tell him. And Aled gets very waxed up about parental obligations and men's rights regarding their children. His brother had a terrible time with his ex trying to obstruct access to his kids. There was all sorts of arguing and fallout. Pretty vicious. Aled spent ages supporting his brother with it. He wouldn't approve at all about the way I helped Cathy and kept Tom in the dark.'

'You'd better tell him. I had to ring him to find out where you were. It's not going to matter to Tom now and he's getting a bit irate about us questioning you.'

'I can handle my husband, thank you very much. Can I go now?'

'Yes, but we'll need a statement from you. We'll be in touch.'

Rain sprinkled his face when Ali closed the window. Lots of food for thought here. Speaking of which, it was time to make inroads on the packed lunch Polly had made for him.

* * *

Belinda ran through the rain to her car. She put her painting stuff in the boot and sat behind the wheel, wiping her face with her hands. She had the jitters now. Things were slipping out of control, and in Belinda's world, that just didn't happen. She'd given Sergeant Carlin a close version of the truth, one that she was pretty sure couldn't be challenged. Cathy had wanted to keep the baby. It was Belinda who'd persuaded her to have it adopted. Why would a bright woman with a promising future and career want to saddle herself with being a single parent? It would be gruelling, expensive and hard on the child. Cathy had held out for a while and then crumbled. Belinda couldn't even recall why she'd been so adamant about adoption now. It was just the way she'd felt at the time. She'd honestly believed it was the right thing. Would she push the same advice now? Probably not, but then society had altered greatly. Back then, women celebrities didn't trot around the world openly acquiring babies, making it all somehow glamorous. Now there was prestige to being a single parent, if you had enough money.

None of it mattered to Cathy or Tom at this point, but Belinda didn't want to be cast as the baddie who'd persuaded a mother to give up her child.

Aled wasn't aware that she'd met Tom at college. There was no particular reason why she hadn't mentioned it, but now she wished she had because that omission just complicated things even more. Generally speaking, she always had the upper hand with Aled, but he could be disapproving of deception, especially after the lies his brother's manipulative ex had told. If he ever discovered that she'd persuaded Cathy to have her baby adopted and deprived Tom of his son, he'd be terribly angry.

She needed Harry to soothe her and rang him.

Harry asked, 'Shouldn't you be in painting class?'

Bless him, she was always in his thoughts. 'An obese policeman interrupted and dragged me out.'

'Oh my God, why? Hang on, I'm out on my bike. I'm just going to move off the path.'

She waited, clicking her nails on the steering wheel.

'What's happening, then? It must have been important for him to barge in like that.'

His voice was so caring, she got a bit tearful. This had all been such a strain. 'I had to tell this sergeant about Tom's son.'

'What changed your mind?'

'I never told you, but I went to Tom's house last month. He needed to chat again and I couldn't refuse. He was very emotional and still angry with me for helping Cathy conceal her pregnancy. The police found my fingerprints there, so I had no option but to explain.'

'Oh, I see. Well, like you said, you had no choice. How did the policeman react?'

'He got very stern. But listen, I said I'd told no one else, because Tom asked me not to. I didn't mention you.'

'OK. I'll keep my trap shut — you can rest assured on that. Are you going to tell Aled?'

'I'm not sure.'

'Probably best to at this point. I can hear the tension in your voice, so I'm sure he will. He'll understand.'

'Thanks, Harry. You are a darling.'

'Always here with a listening ear.'

She smiled. 'Enjoy the rest of your bike ride.'

Belinda sat and considered, then decided to head for the supermarket. She'd cook Aled's favourite tonight, lamb shanks, pour him a few glasses of robust Tempranillo and then when he was full and mellow, she'd explain about Tom.

* * *

Fairlawns clinic was housed in a modern, single-storey building. Lots of steel and shiny glass in blue-framed windows. Inside was shiny too, and airy. Siv and Patrick signed in and were given visitor passes. They waited in armchairs beside a cascade of green plants. Patrick tapped on his phone while Siv flicked through a clinic brochure. There was quite a menu of treatments: intrauterine insemination, fertility preservation, surgical sperm retrieval, hormone treatment and genetic embryo testing were just for starters.

A man and woman were waiting in the next cluster of chairs. He was whistling soundlessly. She massaged one hand with the other and shot Siv a tiny, complicit smile. *She thinks I'm here with Patrick for fertility treatment.* Siv smiled back.

'Do you want children?' she asked Patrick.

He straightened up, tapped his chin. 'Never considered it. Maybe one day, if the time's right.'

183

'I suppose people who come through these doors thought the time was right, but then nothing happened.'

'How about you, guv?' Patrick slapped a hand over his mouth. 'Sorry, I didn't mean . . .'

'It's OK, I raised the subject. When I was married, we did talk about it now and again, but never came to any conclusion.'

'These places cost a fortune, Kitty says.'

Siv had noted a good many 'Kitty says', from Patrick these days. If they stayed together, she gauged it would be Kitty who'd decide if they'd have children. 'I heard back from Kay Turton's solicitor. He confirmed that he visited her the other day and that he'd sent one letter to Glen Belanger. Belanger's the medical director as well as a consultant. The clinic's solicitor replied, saying that the matter had been referred through their complaints procedure. Kay's solicitor believes that she should continue with the process, although he can see that at present, it's the least of her concerns.'

Patrick made a money-shuffling gesture with his fingers. 'He would.'

'There is that, but I agree with him that it's a very serious issue and it raises wider concerns about the way this clinic operates. Maybe there are quite a few other children with unexpected fathers.'

A receptionist glided in their direction. 'Dr Belanger will see you now. Second door on the right. I'll buzz you through.'

The consultant had a large office, painted in a washed blue. Siv made introductions. Belanger shook hands with them both. A confident grip. There was a desk with chairs, but he indicated a corner with armchairs.

'Please, do sit down. Coffee?'

'No, we're fine,' Siv said.

He was a big man, tow-haired and with a blotchy complexion. His dark suit and white shirt were businesslike, the only splash of colour the green-and-white pattern on his tie.

He sat and said, 'So?' His voice was toneless, quiet.

'We're investigating the murders of Tom Pullman and his granddaughter, Lyra, last Thursday afternoon,' Siv said.

'I read about that. Shocking.'

'Kay and Ryan Turton are friends of yours and were clients. They had IVF at this clinic.'

'More acquaintances, to be absolutely correct. I had the occasional squash match with Ryan and Kay sometimes joined us in the bar afterwards. That was when they approached me about their fertility problem and I suggested they make an appointment to see me here. We didn't mix outside of the club.'

As Siv had anticipated, he was drawing the parameters carefully. She was also sure that he'd have spoken to the clinic's solicitor before seeing them. 'But to be absolutely correct,' she echoed, 'Kay and Ryan Turton conceived Lyra Turton through IVF at this clinic, and a DNA test subsequently demonstrated that Ryan wasn't Lyra's father. Something went badly wrong.'

Belanger leaned back in his chair, hitching his right leg across his knee. 'That has been alleged and we received a complaint. I can tell you that we have just written to the Turtons' solicitor, requesting our own DNA test to verify the information we've been sent. That's really the first thing we need in order to investigate. Given the child's sudden, very sad death, we've simultaneously contacted the coroner, asking for DNA to be provided from Lyra Turton — with her parents' permission, of course. We have stressed that we would appreciate their cooperation. Whatever happens now, we need to investigate if something did go wrong at the clinic and report to our governance.'

'So you're questioning the DNA test that Ms Turton had done?'

Belanger canted his head and blinked his sandy eyelashes. 'Ms Turton had a postal test done via a company we're unfamiliar with. We're entitled to ensure that a test is done with proper rigour, to our high standards.'

'And if a test done by yourselves agrees with the one Ms Turton received, that would prove that proper rigour wasn't applied when she had her IVF procedure here.'

He ran a palm along his jaw. 'That's conjecture at present. I'm not prepared to comment further until we have completed our own test, Inspector.'

Siv changed tack. 'Have any other mistakes of that kind been made at this clinic?'

'Not to my knowledge and we've never had any complaints. We have strict procedures and constant cross-checking.'

Siv wondered how many parents would pause to question their child's paternity. So much was taken on trust in this situation. Kay Turton had been particularly perceptive and proactive. 'You're very cool about it, Dr Belanger. The Turton marriage is on the rocks because of what's happened.'

He raised a finger. 'What's *alleged* to have happened. I'm sorry to hear that. We have tried to reach out through our solicitor.'

How Siv disliked that meaningless phrase, *reach out*. She waved a hand at Patrick.

He watched Belanger coast the change of questioner with ease and asked, 'Where were you last Thursday afternoon?'

Belanger raised an eyebrow and reached for his phone, flicking through the screen. 'I was here in my office from two p.m. onwards, writing reports and evaluating test results.'

'What time did you leave?'

'About five thirty.'

'And can anyone verify that you were here?'

Belanger cupped his chin. 'I recall an internal phone call from Fatima Marshall, one of our clinical nurses. I believe that was at about two thirty. We talked for a few minutes. Other than that, I was here on my own, head down, working.'

'Is Ms Marshall here today?'

'I believe she works two days a week, usually Thursday and Friday, so no.'

Siv folded her arms. 'Is anyone else here aware of the issue raised by Kay Turton?'

'I informed my deputy director and fellow consultant. Otherwise, no. Until we have followed due process, there seems little point in worrying other staff. Our work here is highly sensitive. We deal with strong emotions. Anxious staff aren't going to be much use to patients when they're already under stress.'

He had an answer for everything and Siv was fed up listening to him. 'We'll need to get your due process fast-tracked, Dr Belanger. If there was an error, we need to ascertain who the sperm donor was.'

'I don't understand. What has that got to do with your investigation?'

Siv hadn't a clue but she knew one thing — you chased down everything in a murder enquiry. 'It's an important aspect of the whole picture. Can you email me details of your solicitor, and I'd like to see copies of all correspondence to date.'

For the first time, Belanger showed irritation. He flushed and seemed about to object but then said, 'Very well, of course.'

'Thanks, Dr Belanger. We'd like a quick tour of the public areas of the building.'

'Why on earth — oh, if you must. I'll ask reception to show you the corridors and the washrooms. The staff room as well. And by the way, if you want to speak to me again, that's fine, but I'd like my solicitor with me.'

'As you wish,' Siv agreed sweetly and waited while Belanger called reception.

The woman who'd greeted them when they arrived showed them a pleasant, empty staff room and took them up and down four carpeted corridors. They all looked the same, with cream walls and blue carpet, but the one that Belanger's office was situated on led to a fire door with a key code. Outside at the back was a car park. A woman in a nurse's uniform was getting out of a Fiat.

Siv asked, 'Is that where all the staff park?'

'That's right. The front car park is for the public.'

'So you could exit through this door to the staff area?'

'Yes, of course.'

'Thanks. We'll go out this way then, as we're here.'

In the car park, Patrick said, 'Belanger didn't seem too bothered by us. Hope we're not losing our edge.'

'Speak for yourself. He didn't like the idea of us probing the clinic's sperm allocation.'

Patrick was scanning the building. 'No CCTV. After that phone call at half two, Belanger could have come out this way, driven to Cove Parade and back without anyone seeing him.'

'Yeah. But why would he have murdered them? He had no beef with Tom Pullman, and killing Lyra wouldn't have made the complaint go away. If anything, it would draw attention to it. He'd know that DNA would still be available after death. It doesn't add up.'

Patrick shivered in the cutting breeze. 'Should have worn a scarf today. Maybe Belanger had already found out that a sperm mix-up had happened and identified who the donor was. He might have been stressed out about the effect on the clinic's reputation. Fear can make people act impulsively. I'll contact Fatima Marshall and check his phone call with her.'

Siv did her jacket up. 'One thing's for sure, whatever the outcome. Belanger will change squash partners.'

CHAPTER 15

They were all back at the station, drying off from the rain. Ali's jacket was dripping from the back of his chair.

'Why don't you hang that on a hook?' Patrick asked.

'Is it bothering you?'

'It's wetting the floor near my desk.'

'Worried someone's going to think you've got a problem?'

Patrick grumbled, 'I'm not a slob like you. I like to keep things tidy. We've got coat hooks so we can hang our coats on them.'

'OK, OK, no need to get your dander up.' Ali took his sodden jacket to a hook.

Siv listened. They were probably ill-tempered because although this case had plenty of twists and turns, they all seemed to be leading into cul-de-sacs.

'Listen up,' she said, and gave a brief summary of the visit to the clinic. 'I've contacted Fairlawn's solicitor. He said he needed to speak to his client, but didn't see a problem with sharing correspondence about the IVF allegation. He said it's minimal, just two letters so far. One in reply to the allegation, stating they'd want to conduct their own DNA test, and one to the coroner's office following Lyra's death, informing them of the issue. He stated that nothing more will be done in terms of the family for now, pending the Turtons having time to grieve and make a decision about whether or not they want to proceed. The clinic will carry out their own investigation into the matter.'

'I spoke to Fatima Marshall,' Patrick said. 'She confirmed that she had a phone discussion with Dr Belanger about a patient around half two last Thursday. They spoke for five minutes or so. So he could easily have nipped to Seascape if he'd wanted.'

Ali popped a piece of gum in his mouth and described his interview with Belinda Hanak. 'Long story short, Tom Pullman had a shock when his adopted son contacted him. The natural mother's dead. Belinda stuck her oar in back in the eighties and helped Cathy, the mother, with the decision to adopt. She claimed that Pullman gave no clue as to the son's identity and said he hadn't told his daughters. He'd told Belinda that he'd had one meeting with the son. I've gone back over his communications and I can't see anything that indicates sudden contact with a man or any reference to a newcomer in his life.'

Siv watched the creeping puddle left by Ali's coat, then looked up at him. His steady chewing reminded her of a grazing cow. 'Was Belinda telling the truth when she said she didn't know the identity of Pullman's son?'

'I reckon,' Ali replied. 'I put the fear of God into her and I can't see why she'd keep on lying at this stage.'

'Maybe he's the man Pullman was meeting in St Peter's.' Siv stood and helped herself to a bottle of water. 'This investigation has paternity running through it now. Turton's lost a daughter and Pullman's gained a son.'

'Aye, but does it have anything to do with the deaths?' Ali asked.

They were all silent. There was a clang in the corridor. Someone laughed loudly and applauded. Patrick's phone pinged and he read a message intently, saying it was important.

'Brian Gifford's in the clear,' he told them. 'We've had contact from the owner of a silver Honda parked at the

Wherry Cove layby last Thursday. She confirmed that she pulled in to eat a sandwich at three. A man in a blue car with a damaged bonnet arrived a few minutes later and walked along the path to the cove. He was back in about ten minutes carrying something in a plastic bag and drove off. I've checked Gifford's car. It's a blue Skoda with a dented bonnet. This woman said there was another black car parked in front of her, but there wasn't anyone in it. It was still there when she left around three twenty.'

'Contact her to see if she recalls a number plate for the black car,' Siv told him. She scanned the incident board. 'Ali, get in touch with local adoption agencies, see if we can find out anything from forty years ago—'

'Hi, guys.' Geordie Coleman was standing in the doorway. 'Am I interrupting?'

'Come on in,' Siv beckoned. 'We're just finishing.'

He stepped in and put his bag on a chair. He wore a soft brown leather jacket over a white T-shirt. 'I won't stop, got an interview to head to. I just wondered how you're doing. Have the Turtons opened up at all?'

'Someone handed us a way in,' Ali said. 'Turns out they had Lyra via IVF, but there was a mix-up and Ryan's not the daddy.'

Geordie whistled. 'Wow! Quite a blow. Have they been told who the dad is?'

'Not yet. They might never find out,' Siv said, 'but now we understand the marital disharmony and why they were pulling up the drawbridge. We've also discovered that Tom Pullman had an adopted son who'd suddenly popped up and introduced himself. They'd met once that we're sure about, possibly more often.'

Geordie's eyebrows lifted in high arcs. 'Complicated family! Pullman had no clue about this son?'

'Not until he turned up. Unfortunately, we've no information about his identity. They might have met in St Peter's church.'

'Well, you've plenty to chew on.'

Ali muttered, 'Aye, but it's mainly gristle, not meat.'

Geordie asked, 'What about this son's birth mother — do you have a handle on her?'

'Dead,' Patrick told him despondently.

'Bit of a mystery all round then. I'd best get off,' Geordie said, hoisting his bag. 'Don't forget that drink, Ali. I owe you a pint.'

When he'd left, Siv said, 'I didn't realise you two were mates.'

'We have a bevy now and again. Geordie's spent some holidays with relatives in Antrim, so we share a bit of background scenery.'

Patrick was spinning an apple by its stem. 'He dresses a bit casual for the job, doesn't he?'

'He's not a sharp dresser like you, no. He's not keen on suits,' Ali said.

'I reckon he should wear one,' Patrick replied. 'Best to look smart when you're liaising with families, gives them confidence in you.'

Siv laughed. 'You're sounding positively middle-aged today, Patrick, what with coat hooks and smart dressing. Enough of the chat now, let's push on.'

* * *

Siv hid it from the others, but she was restless and unsure where to go next with the investigation. She scrolled through the Fairlawns clinic website and read glowing reviews from satisfied customers. There was no adverse publicity.

Her drab office grated on her, with its jaded décor, musty smell and worn laminate flooring. The best thing about it was the view to the museum and theatre. She shifted things around pointlessly on her desk, tore off a sheet from a notepad and folded a butterfly. As always, the discipline soothed her.

She recalled the first day she'd sat here, anxious, unsure that she was up to the job, feeling like an impostor. Not convinced that she'd made the right decision moving from London. She must have come across as so prickly and tense. The pale, nervy widow. Ali and Patrick had done well to put up with her.

Where does the time go, Ed? Seems like yesterday that we were walking across Greenwich park to the cinema.

There. She sent the butterfly spinning through the air. It caught on top of one of the vertical beige blinds that formed a screen across the wide window between her and the team room. How she hated those institutional, grimy blinds. She'd leave the butterfly there. It might entertain the cleaner, with whom she conducted a daily battle. She drew the blinds across every morning so that she wasn't on view, and the cleaner pulled them back every evening. She'd tried leaving notes, but to no effect. Perhaps the cleaner couldn't read or was just stroppy.

No good sitting here, obsessing about the blinds. She decided to take another look at Tom Pullman's house, now they had the heads-up about the adopted son. A drive through the country lanes would at least give her the illusion that she was doing something useful.

She picked up a coffee and a slice of quiche at Gusto and pulled into a turnoff on the road to Harfield to eat. Drifts of cherry blossom reminded her of the bouquet Fabian had given her. He puzzled her. Maybe he was one of those men with a limited repertoire, who relied on a well-rehearsed script with women. Or was she being harsh, judgemental? She really hadn't a clue. She might ask for Bartel's opinion. The coffee was good, giving her a boost. She finished it and drove on to Pullman's cottage.

When she let herself in, the house was warm and still. Downstairs, she noted that the pie had gone from the kitchen, and the carnations were no longer in their vase in the living room. Kay or Nell must have been here. She inspected framed photos of Pullman and a fair, well-padded woman who must have been his wife. There were several of Kay, Ryan and Lyra and plenty of Lyra on her own, from babyhood onwards. Only one of Nell, Siv noticed.

She headed upstairs and drew a chair up to the filing cabinet in Pullman's study. There were a number of personal documents concerning finances, insurances and guarantees. The man had belonged to a generation that still kept paper records, although his were fairly minimal. When Siv had cleared her father's house after his death, it had taken her days to work through the archive of papers. He seemed to have hung on to every invoice and receipt that had ever come his way. She'd found utility bills and bank statements from the 1970s. There was a shredder under Pullman's desk and she guessed that he'd cleared out regularly. She went through the files but found nothing of interest. What was she hoping for — letters from the long-lost son, with a name and address on? *Fat chance*, she told herself.

She moved to Pullman's bedroom and rummaged through the wardrobe. He hadn't skimped on clothing. There were lots of cashmere sweaters, cotton shirts and cord trousers in mustards and greens. What she considered 'country gent comes to town' clothes. He'd liked his woven ties — a rack of them hung on the back of one of the wardrobe doors. There were a couple with the same attractive horizontal wave pattern, in different colours. She examined one of the labels. *Minstergreen*. It was a popular local conservation charity with an online shop.

The bed was a double with one side pushed against the wall. Siv sat on the edge and switched on the radio. It was tuned to a classical music station. The digital screen informed her that she was listening to Haydn as she searched the two-drawer bedside table. Pairs of glasses, throat lozenges, indigestion tablets, a pair of earbuds, a couple of paperbacks and a crayoned card from Lyra with a drawing of red-nosed reindeer and her haphazard print inside: *haPPy XmAs to PopPA*. Siv pictured her sitting at home at the kitchen table, kicking her legs, tongue poking out as she concentrated. When the adverts came on the radio she switched it off and smoothed the duvet cover.

Downstairs again, she saw that the backdoor key was in the lock. She opened it and stepped out into a pretty space devoted to shrubs and flowers, with an iron table and chairs sitting on a raised central dais. Bags of potting compost stood by the stone wall that divided the house from the neighbour.

Siv crossed to the wall and ran her fingers along the soft green moss growing in the crevices. A woman came out from next door with half a dozen long bamboo canes in one hand and a boy aged about six swinging on the other. She had a resigned expression and wore mucky green wellies paired with a floaty skirt that didn't seem suited to gardening. The boy was just in swimming shorts, despite the nip in the air.

'Hope you don't mind me asking who you are,' the woman said, resting the canes down. 'Stop it, Josh, you're hurting my arm!'

'I'm Detective Inspector Drummond, Berminster police. And you are?'

'Trudy Hampton. I told Kay I'd keep an eye open, after what's happened to her poor dad.' She almost lost her balance as Josh leaned backwards, swinging her arm. 'Josh! Behave! What's wrong with you today?'

Josh laughed and head-butted her in the side. She cast her eyes upwards and ruffled his hair.

Siv asked, 'Did you know Mr Pullman well?'

'We moved in last year and he was ever so helpful. So terrible, what's happened. He'd mentioned Lyra's party and how thrilled she was. I didn't see him that often. He was a busy man, out a lot.' Trudy said this wistfully, like a prisoner who rarely escapes her cell.

'Did you notice any visitors here recently? Anyone you hadn't seen before?'

Josh clutched his mother around the waist and droned, 'Mummummummummummum . . .'

'Josh, give me a break. Why don't you go and see if you can spot Oaky? I bet he'd like some lettuce.' She smiled at Siv. 'Oaky's our tortoise.'

'Don't wanna,' Josh grumbled, clinging to her even tighter.

'We were daft getting him for you, you hardly pay any attention to him!'

'He's *boring*.'

Siv could only agree with Josh that a tortoise would offer limited interest to a small boy. She prompted, 'Visitors?'

'No, not that I noticed. Just Nell, his daughter. She cleaned for him on Wednesdays.' Trudy grinned. 'Mind, Tom said he had to go round after she'd gone and do some of it again.'

'What you *laughing* at, Mum?' Josh rocked his mother from side to side. 'What's so *funny funny funny*?'

'Shouldn't you be at school?' Siv said to him.

He glared at her. 'I had tonsillitis.'

Pity it wasn't laryngitis. 'Oh dear, too bad.'

'He's on the mend now, aren't you, Joshy?' his mother said fondly. 'Got his energy back, more's the pity!'

He shivered dramatically. 'I'm cold!'

'I did tell you to put a coat on.'

'I was too hot inside. Now I'm cold.'

'Josh, go and get a coat or your fleece.'

'Don't wanna. Too tired. *You* get it.'

Trudy rolled her eyes and chuckled. *What's he like?*

Siv enquired, 'Did Mr Pullman and Nell get on as well as you and Josh?'

If Trudy clocked the barb, she didn't show it. 'Pretty well, I suppose. They had a bit of a barney last week, though. He was in the garden and Nell came out. She seemed to be having a go at him. She took one of the terracotta pots and smashed it. I saw him sweeping it up after she'd gone. Cleaners are supposed to remove mess, not make it!'

Josh inevitably interrupted. 'What's a barney?'

'An argument,' his mother said. 'Like you have with me when I want you to put your shoes on but you're stuck to your iPad screen.'

Siv was exhausted just listening to them. 'Did you hear what Nell and her dad were saying?'

'Not really. Tom was shushing her and they went indoors. He'd seen me outside hanging out washing. I suppose he was embarrassed. I heard Nell say something about "three's a crowd" just before the pot smashed.'

Josh stopped squeezing the breath out of his mother, straightened up and stared at Siv. The penny had just dropped that she was a detective. 'Do you lock bad people up?'

'Sometimes.'

'In cells?'

'Correct.'

'Are the cells like dungeons?'

'No, they're not underground and they've got windows.'

'Do the baddies wear handcuffs?'

'When I'm arresting them, if they've been very bad. For example, if they keep annoying and disobeying their mothers.'

Josh poked his tongue out at her.

Trudy giggled. 'Maybe DI Drummond could lend me a pair to use on you. Then I'd get a bit of peace and quiet.'

She'd asked for another head-butt, and Josh duly delivered it to her chest. She let out an *ouf!* Her face creased with pain. Siv couldn't help wondering if she might meet Josh in the station at some point in the future, when he was being booked for assault.

'I'll leave you to your family fun,' she said. 'I reckon Josh is well enough to go back to school tomorrow.'

She locked the house and returned to her car. Time to see Nell again and find out what she'd meant by 'three's a crowd'.

CHAPTER 16

It was the first time Patrick had been in a Catholic church. Because his name belonged to the patron saint of Ireland, people often assumed he was Irish and therefore probably Catholic. His mother had named him after Patrick Swayze, her Hollywood crush. She'd once dabbled in the Baptists and had taken him and Noah to a couple of services but had decided they were *a bit severe*.

Father Murray had called the station to say that someone had information for the police. Patrick walked up and down the aisles of St Peter's while he waited. It was quite ornate. Lots of statues: saints Bernadette, Anthony and Paul, and one of the Virgin Mary surrounded by a floral arrangement. A smell of incense mixed with lilies.

Patrick stood in front of a six-foot plaster statue of St Peter. He carried a bible and was dressed in brown robes, had a white curly beard and a disdainful expression. A large brass halo circled his head. Patrick had noted that all the saints had bare feet. Maybe it had been their thing, like that singer, Sandie Shaw. He supposed that was an irreligious thought and started guiltily as a priest called to him from a door at the far corner.

'Are you the detective?'

'Yes, DC Patrick Hill.'

'Come to the vestry. Den is in here.'

'I'm Father Murray,' the priest said, drawing a chair up for Patrick. 'We don't have a statue of your saint, despite the fact he was a fine man. Sorry about that.'

'It's called St Peter's. Stands to reason it'd need to be called St Patrick's for there to be a statue of him, wouldn't it?' The speaker was a strapping youth with gappy teeth and two rings through each nostril. 'I'm Den, Den Barclay.'

'Den has been helping us out now and again,' Father Murray said.

'Community service, my mate the padre means. He's being discreet, bless him.' Barclay sniggered. 'Listen to me, blessing you! I'm stealing your thunder.'

The priest laughed awkwardly and clasped his hands in front of his scrawny chest. The vestry was dark and narrow with a sink in one corner. It smelled of sweat and soap, reminding Patrick of the changing rooms at school. A vacuum cleaner, mops and buckets and a trolley with cleaning materials took up most of the space. Their three huddled chairs meant their knees were almost touching. A gold-painted angel with a broken wing and brandishing a trumpet stood on a table nearby. Barclay saw Patrick's glance.

'I'm fixing him. I call him Uriel, one of the seven princes of heaven. He'll fly again before too long. Padre, Uriel's been a bit hidden up in that corner of the side chapel. I fancy suspending him from the ceiling over the altar. What d'you reckon?'

'Um, I'm not sure . . .'

Barclay winked at Patrick. 'He'd be amazing, flying over your head with his trumpet while you're doing your hot gospelling.'

'Can we get to why you wanted to see me?' Patrick could barely focus in the gloom. There was one shallow window high in the wall that cast more shadow than light. The priest's face was almost in darkness.

'Go ahead, Den,' Father Murray said.

Barclay flicked one of his nose rings. 'Marina, one of the old dears who does stuff here, had to go for an appointment a couple of weeks ago. Something to do with her hearing.'

'Her eyes,' Father Murray corrected.

'Whatever. Old people all fall apart one way or another. My grandad's had just about everything replaced. I call him the bionic man. So anyway, I stepped in. Came and did the flowers, a bit of cleaning. Rescued poor old Uriel from his niche.'

Patrick recalled the information from Marina Desmond. 'Was this on a Thursday?'

'Yep. I was giving old Uriel a bit of a once-over in here when I heard the church door open. It wheezes a bit.' He demonstrated with a gasping intake of breath. 'I peeked out and saw these two guys come in. One was definitely the old bloke who got whacked.'

Father Murray winced and crossed himself.

Patrick wondered why Murray put up with the man. Maybe it was his Christian duty to let him do his community service at the church. Barclay had landed a cushy number, faffing about with angels and flowers. 'What about the other man?'

'I didn't get much of a look at him. He was behind the old guy and they went in the corner by that water bath thing.'

'Holy water font,' Father Murray corrected.

'Yeah, magic water. Sounds like something from Harry Potter! He was taller than the old guy, had a dark rain-coat with the hood up. Held himself well. Had his hands stuffed in the front pockets of his jeans.' Barclay stood and demonstrated.

'Did the older man have a little girl with him?'

'No kid.'

'Can you recall the date?'

'Yep, twelfth of March. I have to keep records of my hours, see.'

'Did you hear anything they said?'

'Nope, too far away.'

'How long were they there?'

'Dunno. One of my mates rang. They'd gone when I went back out with the hoover.' He turned to the priest. 'It needs some new bags by the way, Padre. Why don't you just get a bagless one? Much easier to empty.'

'Not in this year's budget,' the priest said with regret. He turned to Patrick. 'Has that been of help?'

'Any information could be useful, thanks.' Patrick stood, keen to get back into the light.

'Don't you want to hear how I ended up with this gig?' Barclay laughed.

'No. You seem to be enjoying your punishment, though. I have got a question, Father Murray.'

The priest seemed glad to have more of a role. 'Of course, how can I help?'

'Why have all the statues of the saints got bare feet?'

'Goodness, I've never been asked that before.' He stared up at the Artexed ceiling, as if there might be a divine answer. 'I have to admit I'm not sure. I expect it's to express poverty and humility.'

Barclay tapped his arm. 'I reckon Jesus paid below the living wage. The disciples couldn't afford the sandal leather.' He threw his head back and guffawed. 'Living wage! It's a good one, admit it!'

Father Murray laughed weakly and saw Patrick as far as the main door. 'Den means well. His heart's in the right place underneath that cockiness.'

'Whatever you say, Father. Good luck.'

Patrick heard the door groan behind him as he exited. It must be quite a strain, trying to be holy and charitable all the time. No wonder the priest had a fragile air.

He was pleased that he'd made some progress. Tom Pullman had met a male friend — or his son — in the church on at least three occasions and they had a description, albeit vague. Not that that was much help without a name.

* * *

Siv found Nell Pullman cleaning a large Edwardian house near the hospital. Or rather, from the evidence of a half-full coffee cup, she'd been lounging on the living room sofa with her feet up on a stool reading magazines and eating from an open packet of custard creams. Still wearing the red jeans, now with a creamy stain on the right thigh. Her hair was snagged back in an elastic band, but a shank of fringe kept dropping across her left eye.

'I'm beginning to worry you fancy me,' she said, 'turning up so often. How come you're always so smart, like you've just been ironed?'

Siv sat on a chrome chair opposite the sofa. 'I make an effort every morning.'

'Right. Not much point in me doing that when I'm skivvying. Custard cream?'

'No. What were you arguing with your dad about last Wednesday? And don't bother asking me how I know.'

Nell pulled a pout and rubbed ineffectually at the stain on her jeans. 'It was nothing. He was nagging me, as per.'

'Try again.'

'What, you don't believe me?'

'Like I said, try again.'

'You do fancy me, that's why you like persecuting me. A sort of weird attraction.'

Despite how irritating she was, Siv quite liked Nell. There was intelligence and humour behind the slapdash facade. That's probably why her father had lost patience with her so often. Wasted talent. She decided on a biscuit after all, in case this was a long haul.

'I'd rather talk here, but we could go to the station. You have no alibi for last Thursday, remember.'

Nell huffed, turned and lay full length on her back on the squashy sofa. 'I like this old house. Belongs to a lecturer at Rother College. It's comfy, lived-in. Not like Kay's "look at me I'm smart and smug with it" place.'

Siv took in the crumpled cushions, crammed book-shelves, the piles of *New Statesman* and *Literary Review*. 'It is a

relaxing room, and you clearly find it so. Strikes me sometimes that you don't much like your sister.'

'I don't *dislike* her.'

Siv crunched her biscuit. 'The argument with your dad
annoyed you so much you smashed a pot in the garden.'

Nell gave a deep laugh. 'I've smashed more than that
in my time. He was going on about my education again.
Yadayadayada.'

'What did that have to do with you saying three's a
crowd?'

Nell's head whipped round to face her. 'You what?'

'Oh, do stop stalling.' Siv decided it was worth a punt.
'I reckon you'd found out about your brother. Half-brother.
Were you poking about when you were cleaning? I bet you
have a snoop when you're in other people's houses. I would.'

The shock on Nell's face told her she'd hit home. She sat
upright. 'Shit! How d'you find out about him?'

'A source. You must have been very upset.' Siv weighed
her up. Upset enough to break her father's head as well as
a pot?

'I could do with a spliff now,' Nell said, rubbing her arms.

'You'll have to wait. Did you find something?'

Nell knocked her knuckles together, a sound like tapping tacks into a wall. 'A postcard in his bedside drawer,
picture of the harbour on the front.'

'You told us you didn't clean upstairs last week.'

'I had to use the bathroom. Just took a peek while I was
passing.'

'What did this postcard say?'

'Just a short message. *Hi Dad, see you next week, same place,
same time. Looking forward to it.* It wasn't Kay's writing. I found
Dad in the garden and asked what it was about. He went a
bit wobbly, then came straight out with it.'

'He had an adopted son he'd only just met.'

'Yeah.' Nell was still tapping her knuckles, self-soothing.
It wasn't working, judging by her taut mouth.

'Did your dad tell you his name?'

'No. I insisted, but he wouldn't. He said this new family member was a professional with a good, responsible job. I took that as a snide comparison with yours truly. He was so fucking pleased with himself. Said he'd met this guy recently, but wanted to take things slowly before he told me and Kay. I could see having a son tickled him to bits. I was so mad, I smashed that pot.' She glared at Siv. 'Who did he think he was, keeping that from us? Romancing his new golden boy on the quiet.' She gripped her head.

The woman was an anxiety-prone addict. Siv didn't want her throwing anything. 'Was the postcard stamped?'

'Can't remember.'

'Where is it now?'

'Dad was trying to calm me down. He burned it in the kitchen sink, said that might make me happier. Made me even crosser, like I could be soothed by his little gesture!'

Siv's hopes were dashed. 'Did your dad say anything else about this son — where they were meeting, anything else about him?'

'No. He didn't get a chance. I went home. That's the last time I spoke to him.'

'You didn't tell Kay?'

She shook her head. 'Next thing, Dad and Lyra were dead. Hardly seemed the right time. Anyway, this fine, responsible professional might have been a chancer. I wasn't going to set the hares running and have him try a claim on Dad's estate.'

It occurred to Siv that Nell could have murdered her father so that he wouldn't have a chance to change his will. If that was true, she was now doing a good job of putting herself in the frame, which was an unlikely move. And it wouldn't explain Lyra's death — unless her niece had seen the killing and had to be silenced.

'Maybe you should tell Kay now.'

'I suppose. When I'm ready, I will. Or maybe you will?'

'Unless it turns out to have something to do with the murders, it's not my place to do that. It's for the family to deal with.'

'Yeah, right. I'm knackered,' Nell grumbled. 'I need to go home and rest for a bit.'

'Fine. Nell, if you do recall anything else about this man, call me.'

'I've told you what I can. Piss off and leave me alone. All this is wrecking my head.'

* * *

'And have you been trying your best to follow the rules about diet and exercise?'

Nurse Keene was a tall, terrifying woman with a nose you could launch a small plane from. She was taking Ali's blood pressure in the diabetes clinic. He was convinced she was enjoying pulling the strap extra tight.

'Yes.' He put on his meek voice. 'I've been taking stairs whenever I can and monitoring what I eat. My watch is a big help.'

'Yeeeesss . . .' Nurse Keene pulled her glasses down from the top of her head and entered his BP reading on the computer. 'The watch is fine and dandy as another support, and your wife's very considerate buying it for you, but don't rely on it too much. It's not going to do the work for you.'

'No.'

'You have to maintain and support yourself. Nothing and nobody else can.'

'Understood.'

'Well, you're not bad at all today, so well done. Better readings than at your last appointment.'

He breathed out with relief. 'Thanks.'

Nurse Keene swivelled in her chair and fixed him with a stern gaze. 'Don't forget it's not long since you were in hospital because you got slack. I haven't, and neither has your long-suffering Polly. I hope you treasure the way she cares for you.'

'I do, indeed.'

'Pleased to hear it. Right, that's us done. I can go home now and feed the dog. See you in three months, and don't give Polly or me any more frights.'

Ali escaped from the clinic and did a slow jog to his car, hoping that Nurse Keene was watching him from her window and giving him brownie points. God, she was alarming. He imagined that she'd have a big bruiser of a dog like a Bullmastiff or a Boxer. She'd wrestle with it at home and take it for robust walks. He drove around the corner and fell on his third fag of the day, taking deep, grateful drags. Now and again, he glanced in the rear-view mirror to make sure Nurse Keene wasn't creeping up on him. While he smoked he checked his email and saw one from Siv, updating him with news of another witness at St Peter's and Nell's information.

She ended, *I'm wondering about Nell, but there's no forensic or other evidence against her.*

He replied. *I contacted local adoption service. They ran the name Cathy Newall through their records, but didn't come up with anything. Mind, they lost a load of paper records during an office move and they said that if the adopted child was placed out of county, the records would have been transferred with him.*

Soothed by nicotine, he drove to the White Horse pub and found Geordie ensconced in a corner, drinking a pint.

'Another one of those?' Ali asked.

'Keep it coming!'

Ali bought himself a low-calorie tonic with two slices of lime and another pint for Geordie. He really wanted crisps, but asked for cashews instead.

He carried the drinks over on a tray. 'How's family liaison these days?'

Geordie grimaced. 'I was dealing with a cot death today. Grim, but they were glad to have me there — unlike the Turtons.'

'I can see that still rankles.' Ali opened the nuts and offered the bag to Geordie, who shook his head.

'Well, no one likes to fail, but they were hard work. How's your case coming along?'

'Still no ID on Pullman's adopted son. Nell Pullman has now told us that she'd found out about him, saw a postcard from him to his dad.'

Geordie shoved his old pint to one side and took a sip of his new one. 'Oh, so have you got the card?'

'No, Pullman burned it, or so she says. She's a weasel, that one. We're pretty sure that Pullman and the son met in St Peter's church, at least a couple of times.'

Geordie looked pensive. 'I suppose you could try adoption agencies.'

'I have. Nothing.'

'Nearly a week on and no main suspect.'

'Aye, but don't rub it in. We could do with a bit of luck and no mistake. Siv gets ratty when there's no progress.' Ali pictured her going home to her empty wagon. It couldn't be good for her, living out in the sticks on her own. He'd always had company, coming from a big family and then marrying young. He couldn't stand being on his own for long; it made him anxious.

'She's rated though, I hear — made her mark,' Geordie said. 'Especially now Mortimer's her sort-of stepdad. That must be odd.'

'No love lost there, mate. But she's good, aye. Persistent. Thinks out of the box.'

'You admire her, don't you?'

'Aye, suppose I do. And why not?' Ali laughed. 'She's always straight with me, sometimes to the point of brutal honesty.'

'Well, keep me posted about the investigation. After my failure to engage with the Turtons, I have a vested interest.'

'Will do. I keep wondering about Lyra and why someone would kill her too.'

They both went quiet while a group sat at the table nearby and started a loud conversation about what bar snacks they wanted.

Ali asked, 'See the footie match last night?'

They spent an hour arguing over teams. Geordie was quick-witted and good for a bit of banter. Ali spun his tonic out, pleased with himself for showing such restraint, especially when Geordie fetched a whisky chaser, saying he was getting a cab home.

CHAPTER 17

Siv was sipping coffee and going through interview summaries early the next morning. Ali and Patrick weren't in yet, so she had no interruptions. There were still too many people who could have been at Seascape last Thursday afternoon, and there was no hint of the identity of the man Brian Gifford had seen at Wherry Cove. She was halfway through checking his statement when reception rang to say that a woman called Fatima Marshall was there, asking to speak to her.

Siv took a mouthful of coffee and headed down to reception, where a plump woman in a baggy tracksuit and trainers was sitting, clutching a drink from the vending machine. Siv introduced herself and found an empty interview room. It was the smallest and windowless, painted dark green and brought to mind grim interrogation rooms used by the Stasi, but it would have to do.

'Please, sit down,' Siv told Ms Marshall. The woman was blinking rapidly, so she moved her chair to one side of the table to make things less formal. 'How can I help you?'

'I work at Fairlawns clinic,' Ms Marshall said. Her lips barely moved when she spoke, but her double chin wobbled.

'Yes, I recognised your name. One of my colleagues phoned you.'

'Um, yes, about my conversation with Dr Belanger last Thursday.'

She was in her thirties and carrying the kind of extra weight that blurred her features and her shape. Siv gauged that the tracksuit was camouflage rather than an exercise outfit.

'There's something else you'd like to tell me,' Siv suggested.

Ms Marshall clasped short, pudgy fingers on the table. It rocked a little on the uneven floor and she lifted her hands quickly, as if she'd been burned.

Siv put out a hand to steady it. 'Take your time, Ms Marshall.'

'That man who died, Mr Pullman. You might know this already, but . . . he came to the clinic. Well . . . I only saw his back, but I'm sure now it was him. I wasn't certain, you see, but I saw more photos of him online.'

'When was this?'

'I can't remember exactly. One evening in early March.' It wasn't hot in the room, but she pulled down the zip of her top and fanned herself with her hand.

'Talk me through exactly what you saw.'

The woman blew a little puff of air up her face. 'It was late, about seven in the evening. Dark outside. I was leaving, coming along the corridor near Dr Belanger's office. I saw a man going through his door, then it closed. I wondered about it, because we don't usually have visitors in the clinic at that time. But I was on my way home . . .' She seemed to run out of energy.

'It was just that once that you saw Mr Pullman?'

'Yes. Then when I saw the news details and the Turtons' name, I realised that he was related to a previous IVF patient.'

'Were you involved with the Turtons' treatment?'

'I was, yes.'

'You have a good memory. That was over four years ago.'

'It's an unusual name, and it was a very satisfying treatment because it succeeded at the first attempt. There's around a thirty-per-cent chance of that, so we had reason for being pleased.'

Siv was buzzing quietly at this information, yet she had a sense that this wasn't the primary reason Ms Marshall had come to see her. She was working her lips, as if worried about what else she might say. Siv debated whether to mention the alleged IVF error, but decided not to pre-empt the woman and possibly cloud issues.

'So,' she said, 'everything had gone very well with the Turtons' treatment.'

The woman sounded cagy. 'They were thrilled.'

'Thank you for coming here with this information regarding Mr Pullman. I appreciate that you're worried about it.'

'Dr Belanger hadn't told you, had he, when you came to see him?'

'I can't comment on that.'

'I suppose you'll have to speak to him now.'

'Does that make you anxious?'

Ms Marshall cleared her throat. 'Of course it does. He's my employer.'

'We're talking to him anyway, as part of our enquiries. I won't need to divulge that you came to tell me about Mr Pullman's visit.'

That didn't reassure her, given the miserable expression on her face.

Siv added, 'Is there anything else?'

She shoved her chair back. 'That's all.' She hurried to the door with little steps, yanked it open and was gone.

Siv could only hope that whatever was eating her would bring her back.

* * *

Ali and Siv were sitting opposite Glen Belanger and his solicitor, Noel Ure. They were men of substance, at ease and complacent. Siv couldn't help picturing Kay Turton's anguished face. Both were smartly suited, but Ure had the upper hand in quality of material and tailoring. He had a broad, florid face, piggy eyes and an assured manner. He and his client had met for over an hour before the start of the interview and they'd prepared a statement. The solicitor smoothed it on the table in front of him.

'Dr Belanger has requested me to read a statement that he's written about his meeting with Mr Tom Pullman. He is not prepared to answer any other questions at this time.'

Siv looked at Belanger. 'It might help you if you would. We always appreciate cooperation.'

Ure put a hand up, displaying a gold signet ring. 'Dr Belanger understands that, but he cannot add anything to his prepared statement.'

'Not even if he tries really hard?' Siv asked.

'Please, DCI Drummond.' Ure sounded pained. 'My client is cooperating with you at a very difficult time.'

'Go on then,' Siv told him. It might improve her mood if she antagonised these two, but it was unlikely to be productive.

Ure picked up the sheet of paper while Belanger stared ahead with a face like stone.

'This statement has been prepared on behalf of Dr Glen Belanger of twenty-four, Queen's Crescent, Berminster.

'I can confirm that I met with Mr Thomas Pullman at my office in Fairlawns clinic on the twelfth of March, in the evening. Mr Pullman had phoned me in an agitated state the previous day. His daughter had confided in him about the alleged error in her IVF treatment. Mr Pullman was very upset and talked about going to the press. I tried to calm him and I explained that I couldn't discuss the issues because of client confidentiality. He ended the call abruptly.

'Around seven o'clock on the evening of the twelfth of March, I went to my car to fetch some papers. Mr Pullman was in the staff car park and accosted me. He was in an excitable state and speaking loudly. I thought it best to invite him to my office.

'I met with Mr Pullman there for approximately half an hour. He stated that he hadn't told his daughter of his contact with me, and I informed him that I wasn't comfortable with that. I explained that Ms Turton had consulted a solicitor. I also informed him that I couldn't discuss confidential aspects of his daughter's treatment, but that we would do our utmost at the clinic to establish if the allegation was true.

'Mr Pullman was antagonistic at the start of the meeting, but seemed reassured by my discussion with him, my explanation of our complaints procedure and our clinical governance. He agreed with me that he would inform his daughter and her husband that he had met me. I advised him that I wasn't prepared to see him again while an allegation was being investigated.

'I realise now that I should have told the police about this meeting after Mr Pullman's death. I refrained from doing so because I wasn't sure that he had subsequently informed his daughter, and I didn't wish to cause any further distress or confusion for the Turton family. The meeting had not been significant and did not seem to warrant disclosure. I accept that this was not a correct decision on my part.

'That is the only occasion on which I met Mr Pullman.

'This statement is my full and complete account of my contact with Thomas Pullman. I am not aware of any other information which may be of use to the police in their investigation.'

Siv could tell from Ure's tone that he didn't rate his client's decision to meet Pullman without consulting him. Belanger had remained expressionless throughout. Ure placed the paper down and folded his arms.

Siv spent a few moments adjusting the angle of her notepad. 'It sounds as if you took Mr Pullman to your office because you wanted to steer him away from talking to the press.'

Ure responded, 'As my client has stated, he wished to offer Mr Pullman some support and reassurance at a difficult time.'

Siv turned her chair slightly towards Ali.

He asked, 'Mr Belanger, why do you think that Mr Pullman hadn't told his daughter about his contact with you?'

'Pointless question, Sergeant,' Ure said.

'A reasonable one, surely,' Ali replied. 'Your client would have formed some opinion of Mr Pullman — his motives and his family context.'

Belanger shifted as if he might speak. It would be hard for a man used to calling the shots in his professional life to stay silent. Ure stopped him with a wave of his hand.

'My client has made his statement and now he needs to get back to his work. We're finished here.'

'Not quite,' Siv said. 'Your client has no one to confirm his alibi for the afternoon of the eighteenth of April, and his meeting with Mr Pullman indicates that there was antagonism between them.'

Ure sighed. 'The antagonism was clearly from Mr Pullman, and my client succeeded in offering the man calm, professional advice. He didn't have to invite him into his office. You have no evidence of any kind against my client. Now we really have finished.' He stood up and motioned to Belanger.

'For now,' Siv smiled. 'I'm sure we'll meet again.'

Ali closed the door after them and leaned against the wall, rocking on his feet. 'We didn't get much change there. Belanger was acting out of the goodness of his heart.'

Siv was doodling on her notepad. 'I'll talk to Kay Turton, but I suspect she was unaware that her dad had gone to Belanger. How come we didn't see Pullman's call to the clinic on his phone records? He didn't have a landline at home and the Turtons haven't got one.'

Ali rubbed his back against the wall. 'It's terrible when you get an itch halfway down your spine. Public phone?'

Siv stopped halfway through drawing a speckled bird's egg. 'Hang on, BSS must have a phone.'

Ali pictured sitting with Belinda Hanak. 'There was one on the desk in their office.'

Siv flipped her pad shut and stood. 'Get hold of a call record. If Pullman used that phone to call the clinic, he might also have rung his son from it. You see, we might have got unexpected change from Belanger after all. And stop rubbing the wall, that paintwork's so old, you'll remove a layer.'

Ali turned and touched the dark cream surface. 'Nah, there's so much on here, it'd take a blowtorch to shift it.'

* * *

Siv found Kay Turton sitting in her kitchen, scrolling through coffins online. Her cheeks were tear-stained.

'I'm sorry to intrude, I won't take long,' she said.

'It's a relief to be interrupted. Not quite the shopping I ever expected to find myself doing,' Kay said. 'There's a bewildering variety of shapes and materials, all eco-friendly now. It must have been easier when you just chose wood.'

There was no sign of Ryan. 'Is your husband helping you?'

Kay sounded weary. 'Not really. He talks about getting involved, but whenever I start discussing arrangements, he has to be somewhere.'

'What about Nell? Can she advise?'

'Somehow, things always get more complicated and difficult when Nell lends a hand.' She turned the iPad screen to Siv with a little shudder. 'They're all so . . . *pretty*, considering their purpose. What do you think, willow or wool? I didn't even realise you could have a wool coffin. It says here that they're cosy and warm. As if Dad or Lyra will ever be cosy again. Even the cremation won't warm them. Who on earth writes this stuff?'

Siv was trying not to look. 'I'm not sure what to say. It's such a personal thing.' Ed's coffin had been white cardboard. She had a woozy sensation, wanted to get away from the topic. 'Shall I make you a cup of tea?'

'Yes, thank you.'

Siv switched on the kettle and put tea bags in mugs, glad of the chance to compose herself. When she brought the tea to the table, Kay was staring at the screen with a glazed expression.

She switched the iPad off. 'I'll do it later. I need to decide, though. I keep putting it off.'

'Maybe close your eyes and pick one,' Siv suggested.

'Like pin the tail on the donkey?'

'Your dad and Lyra won't mind. I'd make it easy on yourself.'

Kay took her tea. 'That's kind of you, and sensible too. It's hardly your job to give me advice on the funeral. What have you come about?'

Siv cradled her mug in her hands. 'You did tell your dad about the IVF mix-up.'

'Oh.' Kay sat back. 'I did, yes. I didn't mean to, but I just cracked one evening when he was here and it all spilled out.' Kay seemed to believe she needed to apologise for being vulnerable.

'It's not something to feel guilty about. Confiding in your dad was a natural thing to do. Why did you tell me you hadn't?' Siv was sure she could anticipate the answer.

'I didn't want Ryan to find out. He was adamant that he didn't want it talked about in the family and I'd given him my word.'

Siv sighed inwardly. 'Your dad went to see Dr Belanger. Did he tell you?'

'No! Why'd he do that?'

'Anger, wanting to stand up for you, take care of you.' *Given that he probably realised your husband wouldn't.*

Kay rubbed her forehead. 'What did Belanger say about it?'

'He calmed your dad down, advised him of due process and all that. He's told us they met just the once.'

'Well . . . doesn't matter now. I don't even care much if Ryan does find out. I'm too tired to worry about it.'

Siv drank her tea and saw that Kay's eyes were straying to the iPad. So many secrets in this family: Kay unaware that she had a brother and that her sister knew, Nell ignorant of the IVF blunder, and their father, who was now free of all such problems, playing his cards close to his chest about his son and having contact with Belanger behind Kay's back. And of course, Ryan and his divorce consultation.

'I'll let you get on with your planning,' Siv said.

'Thanks. I need to make a choice, then I might sleep tonight.'

* * *

It was really too warm in the wagon for a fire, but Siv needed to see the glow of flames. She lit the wood burner, unpacked the sandwich selection she'd bought on the way home and poured a glass of akvavit, pausing with the bottle. Had she had one last night? She couldn't remember, but after the sight of those coffins she needed fortifying. She knocked back what she'd poured, shivered with pleasure at the fierce, cold bite and filled the glass.

She sat by the fire with her supper and opened the carrier bag she'd found by the door, assuming it was one of Corran's meal portions that would keep her going later in the week. Instead, she found a large oval box of chocolates, pale grey with a white label.

Boxing Hare Chocolatiers
20 Hand-Crafted Signature Chocolates
Luxury Limited Edition

She opened the card attached to one corner and read the message inside.

Hope you enjoy these. They'll give you energy while you're working hard. Don't forget, all work and no play . . . Lunch on Sunday? Message me and I'll book somewhere. Fabian x

She laid the box on her lap and finished her sandwiches. Then she undid the lid, lifted off the covering paper and selected a strawberry and elderflower. It was delicate and delicious. She followed it with a cardamom orange and licked her fingers.

The chocolates were amazing, finding them by her door less so. It made her uneasy. Annoyed.

How had Fabian traced where she lived? She'd been deliberately vague with him. Then it came to her. Of course. Mutsi.

She put the box aside and picked up her drink. Flowers, now chocolates and on the basis of one meeting. Her phone rang. It was Hope.

'Hi, Siv. Just wanted to ask how your exhibition opening went the other night.'

'It was fine, thanks, lots of people. I couldn't stay long because of work. How're you?'

'Like you, up to my ears in it. Spent the day on a complex dementia case and I'm pretty bewildered myself now. You OK? You sound a bit far away.'

Siv gazed at the chocolates. 'I'm not sure. I had a drink with a man and it's a bit weird.'

'You kept that quiet!'

'I wasn't sure I was going to meet him. Thing is, within days he's given me expensive flowers and chocolates.'

Hope laughed. 'You say that as if it's a bad thing.'

'A bit too full on, surely? And he left the chocolates by my door. I didn't tell him where I lived.'

Hope's tone shifted, became more serious. 'How did he find out?'

'Mutsi, I'm sure. She met him at the museum the other night and she took a shine to him, naturally.'

'Well, then. Nothing spooky. He likes you! Is it mutual?'

'I like him but it's all a bit too much too soon, surely? I haven't even agreed to see him again.'

'Siv, he's keen. Why wouldn't he be? You're gorgeous. Give the man a break.'

'Why am I so unsure?'

'Because life dealt you a shit hand and you were widowed. Anyone would tread carefully after that. Well, except for one friend of mine whose husband died. She slept with any man who came within grabbing distance just weeks after the funeral.' Hope giggled. 'Grief takes many forms.'

'Well . . . I'll mull it over. The chocolates are terrific. Posh, artisan.'

'Sounds like he has good taste. What's his name?'

'Fabian.'

'Unusual. Is he French?'

'No idea.'

'Enjoy the chocs, Siv, and don't overcomplicate it. See how it goes. If it comes to nothing, you'll have had some nice gifts.'

When they'd finished talking, Siv put the chocolates in the kitchen, filled her glass again and sat watching the fire.

She still didn't like the fact that Fabian had been at her door without her consent.

CHAPTER 18

Mortimer had joined them for a morning briefing. His visits to the team were random and always unannounced. Siv suspected he made them when he had a gap in his diary. She watched him help himself to a muffin from the selection Patrick had brought in, baked by Eden. Mortimer never contributed goodies, and she'd heard that he rarely put his hand in his pocket for drinks. If he was that tight-fisted with Mutsi, he might not last long, and then her mother would decamp for more promising pastures. That possibility cheered her, although it would make working with him tricky.

'Don't mind me,' he said, catching a stray blueberry. 'I just need to make sure that all is being done that should be done.'

'We're working our socks off, sir, but we have a disappointing lack of any forensics that might help us,' Patrick told him.

Ali pulled a face at him and mouthed, *Creep*.

Siv took charge. 'Let's focus on what we have. Tom Pullman had a son and he'd met him, probably in St Peter's, at least three times — twice with Lyra present, because she'd told her friend Elsie about it. He visited the church with Lyra on the afternoon they died. Nell Pullman found out about the son but not his identity, or so she claims. Belinda Hanak also knew about him. Kay is unaware. The Turtons had IVF but Kay discovered that Ryan wasn't Lyra's father. She'd started a complaint to the clinic through legal channels and she told her father about the error. Glen Belanger oversaw the IVF procedure. He met with Tom Pullman — he claims just once — and according to his account, calmed him down. Ryan Turton is considering divorce, but hasn't informed his wife yet.'

Mortimer had a disconcerting habit of closing his eyes when he was listening, but he suddenly straightened his sloping shoulders and exclaimed, 'What a family!'

'They have their tricky aspects,' Siv agreed.

He pointed at the incident board. 'What do we know, if anything, about this man Pullman met in the church?'

Ali said, 'He was well set, taller than Pullman, wore a dark raincoat with a hood and had his hands in the front pockets of his jeans.'

'Brian Gifford saw a man sitting on the rocks at Wherry Cove with a hooded coat, could be the same person,' Siv recapped. 'Gifford stole a jug from the Turtons' house on the Thursday afternoon while Pullman was fetching Lyra from nursery. He states he saw nobody else around, but he did notice two cars at the layby near the cove. One is accounted for. Patrick, did you have any luck with the black one?'

Patrick shook his head. 'I asked our witness who was in the other car, parked behind, but she couldn't recall any details.'

Siv stood and went to the board, pointing to the updated list of people still without confirmed alibis. She read it through.

Aled Hanak — garden centre shopping
Belinda Hanak — at home
Nell Pullman — at cleaning job
Harry Hudson — out cycling
Glen Belanger — in his office

Patrick tapped his desk. 'Pullman might have threatened Belanger during that meeting. If Belanger's got something to hide, it could have rattled him.'

'Sure,' Siv said, 'but we've no evidence of that.'

'Nell Pullman's a dopehead with a short fuse and she was concerned about her dad's money if there was another sibling on the block,' Ali said. 'I reckon she could have done it. The way she kicked off at that customer at her stall indicated a lack of control. I still haven't been able to get hold of the guy she cleans for on Thursdays. I called by his house. A neighbour said he's away, wasn't sure when he'll be back.'

'But why would she kill Lyra?' Siv asked.

'Nell had daddy issues, didn't she? He nagged her about her life, job, drug habit, lack of prospects, compared her to her more successful sister. Nell could have been jealous of Lyra — her dad doted on his granddaughter in a way that he didn't on Nell.' Ali was warming to his theme. 'Maybe that grated, and she went round there that afternoon after brooding about the postcard she'd found the day before. Things got hairy and she lashed out.'

'Fair points.' Siv sat down. She appreciated why Ali was going down that road but she wasn't convinced that Nell was their killer. Still, she'd let him follow it up for now. 'I sensed that Fatima Marshall, the clinical nurse at Fairlawns, had more to say but was reluctant. I'll contact her. Ali and Patrick, go back over the people on that list and their whereabouts last Thursday afternoon, particularly Glen Belanger and Nell Pullman. Did we get anything on the BSS landline?'

'I've requested records for the last six months,' Ali confirmed. 'Soon as they arrive, I'll scrutinise them.'

Siv glanced at Mortimer, who was checking his phone. 'Did you want the last muffin, sir?'

* * *

Siv waited in the car park at Halse Woods. It was quiet there, with few cars. The birds were flitting busily in the greenwood.

She'd got hold of Fatima Marshall, who'd reluctantly agreed to meet in her lunch hour. She spotted Kitty, Patrick's partner, trundling a wheelbarrow in the distance. Fatima was late. Maybe she'd changed her mind, although Siv had used that useful, vague phrase, *I don't want to have to question you formally.*

When she saw Fatima driving in, she got out of her car. She'd sit in the woman's passenger seat, ensuring that she couldn't change her mind and decide to take off.

'Thanks for coming,' she said, opening the door and sliding in.

'I can't stay long,' Fatima blurted. She was wearing her clinic clothes, black trousers and a grey tunic with white trim. They gave her a more defined shape, although one of her trouser hems was fraying.

'It won't take long if you don't beat about the bush.'

'Meaning?'

It was said defiantly, but Fatima's nerves were so apparent, Siv could almost hear them jangling.

'Meaning we're talking about two murders and I believe you have information concerning the clinic.'

Fatima stroked a plump arm. 'I need my job. I've three kids to support and their dad skips on the maintenance whenever he can.'

'Tom Pullman and his granddaughter needed their lives. How long have you worked at Fairlawns?'

'Nearly twelve years.'

'Has something been going on there?'

Fatima nodded, her chins quivering. 'I think so.'

'You must tell me.'

Her eyes brimmed. 'I saw a letter on Dr Belanger's desk, from a solicitor. It was about Lyra Turton.'

'You read about the allegation, then.'

'Yes. It might be true.' Fatima opened her window, fanned herself.

Nice and easy. 'I'm listening.'

'We prepare lots of sperm samples in the lab, with handwritten labels of the donor's name. I've been pushing for us to have a barcode system for some time. It's good practice, removes any margin for error. Dr Belanger has said he'll consider it, but nothing happens.'

'So, the wrong name might have been written on a sample.'

Fatima took a breath. 'It's worse than that.' She swallowed, patted her pocket for a hanky.

Siv took a pack of tissues from her bag and passed it across. She'd often found tissues handier than handcuffs.

'Thanks.' Fatima blew her nose hard. 'I . . . a couple of times, I've suspected that Dr Belanger has written new labels on sperm samples.'

'Go on.'

'I wrote the label on Ryan Turton's sample, but when it came to the treatment, I saw that Dr Belanger had redone it. It's happened a couple of other times as well, when I've been on duty with him. My writing is perfectly clear.'

'You never asked him about it?'

'He's not the kind of man you question. He's very domineering and cutting if you don't jump when he tells you to. I've seen him make colleagues cry.' She sniffed. 'There's other stuff as well. I've heard him make comments now and again about the female patients. Saying they're pretty, sexy or fit, things like that. Throwaway remarks, but distasteful. And I can't prove that he changed the labels, but I'm certain because they were labels I'd definitely prepared.'

'Can you think of a clinical reason that makes sense, one that would explain his actions?'

'No. There shouldn't be any need to do that. The label should remain the same until the sample is used or destroyed.'

Siv recalled an evidence bag that a colleague had once tampered with, to cast confusion in a drugs operation. He'd altered a handwritten code. She could only come up with one reason why Belanger might have meddled with labels. 'What do you make of it then — why would Dr Belanger do that?'

Fatima turned her head to the window. 'I've no idea.'

'Fatima, come on, stiffen your backbone for me here. You're a clinician, meaning you have experience and skills. I'm adding two and two, so I'm sure you can.'

Fatima turned around reluctantly. 'It could mean it was a different sperm sample.'

'Dr Belanger was deliberately mislabelling the samples.'

'Perhaps.'

Anxiety was making her breath hot and sour. Siv inched back a bit. 'Fatima, did you ever suspect it might be Dr Belanger's sperm?'

The woman gave the tiniest of nods. 'Why else would he have rewritten the labels?'

Why would a doctor do that? Grandiosity, a God complex, a warped sense of humour, just because he could?

'You're going to have to give a statement. Not right now, but in the next couple of days.'

Fatima said miserably, 'He'll find out, won't he?'

'That depends on the reason Belanger was changing labels, but as you can't think of a good one, it might be malpractice. Have any other staff suspected this, or witnessed labels being altered by him?'

'I can't say. I've never mentioned it to anyone. I'll get into trouble for not flagging it before now.'

'I can't make any promises about what will happen. If you're frightened of him, you'll need to say so in your statement. Clearly, you're not the only staff member who is.'

'I just don't want to see him at the moment,' Fatima murmured.

'Call in sick,' Siv said. She'd started to get impatient. She understood that a man like Belanger could be overwhelming to subordinates. But if Fatima's allegation was correct, there might be a number of families who were in for a terrible shock and ongoing suffering. The woman should have spoken up about his suspected malpractice.

Siv returned to her car. This kind of allegation was a first in her experience. She wasn't sure that it constituted a crime. She headed for Mortimer's office when she got back to the station. As she opened the door, she heard him on the phone, talking about carpet, and guessed that Mutsi was bending his ear about the décor at Clifftop.

'I have to go,' he said when he saw Siv. 'Yes, of course. Yes, me too.' He seemed a bit red about the ears.

'Sorry to interrupt, sir, but I need to run something past you.' She explained the conversation she'd just had with Fatima.

He frowned. 'We need to tread carefully with this. I suppose it's medical malpractice if it's true. These cases are dealt with by the governing authority in the first instance.'

'It strikes me as a kind of arms-length rape,' Siv said.

'Yes, well, for heaven's sake, don't use that word with Belanger or his solicitor! At present, it's an allegation, nothing else. Does this nurse seem reliable?'

'Yes. She's worked at the clinic a long time. She was reluctant to make the allegation because Belanger's a difficult boss and she's worried about her job. She also commented that he sometimes made improper references about his female patients' appearance. If he has substituted his own sperm in some samples, it sounds as if he might have selected the ones he judged attractive enough to receive it. Perhaps he liked the idea of his progeny having pretty mothers.'

Mortimer squirmed. 'How appalling.'

'A DNA test for Belanger would help, because it would prove if he's Lyra's father, but we have no reason to request it. No unidentified DNA was found at the Turtons' house.'

Mortimer said, 'Of course, if this is true and he's done it once, he's probably done it on other occasions.'

Siv noted that the picture of Lake Keitele was crooked again. The ancient station building probably had shallow foundations and subsidence. She got up and pushed her chair in. 'I'd like to rattle Belanger, get him in again and put the allegation to him. After all, if it's true and he is Lyra's real father, he had a lot to lose if it got out, and Tom Pullman was making noise. That gives him motive.'

Mortimer shifted uneasily. 'Very well, but go carefully. It would help if his car was on CCTV anywhere near the Turtons' house last Thursday.'

'I'll check in with Ali and Patrick before I call Belanger.'

CHAPTER 19

Harry Hudson had been brooding. He was a law-abiding man, liked things straight and believed that the police generally did a good job. He'd been fretting because he might have remembered something relevant to Tom Pullman's death. It had only come to him in the last week, a shadowy recollection from an iron-cold night in early January that gradually grew clearer. He'd realised there was a chance that his memory of that night was connected to Pullman's son. It was the kind of thing he'd usually discuss with Belinda, but she had plenty on her plate and she'd been away for a fortnight in the Maldives with Aled in January. Also, if he told her, she'd try to dissuade him from talking to the police and he'd buckle under her sway.

There was a time to stay silent and a time to speak up. That sounded biblical, but it was a maxim that fortified Harry as he debated what to do.

He'd turned it over in his mind for several days. The police were aware of Tom's son now, and Belinda had informed them of her involvement on that score. If he spoke to them and phrased things carefully, it couldn't get her into any trouble, so that wasn't an obstacle.

He came to a decision and cycled to the police station on Thursday afternoon, where he asked to speak to DC Hill.

By now he was quite fired up at helping a murder enquiry, enough to ignore his grumbling knees. After twenty minutes, a cup of metallic-tasting tea and a KitKat from a vending machine, the young detective appeared. He exuded a youthful vigour that caused a pang of envy in Harry's chest. His joints were aching today, and he'd have given anything to be supple again.

'Mr Hudson, hello. You wanted to see me?'

'That's right. I remembered something, reckoned I should tell you.'

DC Hill led him to a room at the end of a corridor and pulled a chair out for him at the table. Harry liked that courtesy. The detective sat at a diagonal with his hands in his pockets.

'Off you go then, Mr Hudson.'

'Back in January — I'm pretty sure it was the seventh — we had a BSS talk in the evening. It was one of the ones that are open to the public. The topic was *Meet the Brunels*. Tom gave the talk, and it was good. He always did his research thoroughly. About twenty-five people came.'

DC Hill said, 'OK, yes. Was this talk at the library?'

'That's right, in one of our rooms up the top. It was nearly all older people, as usual, but there was a chap sitting right in the back row who was much younger. I didn't notice him at first, because I was on a side chair up at the front and I didn't have my distance glasses on. When I did spot him, I remember thinking it was good to have a bit of young blood for a change.'

The detective was looking a tad bored. Harry lost his bottle. He shouldn't have come. 'This is probably a waste of your time.'

'Not at all.'

'Right. Well, at the end of the talk, when we were dispersing, I noticed this chap out on the landing, speaking to Tom. Tom was all smiles. He always loved the chance to talk about BSS and what we do.'

DC Hill straightened up. He would be wondering, as Harry had when the memory returned, if this had been the adopted son turning up on that frosty night.

The detective asked, 'How long did they speak for?'

'No idea. I went on my way. Tom was in charge of locking up that night.'

'Can you describe this man?'

Harry had been making an effort with this and he narrowed his eyes in concentration. 'Quite tall, short fair hair, good pair of shoulders on him. I didn't get much idea of his features. He had a dark coat with a hood.'

'Did you hear him at all?'

'No, I wasn't that near.'

'Have you seen him since, or did Mr Pullman mention him?'

'Sorry, no. I forgot all about that night until a couple of days ago.'

'What about other people at the talk — would they recall this man?'

'I doubt it. He was seated right near the door and people were keen to get away at the end. It was a bitter night. I was surprised that so many people came out in the cold.'

'Was Belinda Hanak there that night?'

Harry was relieved to be able to say, 'No, she was on holiday.'

DC Hill drummed his fingers on the table. 'Mr Hudson, I'd like to get one of our officers to do a composite sketch with you, try and see if we can put together a face.'

Harry got panicky. 'I really didn't see him close up and my eyes aren't what they used to be.'

'We can work with impressions to start with. It's amazing what people remember, once they get going.' The detective smiled encouragingly. He was a kindly young man. 'It's not a test, not a pass or fail. Just whatever you can come up with for us. It might be a tremendous help.'

Harry was reassured. 'Is this like an identikit?'

'Exactly, using a computer. We have a special software programme now.'

That sounded exciting. 'D'you mean right away?'

'I'll see if my colleague is available. If not, I'd like to get it done as soon as possible. That OK with you?'

'Fine with me. Anything I can do to help.'

'You sit tight. I'll get someone to fetch you a cuppa.'

Harry sat tight, pleased with himself. His gardening and cycling were satisfying enough, but it was good to be part of something different, ring the changes. It was all very well keeping Belinda's confidences, but when all was said and done there was a murderer on the loose.

He wouldn't tell Belinda about today, though, or helping with this composite. No point in rocking the boat. It would be the first secret he'd ever kept from her, and it gave him a little kick of excitement.

He waited, hoping that the next cup of tea wouldn't be from a machine.

* * *

It was seven that evening before Siv and Ali sat down again with Glen Belanger and his solicitor. This was going to be thorny, so Siv asked Ali to let her do the talking. They'd found no sign of Belanger's car on CCTV last Thursday afternoon — an absence of evidence that simply meant he might have been clever enough to take back roads, and he was an astute man. He and Ure hadn't prepared a statement this time, but clearly Ure had said he'd speak. He took out a leather folder with a notepad and a Mont Blanc pen.

'We just wanted to explore a few issues with you,' Siv said.

'Of course, Inspector. How can we help?'

'Serious allegations have been made to us by a member of staff at Fairlawns clinic. We've informed HFEA, the Human Fertilisation and Embryology Authority.' Siv paused for effect.

Belanger stiffened slightly and touched his tie knot.

'What is the nature of these allegations?' Ure spoke smoothly, uncapping his pen.

'That Dr Belanger wrote new labels for sperm samples on several occasions. This is contrary to protocols. Also, that he used inappropriate language regarding some of his patients.'

Ure made a note in a smooth, flowing hand. 'And who has made these allegations?'

'I can't divulge that. I can say that one of the sperm samples that Dr Belanger is alleged to have altered the label on was Ryan Turton's.'

Belanger flicked a glance at Ure.

'Well,' Ure said, 'as you've pointed out, this is a matter for HFEA, not the police.'

'In the first instance,' Siv agreed. 'Depending on their investigation, there could be criminal proceedings. You seem a bit concerned, Dr Belanger. I'm not surprised — first an allegation about a sperm mix-up and now this.'

Ure said crossly, 'Apart from throwing allegations around and scoring points, what is the purpose of this meeting?'

Siv was on dodgy ground, so she kept her voice firm. 'The point of this interview is that an allegation had been made regarding Dr Belanger's clinic and Mr Pullman's family. Dr Belanger met Mr Pullman, who had threatened to go to the press, and he has no one to confirm his alibi for the afternoon of the eighteenth of April.'

Ure capped his pen and leaned back. 'And that's it? I'm amazed that you've wasted our time with this.'

Belanger had started shifting around. 'These new allegations — are they from Fatima Marshall?'

Ure put a cautioning hand on his arm. 'I'd like to consult with my client.'

'Sure, we'll give you ten minutes.'

Siv and Ali went out to the small courtyard at the back of the station.

Ali sat on a bench and lit a Gitane. 'Second of the day.'

Siv walked up and down. The air was nippy, with a promise of rain.

'We've nothing really,' she said, sounding glum. 'I was hoping to rattle Belanger into dropping his guard, but we'll go back to some bland statement. The HFEA might well suspend Belanger now, pending investigations, but that does nothing for us.'

Ali took a deep drag on his cigarette and blew a twisting smoke ring. 'Even if he's the daddy to half the kids in town, it doesn't make him a murderer.'

'But it might unnerve him, make him do something stupid, trip himself up.'

Ali gave her a long-suffering look. 'He doesn't strike me as the type. And medics close ranks. I wouldn't be surprised if he isn't even leaned on to provide a DNA sample. My money's still on Nell, so I'm on her tail.'

Siv frowned at him, but he was gazing up at the patchy grey sky. He finished his cigarette while she walked up and down, kicking gravel aside. When they went back to the interview room, Belanger had regained his poise and Ure had a smug expression.

'My client believes that these allegations concerning labels and inappropriate remarks have probably been made by Fatima Marshall. He had reason to admonish Ms Marshall several months ago, about repeated late arrival for her shifts and lack of attention to her uniform. My client is concerned that these are malicious allegations and he's sure that this will prove to be the case.'

Belanger smiled now. 'Sorry to disappoint you, Inspector.'

Ali said, 'You seem to take the prospect of being suspended from your profession with great equanimity.'

'That's because I'll be exonerated by any enquiries,' Belanger bit back.

'That completes our business here,' Ure said with satisfaction.

He beckoned Belanger and they sailed out of the room on a wave of aftershave.

'Nice try, Ali,' Siv said.

'He's as slippery as a jellied eel, that one. They're disgusting, by the way. Have you ever eaten them?'

Siv had to smile. 'No, but speaking of food, I need a meal. Want to come to Nutmeg? I'll see if Patrick's still around.'

Ali smacked his hands together. 'Aye, let's do that. We'll get mates' rates from Pol.'

* * *

In Nutmeg, they polished off Polly's special of the day, pea and ham risotto. Ali did a little drum roll on the table, leaned across to Patrick and produced a coin from behind his ear.

'Abracadabra!' He flourished the ten pence piece.

Patrick gaped. 'How'd you do that?'

'Dotty Debbie inspired me to watch some YouTube videos. It's not that difficult. I've been practising on Polly. I might move on to a card trick next.'

'Maybe you can magic us a murderer first,' Siv told him, impressed by his sleight of hand.

Patrick eyed the dessert menu while Ali regarded it longingly and Siv ordered coffee. Ali's phone rang and he slipped outside to take the call.

'This guy Harry Hudson told me about must be Pullman's son,' Patrick said. 'Black hooded coat again, well built. Pullman told Belinda that he got in touch in January. Maybe that BSS talk was the first meeting.'

'His son doorstepped him at a public event? I suppose it might make sense, if the man was anxious about his dad's reaction. You'd think he'd have written to him first, but there was no correspondence at Pullman's home.'

'Pullman might have got rid of it, especially if he suspected Nell snooped through his things.'

'When will the composite picture be ready?' Siv asked.

'Tomorrow morning.' He glanced over her shoulder. 'Ali's got a spring in his step.'

Ali was back, waving his phone. 'That was Johnstone, the guy Nell cleans for. He'd been on a business trip to the States, left that morning, Thursday the eighteenth, got back today. His mum told him that she visited his flat last

Thursday evening and Nell hadn't been in. The place hadn't been touched, rubbish unemptied and no vacuuming done. The mother had to clear up the stuff from a dinner party he'd had before he went away. He picked up my messages and read about the murders when he got back, realised we might be checking on people for last Thursday afternoon. He works in security. Guess he has a nose for this stuff. Nell had been in today because the post was on the kitchen table and the dishcloth was wet.' He winked at Siv. 'I've been keeping Nell in the picture. Now we've got her in our sights. Bring her in tonight?'

Siv checked her watch. It was gone ten o'clock. 'She'll probably be outside of several spliffs and not fit for interview. First thing tomorrow. And stop smirking: that's an order.'

CHAPTER 20

Siv and Ali arrested Nell Pullman on suspicion of murder at 8 a.m. She was in bed when they arrived and it took fifteen minutes to rouse her. At the station, she refused a solicitor.

'You're out of your fucking minds. Bunch of tossers. No, I don't want a solicitor. I've done nothing wrong. I can say no comment on my own without some posh twat sitting beside me.'

She had blueish shadows beneath her eyes. Her hair was loose and tangled, with a pillow feather stuck on the crown of her head. Ali fetched her coffee. She gulped it down and asked for another.

'And can I have a biscuit or something? I've had no breakfast. I bet you're not allowed to question me on an empty stomach.'

They gave her a couple of croissants, another coffee and water for good measure. Siv told Ali he could lead on the interview. He'd be a good match for Nell.

But Nell attempted to lead it herself. 'It's no good you lot saying my prints are in Kay's house. Of course they are — duh! I visit there, don't I?'

'That's no problem,' Ali said. 'Is that coffee hot enough? The machine's a wee bit dodgy sometimes.'

'What? Yeah.' She eyed him and tore at her second croissant.

'Let's go back to last Thursday, the eighteenth of April. Where were you that afternoon?'

'I've told you this. Cleaning.'

'At the Johnstone house near the harbour?'

'Yep.'

Ali tutted. 'Thing is, Mr Johnstone has told us you didn't clean that day. His mother went to the house that evening and found it in a mess. She did the cleaning.'

Nell swallowed and rubbed her fingers together. 'No way. She must have mixed up her dates. I left it all neat and tidy.'

Ali found it hard to believe that Nell the cleaner ever left anywhere that shiny. 'No, there's no doubt. You see, Mr Johnstone had had a dinner party on the Wednesday evening before. He left for Philadelphia on Thursday morning and he wrote you a note, apologising for the extra mess and asking you to clear it up. It hadn't been touched.'

Nell drank coffee. 'Bugger.'

'Exactly.'

She pulled a sour face. 'That place isn't usually untidy. He makes so little mess, it's a doddle of a job. I went yesterday and it was amazingly ship-shape.'

'I expect his mum's thorough, unlike you. So, you lied to us. Where were you?'

She twiddled a strand of hair. 'I was in bed all day.'

'Why was that?'

'I got a bit out of it the night before, after the argument with my dad. I was upset, I took meds, smoked weed and drank too many lagers. Overdid it all round. Felt rotten the next day. I was asleep when Kay called me to tell me what had happened.'

Ali sneered, 'You expect us to believe that?'

Nell finished her coffee. 'Believe what you like. I'm telling you: I was in bed all day long.'

'Why didn't you just say that to start with?'

'Seemed easier to tell you I was at work. Either way, I didn't have an alibi and you lot start making mountains out of molehills.'

'It's a very serious offence, to lie to police in a murder investigation.'

'I'm sure, but I bet people do it all the time. I mean, no one's expecting their dad and their niece to get murdered while they're having a crap day and lying low under the duvet, are they? No one's expecting to have to provide an alibi because they had a rough day.' She gave a nasty grin. 'I bet both of you have had days when you were skiving and you wouldn't have wanted to explain yourselves. You're only human, even if you try to conceal it!'

'I'm not buying it,' Ali said. 'You'd argued with your dad the day before and you were worried about this brother appearing on the scene. You went to Kay's house to pick a fight with your father. We've seen your temper, remember.'

Nell spat, 'Oh, get real. I was out of it all day. I couldn't have picked a fight with a gnat.'

Siv believed her. She imagined that Nell probably had quite a few days like that. She gestured to Ali, and suspended the interview.

In the corridor, he said, 'It's bullshit from beginning to end!'

'I reckon she's telling the truth. And we've no hard evidence. Unless she confesses, what do we do?'

Ali bashed the wall with his fist. 'Let's hang on to her a bit longer at least, let her cool her heels. I'll go back to her street, ask around the neighbours. Someone might have seen her go out.'

He was clutching at straws, but Siv said, 'OK, I'll give you the rest of the day, but I don't want to keep her here too long. Can't afford all the coffee, apart from anything else.'

Ali wasn't smiling when he stomped away.

* * *

236

The composite sketch was ready. Siv stared at it on her screen. A squarish face with regular features, blank and bland. Mr Anybody. She'd tasked Patrick with publicising it, although she didn't hold out much hope that it would lead anywhere. She'd also asked him to run it by the people who'd attended Tom Pullman's talk in January.

She emailed it to Belinda Hanak and phoned her. 'Are you at home?'

'I am.'

'I've sent you an email with a photo. Can you see if you recognise the man? I'll hang on.'

Siv put a printed copy of the photo on the incident board while she stood back and waited. Was there something familiar about the shape of the face and the hair? Probably wishful thinking.

Belinda came back on the line. 'I've never seen this person. Who is he?'

'Someone we're interested in.'

'Is it Tom's son? Doesn't look like him, or Cathy.'

'I can't comment on that.'

'But how did you get it? Have you found someone who's met him?'

'I'll leave it there. Thanks for your help.' *See, Belinda, you're not the only one who can hold back information.*

Siv took the picture down to Nell in her cell. She was lying on her back, dozing, her ankles crossed.

'Having sweet dreams?' Siv asked.

'Ha ha. How long am I going to be here?'

'Not sure yet. Do you want to contact Kay or a friend?'

'Not bloody likely. I can tell you don't believe I did it. Your mate Ali doesn't like me. He shouldn't let personal animosity get in the way of his professional judgement.'

Siv was minded to agree, and once again, she reckoned that Nell must work hard at muffling her quick brain. 'Never mind that for now. Do you recognise the man in this picture?'

Nell made no effort to get up. She held the image near, then further away. 'Nope.' She gave a little chuckle. 'Should I? Quite tasty.'

'Thanks anyway. Lunch will be here soon.'

'Terrific. Tell them not to wake me if I'm asleep.'

Back at her desk, Siv went over the scant information they had about the man who might be Pullman's son. Ali had left her a note to say that few calls had been made from the BSS landline, mostly to and from members. Tom Pullman had made one call to Belanger in March. She ran her hands through her hair in exasperation. They had to be able to track this man.

The paper butterfly she'd made was still clinging to the top of the blind. As she contemplated it, an idea came to her. An office wasn't just used for phone calls. She rang the BSS number. Jill Bartoli answered and confirmed that she'd be there for the next hour or so. Siv told her she was on her way.

She grabbed her coat and walked to the library, a couple of streets away. It was good to be out in the warm sun. Jill Bartoli was on the top floor of the library, sticking up posters.

Siv introduced herself. 'I expect Tom Pullman spent time here in the office.'

'Oh, yes. A couple of hours a week, usually.'

'I'd like to go through the desk drawers, filing cabinets and so on. Also, can you pin up this picture for me? We'd be interested to hear if this man seems familiar to anyone in BSS.'

'Certainly.' Jill tapped the picture. 'Is he in trouble?'

Siv smiled. 'I'll press on. Can you give me ten minutes on my own in there?'

'Maybe I can help. We keep all the membership and financial records online, of course. Are you after something in particular?'

Wish I knew. 'I'll be fine on my own.'

'Very well. I'll be around.'

Siv sat at the old-fashioned teak desk first, slipped gloves on and went through the drawers on the left-hand side. There were stacks of printer paper and cartridges, envelopes, rubber bands, books of stamps, a large stapler and various pens. She turned to the four-drawer grey metal filing cabinet. It was full of copies of talks that had been given, filed alphabetically, resource materials and a number of old-fashioned thank you letters. Siv paid particular attention to the folder with those in, but they all referred to talks, walks, garden parties and exhibitions attended: *So pleased that we came to the inspiring presentation . . . the cakes were absolutely delicious and you were all so hospitable . . . I was very impressed with the quality of the tapestries on display . . .* She flicked through brochures and leaflets, raising dust.

She found it at the back of the bottom drawer, in a folder labelled *miscellaneous*. A folded letter, tucked into a booklet on home-brewed beers. Siv opened it and placed it on the desk. Why had Pullman hidden it away here? Purely because of Nell's prying eyes?

Dear Mr Pullman,
This letter will come as something of a shock to you.
It's hard to know where to start. I suppose with telling you that I'm your son. My mother was Catherine Newall. She gave me up for adoption soon after I was born. I suspect that you might not have been party to that.
I would like to meet you. Just to see you and see how we get on, what we make of each other.
Perhaps a brief meeting to start? I've given this some thought. It would be easier for us both if it's somewhere public but not too much so. I'll be in St Peter's church next week on the twentieth at 14.30. It's a quiet place to meet, where we can be undisturbed.
I do hope you'll be there. I'll understand if you're not, but disappointed also. It's a lot to absorb. I'm sure you'll have many questions. I have so many too. Maybe we can help each other answer them.
Best wishes,
Francis.

It would have been better with a date, address and a phone number, but Francis was being careful, taking tiny steps. It was a brave move and he'd have been worried about rejection. He was opening up the territory and being careful not to scare the father he so wanted to meet. Perhaps also, by not giving any contact details, he was hoping to ensure that his father would turn up. It would be hard to ignore such a request if you had no other way to respond.

She read it again. The handwriting was small and even. It was well written, carefully worded, articulate and with a kind tone. The man who'd penned it was educated. He was also local, or had scouted the area and established that St Peter's was a handy and discreet meeting place. Siv slipped the letter in an evidence bag, hoping there might be fingerprints other than Pullman's.

Jill Bartoli was loitering outside the office, holding the picture Siv had given her. 'Did you find anything, Inspector?'

'I left everything in order, thank you.'

'I'll put this picture up in the office. I have a funny feeling that I've seen this man. Something about the shape of the head and the hairline. But I can't think where.'

'If it comes to you, please contact me.'

'Inspector, is it true that Nell Pullman has been arrested?'

Siv had turned to go but she stopped in her tracks. 'Who told you that?'

'One of her neighbours works in Aldi and saw her leaving with you in a police car. I was shopping in there this morning. Surely his own daughter didn't have anything to do with Tom's murder?'

Siv noted the glint of anticipation in Jill's eyes. 'Please don't spread rumours. I'm sure you don't want to cause any extra distress for Tom's family at such a difficult time.'

'Oh heavens, no, of course not.'

'Good, because it would be incredibly unkind. You wouldn't want to tarnish the BSS reputation.'

'No, absolutely not.'

Siv left her with that to chew on.

* * *

Belinda was confused and upset. The planned evening with Aled, with her beautifully cooked lamb shank and expensive wine, hadn't gone well. When she'd told him about Tom, Cathy and the adoption, he'd gone very quiet. He'd barely touched the crème caramel she'd prepared, had gone to bed early and turned his back. That just never happened.

Since then, he'd been freezing her out, answering in monosyllables. At breakfast this morning, he'd shouted at her when she asked if he wanted grapefruit.

'Grapefruit! I've never liked blasted grapefruit, but you insist on buying it!'

'But it's good for you, full of antioxidants and fibre—'

'Oh, do put a sock in it! You're so full of it, aren't you? You love telling people what to do. Did you tell Tom that it was good for him to have been deprived of his son?'

'There's no need for that tone.'

'Yes there bloody well is. I can't believe you did that and never told me, even when you saw me so upset about my own brother's situation. Didn't you have regrets or doubts about what you'd done? A man was denied his son. All those years of fatherhood gone, giving him no rights, no say in the matter.'

'I can only say that it seemed the right thing to do at the time. You weren't there, Aled, you don't understand all the circumstances.'

'You could have tried me, explained it. All your guff about never keeping secrets. Yeah, as long as it's on your terms.'

'But, Aled, it was a delicate matter, you must see that.'

'Not for Tom, though. He never got to decide if it was any kind of matter. And how come you never told me that you and he were friends at college?'

'It didn't seem important.'

He'd made a scornful noise deep in his throat.

'It was a long time ago. I got involved in a very difficult situation and did the best I could. You might try to show some understanding.'

'Don't, Belinda. I'm so shocked by what you've told me I'm not sure I know you anymore.'

'Don't be so horrid!'

'Why not? I've had enough of you right now.'

'But we have to talk about this.'

'Really? What about your other confidant? I'm sure you'll be on the phone to your little pet soon to tell him how horrid I've been. Darling Harry. Your face! You'd no idea that I'm up to speed on your calls to him. You see, you're not as good at keeping secrets as you imagine.'

She'd been struck dumb. Aled had taken his coffee to the garden shed, and next thing, she'd heard him leave in his car. That had never happened before. They always discussed their day at breakfast, and if they weren't going out together, talked over what the other had planned.

His anger had left her shaken and furious. How dare he speak to her like that! Just as well she hadn't told him the whole story, that she'd persuaded Cathy not to keep the child. And how had he found out about Harry? He must have listened in to some of her calls, or checked her phone. That was underhand. What a horrible sneak!

She'd tried calling Harry, but he wasn't picking up and that was irritating her even more. He was always there when she needed him. Contrary to his familiarity with her timetable, she had no idea how Harry's days were organised, had never given it a moment's thought.

In the bedroom, she brushed her hair to calm herself, long smooth strokes from the front, through the crown and down her neck. Her hand shook.

Aled had probably gone to see his brother, who'd never found himself another partner. But then, what woman would want him, given the way he bored on about the injustices of the courts and the machinations of his ex? They'd be sitting hugger-mugger right now, swapping misery stories.

She put her brush down.

No one had ever told her to shut up.

She sat on the side of the bed, feeling old.

She had no idea how to handle this unfamiliar Aled.
The world suddenly seemed alarming.

* * *

They let Nell Pullman go home around five o'clock. Ali had returned with no new evidence, other than that her downstairs neighbour had said he reckoned he'd heard Nell flushing the loo last Thursday afternoon. It was above his kitchen and her plumbing made a real racket, interfering with the jazz he'd been listening to on the radio. He couldn't be sure of the time, only that it had been after three, when he'd got home.

Ali wasn't often crabby, but this had put him in a sour mood. 'I'm sure it's her, but we'll never nail her.'

Patrick patted his shoulder. 'Don't let it get you down.'

'Why don't we all head home,' Siv suggested. 'Get some rest, be back fresh as daisies tomorrow. Is Polly working tonight?'

'No,' Ali said.

'Go to the cinema or something, then.'

'Aye, maybe.'

Siv recalled that the cupboards were bare at home, so she stopped at a supermarket for supplies, chucking cheese, bread, milk, sliced ham and a bag of apples in a basket. She'd just negotiated the vagaries of the self-checkout, which objected to her wedge of cheddar, when her phone rang. She plonked her bag on a bench by the wall and sat beside it.

'DI Drummond, this is Jill Bartoli. I've had an idea about that picture.'

'Yes?'

'It was last week, after the murders.'

She listened as Jill described a visit she'd made. It took her ages to get to the point, but Siv waited patiently. When the conversation ended, she put her phone in her bag and sat for a few minutes.

This was astonishing. Was it really possible? Neither she nor her colleagues had seen it in the composite. Should she call Mortimer immediately? No, she'd drive home, review the information and do some research.

CHAPTER 21

Siv made a toasted sandwich. While she watched it steam, she examined the composite face again, in the light of Jill Bartoli's call. She recalled a man standing, the way he held himself. There was a vague likeness, but it was tenuous. She lifted the sandwich from the toaster with a fork and her hands stilled, cheese dripping onto the plate, as she pictured the Minstergreen ties she'd seen in Tom Pullman's wardrobe. Had that figure she'd visualised been wearing a similar one? She closed her eyes and was almost certain that he had.

Siv put the sandwich on the plate, rang the station, had a chat with the duty desk and asked her colleague to find an address, made a note of it.

She ate her sandwich standing, staring out of the narrow kitchen window. Definitely no akvavit tonight, she needed a needle-sharp brain. The dusk was deepening, the wind rising. She heard it slap the sides of her wagon. The trees were dark moving shadows. She should probably call Mortimer, enlighten him about this turn of events and her suspicions. Before she could do that, her phone rang again. It was Kay Turton.

'I'm sorry to ring you, but I've had the strangest call from Nell. She sounded odd.'

'When was this?'

'About ten minutes ago. Maybe she's had too much weed. It can send her that way sometimes, depending on the mood she's in when she smokes it. She said she was at the nature reserve and someone was following her. I was asking her exactly where she was when her phone cut out. I tried ringing again, but it went to voicemail. What's she doing out there at this time of night? The weather's turning nasty.'

Siv thought of the address she'd just been given by the duty desk. Alarm fluttered in her throat. 'Does Nell know anyone who lives out that way?'

'Not that I'm aware of.'

'Leave it with me. Stay by your phone in case Nell calls you again, and if she does, ring me.'

She snatched up her car keys and her coat, phoning Ali as she hurried out. 'Get hold of Patrick and meet me at Bere Marsh reserve. Not the main car park, at the entrance to Stony Ridge Spinney, on the western side. Nell Pullman's in trouble and I can guess why.' She explained as she drove fast, her blue light flashing. Ali lapsed into an astounded silence. 'Got all that?'

'Aye, on it, be there soon.'

Siv had been to Bere Marsh Nature Reserve many times. It was a large, wild area of interconnecting lakes and ponds, with a wildflower meadow, bird sanctuary and hides. It took a good hour to walk all the way round. Part of the site had once been a reservoir and was now called Makin Mere. A lodge sat up on a bank near Stony Ridge Spinney, where the reservoir keeper used to live. Siv had often tramped past it and she'd noted last year that it was being renovated and then had a 'To Let' sign by the door.

While she drove fast through darkening streets, she remembered Nell's amused expression in the cell when presented with the composite picture. *Oh, Nell, what have you done? I bet you were comparing the real face to the composite. You must have been on the phone to him the minute we let you go. Did you want to be the clever one in the family for once?*

245

The wind was gathering force now, buffeting the car and sending rubbish skittering along pavements. A dustbin lid wheeled across the road, making her swerve. She gripped the wheel and concentrated.

Stony Ridge Spinney was a dense stretch of woodland, filled with oak, ash, beech and hazel trees. You could only access it by foot from the road, down a narrow track that cut along the edge and wound past the keeper's lodge. Siv pulled up at the gate set in a stile and saw Nell's battered blue scooter parked beneath an oak. She took her torch from the glove compartment and ran from her car, playing the beam over the scooter. No bag, no phone. She touched the engine. Just warm.

She couldn't afford to wait for the others. She set off running along the track, her feet crunching on flying leaf debris. The dark was intense now, the silence profound except for the wind gusting through the trees, working itself into a gale. She didn't call Nell's name, not wanting to alert the man who almost certainly had her. Half a mile down the path, she saw the keeper's lodge. A light gleamed comfortingly in the downstairs window.

Siv slowed, switched off her torch and walked up the stepped path to the lodge. The wind pushed at her back, like a bossy bystander. It was a Victorian brick-built house with a steeply sloping roof and a deep, arched porch over the front door. A black car was parked to one side by a beech hedge. There must be some vehicle access to the lodge from the back. Siv edged past the car and approached the front window from the side. There were no nets or blinds at the window — you'd have no need of privacy here — and the curtains weren't drawn.

She stopped, the rough chill of the brick against her hand, and glanced through the window into a living room. No one was there. A lamp glowed on a bookcase and the door was slightly ajar. There were two sofas, a coffee table with a can of beer, a plate with a half-eaten pie. One glass. Newspapers lay in an untidy pile beside the plate.

Siv ducked below the window and crossed to the other side of the house. There was a tall, solid wooden door for side access.

She tried the handle, but it was locked and she didn't want to attempt to climb it and make noise. She returned to the white front door and turned the knob. It opened and she stepped into a dark hall, stood and listened. No sound. A thin wedge of light spilled from the living room door, illuminating a coat rack and an old-fashioned stand with a mirror and drawers.

Siv glanced into the living room as she passed, then continued down a passage and through an open door into a kitchen. She switched on her torch to low beam and saw a small, newly renovated room, with fitted cupboards. Swiftly, she moved back to the hall and climbed the stairs, guessing correctly that they'd creak. Each time, she stopped and listened. Upstairs, she found a bathroom and two bedrooms, one with a double bed and a wardrobe, which she opened, the other containing a few stacked boxes, a weight bench and a rowing machine. The wind roamed around the house, knocking and rattling, sneaking through crevices in the single-glazed windows. The curtains shivered in a draught.

The man who lived here had been disturbed while eating and left in a hurry, forgetting to lock the front door.

Siv ran back down the stairs and left the house, carrying on towards Makin Mere with her torch on full beam. The wind was roaring now, snaking around her, lashing and tugging at her. As she drew near the deep, still waters, she saw a shape along the bank to her left, kneeling over something on the ground. The crescent moon threw a faint glimmer on the scene. Siv glanced back along the path behind her. Where the hell were Ali and Patrick?

She approached quietly, then shone her torch full on the man. She saw that Nell was on the ground, still, face-down, her wrists and legs tied.

'Stop! Police! Stop now!'

He turned and then rose slowly. The wind whipped his hair, made him rock slightly. He stepped away from Nell, walked towards Siv and stopped near her.

'No troops with you, DI Drummond?' He had to shout, his words flying away.

She was fearful, but yelled with certainty, 'They're here, don't worry.'

'Can't see them. You came riding to Nell's rescue in a hurry. Mistake.'

'Is she dead?'

'Not sure, but she will be soon, so that's immaterial. Just Kay left, then. I might off her too.' He spoke as if he hadn't a care in the world.

He's going to shove Nell in the mere and me too, if he can. She needed to keep him talking. The noise of the gale was distracting, filling her ears, and her voice strained. 'I might get why you killed your dad, but why Lyra? She hadn't done anything to you.'

'Ah well, you never heard Tom, my darling father, singing her praises. You'd think he was the only man ever to have a grandchild and that she was the only child ever to have a birthday. He informed me that having reflected on matters, he didn't want to pursue a relationship with me and he had to get Lyra home for her party.'

He was so close, she saw his spit fly through the air as he shouted. She struggled to keep her torch stable, the beam fixed on him, but the mauling wind made it difficult. 'He told you in St Peter's on that Thursday afternoon?'

'Exactly so. While Lyra pranced and prattled, wanting to be the centre of attention. One of those indulged kids who believes they're God's gift.'

'And no one ever indulged you?'

'Don't come the shrink with me. You have no idea.'

'I'm sure I haven't. You must have been very angry when your dad dismissed you like that.' *Come on, Ali!*

He blinked, the stormy air teasing his eyes. 'Tom said there was a lot going on in the family, he didn't want to distress his daughters and he needed to focus on little Lyra. Then he went on about her party. He'd indicated that he wanted to include me in his life, that there'd be a future. I thought he liked me, respected me even, then he made me feel that high.' The man held his fingers centimetres apart. 'I was opening up my heart to him and he was focused on cake and balloons and some poxy magician. So I decided: fuck him and his little pet, I'll give the family some distress to remember.'

Siv tried to keep her voice steady. 'You went to the house and murdered Tom and Lyra because you'd been hurt and insulted.'

'That about sums it up, although I'd say the hurt and insult stretches much further back. Forty years.'

'That's why you shoved the cake on his mouth after you killed him.'

'I reckoned he deserved a piece. He'd told me about the effort he'd gone to over it and how amazing it was. How much Lyra *loved* it.'

He wore such a strange expression — a mixture of anger, spite and pain. She kept playing for time. 'No matter how distraught you were, it must have been hard, murdering a little child. Lyra hadn't done anything to you.'

The man flinched imperceptibly. 'I did try to reason with Dad again when I got to the house. I wanted to give him another chance. I did my best, but he blew it. Behaved as if I was taking up his precious time and he had more important things to do. Did he expect that I was just going to vanish because he clicked his fingers?' He glanced quickly at the turbulent mere. 'He'd never given me anything except false hope and crap about making up for all those lost years, and Lyra had a house full of goodies and all his attention.'

'Your dad did give you a tie, though. One of his Minstergreen ones.'

'Well spotted. That was during the brief phase when he was saying to just give him time, we could sort everything out and be one big happy family.' He wagged a finger. 'You deserve your reputation, Inspector. Not that it's going to benefit you now, here with me. Just us two and the stormy night and the lovely mere, waiting for you. You and Nell can keep each other company.'

'Don't be daft. Every police force in the country will be after you. You'll be caught in no time. No point in adding to the crimes you've already committed.'

'I'm minded to finish what I've started and take my chances.'

Siv's eyes were gritty. She pushed her hair away from them. Where were bloody Ali and Patrick? If Nell wasn't dead, she'd need urgent medical attention. She took a step back and said, 'Geordie Coleman, I'm arresting you on suspicion of the murders of Tom Pullman and Lyra Turton. You do not have to—'

He lunged and threw a punch into her jaw that sent her reeling. She fell to the ground, her torch clattering from her hand. She managed to yell *help!* but before she could get up, Geordie's hands were around her throat, his knee pressing her down, his meaty breath in her nostrils and then everything dimmed.

* * *

Ali and Patrick pulled in behind Siv's car and ran along the same path.

'Are you sure she's got this right?' Patrick yelled. 'I mean, Geordie? He's well respected.'

'What she said.' He'd have sworn that Geordie was a good egg, reliable, but the guv's instincts were usually spot on. 'She should have waited for us. If it is him, he's a fit guy and he won't take to being cornered.'

'What a bloody awful night!'

'Aye, it's wild, all right.'

Ali was puffing, while Patrick ran smoothly, his breathing easy. *Let the guv be OK and I'll give up the fags tomorrow.* He swung his torch towards the keeper's lodge. 'Guv said that's where Geordie lives. Let's take a gander.'

They looked through the window, tried the side door. A bat whisked past, making Ali jump. Despite his country upbringing, he wasn't keen on the dark and things that scurry in the night.

He whispered, 'Car's there. Geordie must be around.'

Patrick was about to reply when they heard a faint shout.

'Down by the mere,' Patrick shouted, taking off into the night, arms pumping.

Ali panted behind, doing his best to keep up, lowering his head. The bloody wind had changed direction and was pushing him back. Patrick had a good half minute on him by the time he reached the mere. He heard several loud shouts. When he gasped to a stop, he saw Siv lying on the ground, a shape in the churning water and the back of Patrick's head as he chased a figure around a bend in the path.

He knelt beside Siv, found a pulse, radioed in for an ambulance and turned again to the roiling mere. The shape had vanished.

Ali took a run towards the edge and dived in. He'd learned to swim in a remote lake as a child, but the cold still jarred him. He took a breath and went under. He twisted and turned in the dark, the water pushing and pulling at him, came up for air, went back down. Then he saw her a few metres away, her white shirt glimmering. He swam hard, caught her and headed to the surface. It seemed to take years to get to the side and she was a dead weight. He had a pain in his chest and it was hard to keep Nell's head above the thrashing waves. Oh God, why wasn't he fitter? Finally, he pushed her up the bank and dragged himself out, spitting water and gasping for breath through heaving lungs.

He glanced at the guv and saw that she'd moved a bit. He put Nell in the recovery position, watched mere water spill from her mouth. A pulse fluttered. He ran back to Siv, checked her again, heard a little moan. 'It's OK,' he said, 'ambulance coming. I've got Nell out. Won't be long now.'

He returned to Nell. Her pulse beat weakly and he shook her, calling her name, telling her help was coming. He rocked on his knees and shivered, teeth chattering, waiting for the ambulance.

The storm raged and roared. The sky was racing with furious, hurtling clouds. He'd never been lonelier.

* * *

Siv came to with an oxygen mask on her face and a horrible pain in her throat. Lights were flashing and she could hear voices. She pulled down the mask and raised her throbbing head. Ali was sitting opposite her, wrapped in a foil blanket.

'What?' she croaked.

A paramedic loomed over her. 'Quiet there. Mask back on, please.'

Siv beckoned Ali with a finger. Her arm was so heavy. He leaned over. His cornrows dripped with water and he smelled brackish.

'I got Nell out,' he said. 'She's alive — just — and away to hospital. Patrick took after Geordie, but he lost him.'

The paramedic had turned her back. Siv yanked the mask down again. 'Kay. Get someone there.'

'Geordie might head to her?'

She swallowed and groaned. 'Possible.'

Ali leaned out of the door of the ambulance and yelled for Patrick. Siv sank back and closed her eyes again. The paramedic adjusted the mask. Her hands were beautifully cool.

* * *

Kay had completed the funeral arrangements. Numb exhaustion overwhelmed her. Maybe she should go and search for Nell, but her car was out of action and anyway, DI Drummond had told her to stay put. She craved a hot bath, but she'd have a glass of wine first. In the kitchen, she poured some, switched on the outside light and looked out of the window. What a night! Everything in the garden was shaking in a bizarre dance. A couple of tubs had blown over and were rolling around, and broken branches from the apple tree were strewn on the lawn. Let the weather do its worst; she couldn't care less. She pulled the blinds down, shutting out the turmoil, took her wine and the bottle to the living room and sank down on the sofa. Ryan was away for the night. Working, he said. She didn't care much. He'd told her that morning that he wanted a divorce. Nice timing, not even waiting until after the funerals, but not such a surprise.

The ugly jug that the police had returned stood beside the wine bottle on the coffee table. How she loathed it. As soon as she had time and energy, she'd sell it or, even better, give it to charity.

She tried Nell's number again and got voicemail. Then she called DI Drummond. Same response. She couldn't work out what Nell was up to, but her sister was always unpredictable. Maybe she'd got high and decided to go and hug some trees. Sometimes she took late-night swims in the sea when she was relaxed and carefree, but surely not on a night like this. It was typical of her to cause worry at such a difficult time. Why couldn't she ever offer support and comfort? Kay was annoyed with her now, but anxious too. She'd give it another ten minutes, then call the police station.

The bell rang and she hurried to open the door. DC Coleman was there. She glimpsed a taxi leaving behind him and was puzzled, but she stepped back and gestured him in with relief.

'Have you got news of Nell?'

'I have,' he said, sounding rushed.

'Come on in.'

He stood in the hall. She smelled sweat. It was acrid, unpleasant. His eyes were odd, vacant and his hair was tangled.

'Is your husband here?'

'No, he's away tonight. Why did you come in a cab?'

'Problems. I need to borrow your car. It's a police emergency.'

'Borrow my car? It's in the garage until tomorrow, brake pad problems. Where's Nell? Have you found her?'

He stared at her, licked his lips, then seized her roughly by the arm and shoved her into the living room.

'What are you doing? Let me go!' She tried to get away from him, but his grip was fierce.

'Shut up.' He slammed her onto the sofa and leaned over her. 'Stay there and don't move.'

'What's happening? DC Coleman!'

He snatched up the bottle of wine and gulped from it. 'Where's your dad's car?'

'Back at his house.'

'Fuck.' He banged the bottle down and it fell on its side, a red river flowing over the table.

Kay rubbed her arm. She sensed a rage in him. Something was horribly wrong. He saw her glance at her phone on the table, picked it up and threw it across the room.

She moved back into the sofa. 'Please tell me what's happening.'

'Nell's dead.'

'But how? Where did you find her?'

'I killed her. Chucked her in the mere.'

Kay froze. This man was deranged. 'I don't believe you.'

He grinned at her. 'Don't you? You should. I killed our dad and Lyra too. I might have you in my sights now.' He pointed at her. 'If you could see your face!'

She was in a mist and worried she might be sick, tasting the acid wine in her throat. She swallowed. '*Our* dad?'

He sat beside her, breathed in her face. 'Yep. He was my dad too. I found him and he led me a right old dance. Said to give him time to adjust but yes, he'd like me to be part of the family. Then he changed his mind. Didn't want to worry his precious daughters and darling Lyra. Can you imagine what that was like?'

'I don't understand . . .'

'No. Your sort wouldn't. You've always been loved and wanted, haven't you? You had a lovely childhood out in Harfield.'

'Yes.'

'Yeah, and now you've got this cushy house to come home to.'

She flinched away from the hot rage beating from his body, began to grow angry. Who was he, barging into her home? 'Am I supposed to apologise for these things?'

'No, no apology needed. At least you've got a bit about you, unlike your waster of a sister. That was hard to swallow, that Tom preferred that druggie to me! The charlady with the dope habit who was on the make!'

What on earth was he going on about? 'But . . . when did . . . who's your mum?'

'Dead. Bit of a fling for Dad, as far as I can work out.'

'Why should I believe you?'

He laughed. 'I don't care if you do or not. I'm going to call a taxi.'

What's he going to do to me? 'Are the police after you?'

'Shut up.' He pressed close to her, put a hand around her throat, tilted her head back. 'You've got gumption, even if you did marry that prat.'

He clamped a hand over her mouth, hooked his phone from his pocket with the other and called a cab. Keeping his hand in place he said softly, 'I'll have to tie you up, Kay. Sorry, not very brotherly. We'll go upstairs now and I'll leave you good and secure.'

She didn't believe him. He was going to kill her; she was sure of it. He was mad; he'd killed Dad, Lyra and Nell and he was going to kill her. Fear and rage swept through her. 'For God's sake, I've lost my dad and my child! You're telling me you murdered them and my sister. Why?'

'Haven't got time for all of that. Come on, upstairs.'

As he tugged her, there was a noise outside, like something sliding. Coleman sat forward, alert, his grip on her loosening. Kay eyed the hideous jug. She was sick of men disrupting her life, trampling all over her, treating her as if she was disposable. That arrogant bastard Glen Belanger, her traitorous shit of a husband and now this sweating madman. She grabbed the jug and brought it down with as much force as she could on his turned head.

He slumped, cracking his forehead on the table. She leaped up and ran from the room, yanked open the front door and sped down the drive straight into a policeman's arms.

CHAPTER 22

Siv discharged herself from hospital at two in the morning and got a lift home from a uniform constable. She'd no idea what had happened to her car. In her wagon, she took two painkillers with a glass of akvavit and fell on her bed fully clothed, where she slept blissfully until Patrick rang her at eight the following morning.

'I've got your car, guv. How are you doing?'

She gingerly tried her voice out. 'Whispery, and I have a lovely bruise. I heard you collared Geordie.'

'Yep. He'd managed to get to the back door of Kay's house but I'd run round the side and I didn't mess up the second time. He was treated in A&E, no concussion. A doctor's checking him at ten this morning to make sure he's fit for interview.'

'Can you come and collect me? If not, I'll call a cab.'

'You sure you should be at work?'

'Come and get me in half an hour.' She wouldn't be allowed to interview Geordie because of the attack, but she wanted to observe. No way was she missing that.

The wind had died. When she opened the curtains, there was a hazy sun in a wan, watery sky. She spent a couple of minutes under a hot shower, dressed herself in a black suit and debated whether to wear a scarf around her throat to conceal the bruise. She decided against it. If Geordie saw her, she wouldn't give him the satisfaction of hiding in any way. She made and sipped a cup of tea. It hurt, but it went down, so she ate a yogurt, realising that she'd need invalid food for a couple of days. Then she phoned Ali.

'Guv, how you doing?'

'I'll live.'

'I'm on my way to the station. The roads are filled with debris after last night.'

'You OK after your swim?'

'Nothing a hot bath and a bit of shut-eye couldn't cure. I just checked on Nell. She's hanging in there. Kay's with her.' He laughed. 'I'm glad the ugly jug came in handy.'

'Patrick's fetching me. See you soon.'

'You sound as if you've been chewing wasps.'

'Thanks.'

'I guessed you'd come in. Pol's made you a wee flask of hot lemon and honey, I've it with me.'

Her eyes grew moist. She was absurdly grateful. *Just shock.* 'Great.'

At the station, she was glad of the soothing drink, which Ali had left on her desk. Mortimer appeared briefly in her office, dressed in jeans and polo shirt.

'We were supposed to take the boat to Broadstairs for the day, but I've postponed. I wanted to make sure you're all right and stay local, in case I'm needed. Your mother was very worried when we heard the news last night.'

'I'm fine,' Siv said. 'I just wish I could interview Geordie.'

'Absolutely not. Ali and Patrick can do that.' Mortimer crossed to her window, his rubber-soled deck shoes squeaking on the floor. 'This is hard to credit. One of our officers — and a very popular one too.'

Siv suppressed a laugh, holding her throat. As if popularity bestowed some kind of special dispensation, automatically made someone squeaky clean.

Mortimer hadn't noticed. 'We were harbouring a killer in our midst. The press will have a field day, they'll be all over it and milking it for all it's worth. Bad coppers make for good headlines. I've already had the chief constable on the phone. I'm meeting him later today to plan damage limitation.'

She'd been wondering how long it would take Mortimer to get to the bad publicity angle. 'It's not good for community relations, certainly. It's a shock for everyone. Colleagues' morale will be affected. How long had Geordie worked here?'

'He transferred from Liverpool ten months ago.'

'Maybe he wanted to move here because he'd established that his father lived nearby.'

'That's a reasonable assumption. What a complete and utter nightmare. I'll be in my office for a while talking to press liaison, in case you need me.'

Ali was fired up about the interview when she saw him. 'Geordie's got a solicitor with him. How come Jill Bartoli recognised him from the composite and none of us did?'

'No idea. Maybe she's got a good eye, because it's not that much of a likeness. Luckily for us, she saw Geordie last weekend, at the Turtons' house. She'd called round with a condolence card and he was there. She commented on how mannerly he was.'

'And I sat having drinks in the pub and chatting to our polite murderer,' Ali grumbled.

'Yep, and he was able to get regular updates about the investigation from us.'

'Wee bastard. He must have been laughing at us.'

'As long as we have the last laugh, Ali. Let Patrick lead in the interview, as you and Geordie have previous.'

Siv took her flask of drink to the observation post. Geordie looked remarkably well rested when he entered the interview room accompanied by his solicitor. He had a small, taped cut on his head, where he'd connected with Kay's coffee table.

Ali conducted the preliminaries while Patrick opened his notepad.

The solicitor glanced at Geordie. 'My client is accepting responsibility for the murders of Thomas Pullman and Lyra

Turton and the attempted murder of Eleanor Pullman. Also to grievous bodily harm in relation to Detective Inspector Siv Drummond and assault on Ms Kay Turton.'

'Quite a list,' Patrick said. 'Depending on what happens with Nell Pullman, we might be adding another charge of murder.'

The solicitor softened her voice. 'My client hopes that by confessing and thus avoiding expense and suffering to witnesses, the court will be able to consider awarding a discount on sentence.'

Geordie glanced towards the observation window. 'I'm sorry about DI Drummond. She was in the wrong place at the wrong time. I hope she's OK.'

Siv touched her neck. *Right place, right time, as far as I'm concerned.*

'When did you decide to murder your father and Lyra?' Patrick asked.

'That Thursday afternoon. He wound me up. I was furious with him. I just lost it, picked up that pan from the cooker.'

'How did you get in touch with him?'

'I'd got hold of my adoption papers and I traced him. That's when I decided to ask for a transfer here. I scouted him out at one of those BSS talks in January. I wanted to see what he was like, get the measure of him. He thought I was just an interested member of the public. He was engaging and friendly, seemed like I could approach him.' He clasped his hands together. 'It's a nerve-wracking business searching for a birth parent, I can tell you. I got his address and wrote later in January, told him who I was and suggested we meet at St Peter's. I'd driven past it a couple of times and I called in one day. It was quiet, handy.'

'We've seen that letter,' Patrick said. 'Why did you sign it Francis?'

Geordie's voice was detached and flat. 'That was what my birth mother called me. I was Francis Newall for a short while until my adoptive parents in Liverpool renamed me.'

'Go on.'

'I'd no idea if Dad would turn up at the church, but he did, and we took it from there. When he said he'd never been aware of my existence, it was a relief to confirm there was nothing he could have done about my adoption. That cleared the air a bit between us. Then I met him half a dozen times or so, in St Peter's and twice by the river. He was a bit formal to start with and cagy, but he slowly warmed to me. Seemed chuffed to have a son, after the initial shock. We chatted about lots of things.' Geordie's voice thickened. 'I liked him, found him good company, wanted to get closer. I had no siblings, so it was good to hear that I had ready-made sisters. Lyra was with him a couple of times and she was a bit of a pain, interrupting and grabbing the limelight. Dad talked to me about Kay and Nell, described Kay's lovely house by the coast — I drove past it a couple of times, saw her once getting out of her car. Nell sounded a bit of a mess. Tom worried about her and was frustrated by her.' Geordie drank some water, touched the cut on his head and winced.

Patrick was finding the story affecting, despite himself. His own dad had died when he was a child and he'd always felt the lack of him. 'It sounds as if the contact with your dad was going well. You must have been hopeful.'

'I was, I was indeed. We'd skirted around when I could meet Kay and Nell and I reckoned he'd say soon. I'd got the impression he might ask me to his home.'

'So things went wrong in St Peter's on that Thursday?'

Geordie laid his hands flat on the table. 'Tom told me he couldn't carry on seeing me; it just wouldn't work. Kay had problems that he couldn't tell me about and introducing me into the family would cause too much difficulty. I wasn't prepared for that at all. He'd been giving me quite opposite messages. I really liked him, hoped he liked me. He wasn't even saying hang on a few months. Just wanted to cut me off. How do you do that to your own son?' He took a shuddering breath.

His solicitor asked, 'Are you OK? Do you need a break?'

He shook his head at her, set his jaw. 'I want to get this done. My adoptive parents weren't unkind, but there wasn't really any affection. We just didn't gel, had nothing in common. I was always like an interloper. I had a real connection with Tom — same sense of humour and take on the world. I'd let my guard down with him. Then suddenly, he was going on about Kay, Nell and Lyra as if I didn't matter. I was disposable — again. First, my mother had got rid of me, now him.' He pressed down on the table. 'When he drove away from the church I saw red. He'd led me up the garden path, big time. I went down to Wherry Cove for ten minutes or so, sat there mulling it over, trying to get my head around it all. The sea usually calms me, but not that afternoon. I decided to walk up to Kay's house to try and persuade Dad, give him another chance, but he was insistent that I go away and leave his family alone. As if I wasn't his family! There was all this party stuff in the kitchen, a beautiful cake. He could have invited me, made me welcome, a part of things — but no, that wasn't going to happen. So I slipped on some gloves, picked up the pan and hit him. I cut a slice of cake and smeared it on his mouth.'

Patrick asked, 'And Lyra?'

'I might not have killed her, but she was dancing around on the lawn in her oh-so-special party dress, singing at the top of her voice. She really annoyed me. I walked up to her and she said something about *why wasn't I in the church?* Then she was insisting I sing some silly song with her. I wanted her to shut up, so I made sure she did.'

There was bitterness in his voice. Watching, Siv was chilled. It must have been hard when his father, a powerful figure in his life, slammed the door on him after opening it.

'What happened with Nell?' Patrick asked.

'She was as irritating as Lyra. When she rang me last night, she told me she'd found the postcard I'd sent Dad. He gave in when she quizzed him about it, named me and said I was a police officer. He made her promise to keep it to herself while he worked things out. She'd located me on social media, and then the next evening, there I was, turning up as family liaison. Nell decided to stay quiet about me, see how things panned out. Then she saw that composite, so she reckoned you'd be on to me some time soon.' Geordie started to flag, rubbed his eyes. 'She was dead cocky on the phone when she told me, and she said that if I paid her, she'd keep quiet about me. Stupid cow. She was even dafter than Dad let on. I told her to come and meet me at the lodge, but I waited for her in the trees and dragged her down to the mere. You've got the rest. I wouldn't have killed Kay, by the way. She seemed nice. Gutsy too.'

'I'm sure she'll be grateful when we tell her that,' Patrick said. 'It was handy for you, being the FLO.'

'Certainly was. I put my hand up for it and it gave me an in to the investigation. I was fascinated when I heard about the Turtons' IVF disaster. That's why I wouldn't really have harmed Kay. She'd been through enough and she's married to that pillock of a husband. I went to hers because I was in a panic and I needed a car.' He glanced at Ali. 'My chats with you were handy too.'

'Yeah, so I gather,' Ali said. 'Thanks for playing me. You haven't asked how your sister Nell is.'

Geordie said without emotion, 'She'll live or she'll die. Nothing I can do about it. My head's throbbing now, I could do with a break.'

Patrick wound things up for the time being. The solicitor put a hand on Geordie's shoulder, but he shook it off.

Siv wondered at his contained, matter-of-fact manner and reckoned it wouldn't last. Emotions must be swamping him, even if he was doing a good job of suppressing them. He'd found the father he'd needed and the family he'd searched for and had killed two of them, possibly another. Kay might be the only one left standing. Surely that realisation would hit home at some point and he'd crack up. Probably during a long, lonely night in a cell.

She'd make sure he was referred for psychiatric assessment.

* * *

Siv returned to the hospital, buying anaesthetic lozenges in the pharmacy on the ground floor. Kay Turton deserved an update about her family history before any rumours could reach her. She arranged to meet her in the café and waited by the trays in the spacious, warm room. A text pinged on her phone, from Fabian.

Your mum told me what happened last night. Hope you're OK. Call me later. I make a good nurse. Don't forget that offer of dinner tomorrow, sounds as if you deserve it. F.

Bloody Mutsi, interfering as usual. She'd even managed to swap contact details with Fabian. Siv put the phone away when she saw Kay arrive. At the counter, they both selected large mugs of hot chocolate, which Siv insisted on buying. They sat by a window facing a pond with benches around it. Kay's shirt was crumpled, her hair uncombed.

Siv asked, 'Have you slept at all?'

'Snatches. I was too wired.'

'Is there any news of Nell?'

'They're more positive about her this afternoon, so I'm hopeful. I heard about what happened to you. I'm so sorry. You sound very faint and that bruise is nasty.'

'I'll be fine.' Siv unwrapped a lozenge and felt the benefit of its comforting ingredients immediately. 'I wanted to speak to you in person. I understand that Geordie Coleman told you last night that your dad was his father.'

'DC Hill confirmed that it was true when I asked him. But then I had to get here, for Nell. I've been going over that in my head. I replay Coleman's words, but then I wonder if I dreamed them. It all seems like a hideous nightmare now.'

Siv explained, while Kay blew on her drink to cool it and took little sips.

'Nell knew, then. I'm the only one who was in the dark.'

'She'll have to tell you her version, but your dad asked her to keep it quiet when she questioned him about the postcard.'

'But she was attempting to blackmail Coleman.'

'Yes. That's why she ended up left for dead.'

'I'm so furious with her. Why didn't she tell me about Geordie when Dad died, instead of keeping it to herself?'

Siv had been giving that some thought. It was hard to guess what bizarre plan Nell might have been cooking up. 'We'll establish that when she can talk to us. Maybe she was playing him and after he'd paid up she'd have told you and come to us.'

Kay said bitterly, 'Maybe. I can tell you this, I'll have the truth from her. I'm not putting up with her usual vagueness and avoidance tactics. I'm glad she's going to pull through this, but I'm not sure I'll like her much.'

'I wanted to tell you that we've charged Geordie Coleman and he's confessed. I'm sorry that our own colleague, the man we sent to help you, turned out to be the perpetrator. It's hard to find the words.'

'It's not your fault. It's down to you and your colleagues that Nell is still alive — and maybe me too. He came to my house with flowers and stood in the kitchen with me when he'd murdered Dad and Lyra just days before! I do believe he'd have killed me. He was . . . intense, a bit crazed.'

'You must be shell-shocked. It's a lot to take in.' Siv spooned some of her chocolate to her lips.

Kay was silent, gazing through the window. After a while she said, 'There is some more positive news in the midst of all of this.'

Siv croaked, 'What's that?'

'My solicitor rang me earlier. Glen Belanger has been suspended pending investigation of misconduct. Did you have a hand in that?'

'I can't comment, Kay. But let's just say it seems a fair outcome.'

'Agreed. Also, Ryan's moved out. He told me he wants a divorce, so I rang him this morning and I said he could pack his things and go. After last night, I'm not taking any more crap. I've had it up to here with being deceived. I expect he'll stay at the Dovecote, having room service.'

She was a strong woman, but Siv didn't say so. She'd hated it when people had told her that after Ed's death. It was like an extra responsibility, a role she had to fulfil, especially on days when she felt as weak as a kitten.

Kay pushed her chair back. 'I'm going to pop in to see Nell again, then I'll head home for a shower and some clean clothes. Take it easy, Inspector. You're worn out.'

Siv sat and finished her drink, her head nodding, almost asleep.

* * *

Siv arrived home in the dark. She'd stayed late at the station, wanting to make sure that everything was in order and Mortimer kept up to speed.

She ached all over now, a bit shaky and her throat was closing up. Driving was an effort and she had to focus carefully on the roads. She was anticipating a lovely cold glass of akvavit and bed. Maybe a glass in bed. Bliss.

As she drove slowly down the track, she made out a figure sitting on the steps of the wagon. If this was Fabian wanting to play nurse or bringing her more flowers or chocolates, she'd tell him where to go. Company was the last thing she wanted. She pulled in and saw the figure stand, realised it was too small for Fabian.

She slammed the car door, took a step forward and saw Rik, dressed in black and wearing a baseball cap.

'Hi, Siv. Hope you don't mind me waiting.'

Her first reaction was that her sister now had a Kiwi twang. 'How long have you been here?'

'Hour or so. I got a cab from town.'

Siv croaked, 'But how? I mean, why?'

'I'm wrecked, sis. Can we just go in?' Rik picked up a large holdall. 'I'm kind of asleep on my feet.'

'Of course, yes, sorry.'

Siv went up the steps and unlocked the door, switched the light on. 'Put your bag down. I'll fire up the stove. I suppose I should say welcome home.'

She turned to Rik, expecting a witty comment about her rasping voice and her bruised throat.

Rik burst into tears. Rik never cried: she was made of steel. A stunned Siv took her bag, guided her wordlessly to the window seat.

She went to the fridge and poured two drinks.

It had been a long day and it was going to be a longer night.

THE END

Thank you for reading this book.

If you enjoyed it please leave feedback on Amazon or Goodreads, and if there is anything we missed or you have a question about, then please get in touch. We appreciate you choosing our book.

Founded in 2014 in Shoreditch, London, we at Joffe Books pride ourselves on our history of innovative publishing. We were thrilled to be shortlisted for Independent Publisher of the Year at the British Book Awards.

www.joffebooks.com

We're very grateful to eagle-eyed readers who take the time to contact us. Please send any errors you find to corrections@joffebooks.com. We'll get them fixed ASAP.